To Joan—

A MATTER
OF
HONOR

Enjoy the read!

George R. Hopkins

George R. Hopkins

A Matter of Honor is a work of fiction. Names, characters, places, and incidents are the product of the author's imagination or are used factiously. Any resemblance to actual events, locales, or persons, living or dead, is entirely coincidental.

This book may not be reproduced, transmitted, or stored in whole or in part by any means, including graphic, electronic, or mechanical without the express written consent of the author except in the case of brief quotations embodied in critical articles and reviews.

To

Diane

In the road of life it's not where you go but who you're with that makes all the difference.

Honest and True

He who pursues righteousness and loyalty finds life, righteousness and honor.

Proverbs 21:21

Other Suspense / Thriller / Mysteries

In the Priest and the Detective Series

By George R. Hopkins

Blood Brothers

Collateral Consequences

Letters from the Dead

Random Acts of Malice

Unholy Retribution

Chasing the Devil's Breath

The Staten Island Butcher

All of these mystery/thrillers can be ordered from your local bookstore and are available at Amazon.com, BarnesandNoble.com and in Kindle editions.

Preface

Cartagena, Colombia

Crack!

It sounded like a shot as her yardstick slammed down on the desk. Everyone in the classroom jumped. Eyes shot up to Sister Magdalena Albatross. Beneath her white coif, her eyes danced with fury as she looked down at the open drawer of her desk. The whiskers on her chin seemed to quiver with her rage. "Who did this?" she screamed.

Silence fell on the class. "Who did this? I am warning you. You will all pay for this? Who did this?"

A small boy called out from his seat in the back of the room in perfect English. "Who did what, Sister?" He smiled and added, "We don't know what you're talking about."

A muffled giggle rippled through the classroom.

"You did it, didn't you, you little heathen piece of trash!"

"That's not a very Christian thing to say, Sister."

Sister Albatross wobbled down the aisle and grabbed the small boy by the ear and dragged him to the front of the classroom. "Don't lie to me, you filthy, little street urchin! You did this, didn't you?"

1

The boy looked up at the looming figure in black. He yanked his head and pulled away from her. "Get your smelly hands off me! You don't scare me, old woman!"

Sister Magdalena's fist squeezed the yardstick and lashed out at Chico. He ducked and the yardstick splintered in half as it hit the chalkboard.

"Careful, Sister. You could hurt someone with that stupid stick!"

The class started to laugh as the boy danced in front of Sister.

The nun's face turned beet red. She held up a shaking finger and pointed to the door. "Get out of my classroom, you insolent gutter imp! Go to the principal's office! I will have no more of your mischief in my classroom!"

The boy retreated to the door and then turned. "Sister," he asked, "may I take my snake with me?"

The remnants of Sister Magdalena's broken ruler careened into the door as the boy quickly disappeared into the darkness of the hallway.

* * * *

Chapter 1

Staten Island, New York

Father Jack Bennis sat at his desk in his room at St. Peter's rectory. His body ached. It had been a long day. He emptied his pockets. There were the pink Connemara rosary beads his mother had given him when he joined the Army. That seemed like such a long time ago. He placed the rosary beads next to his wallet and keys. He looked at the keys and remembered his assignment to lock up the church at night and open it in the morning. He checked his watch. It was late. He should have locked the church doors already, but his conference with Roberta and Jack O'Hanlon had taken longer than expected. They were a young, concerned couple who were worried about one of their neighbors.

He reached into his pocket and withdrew two crumpled unopened letters. His brother had given him the letters a few weeks ago, but he never opened them. They were both from Colombia, South America. One was typed. The other was handwritten. He hesitated opening them. Could one be from María Isabelle, the woman who was wounded in Mompas, the woman whose brother was a drug lord in Bogotá, the woman he was in love with? He thought the distance between them would lessen his love for her. It hadn't.

His hand shook as he opened the typed envelope first. Maybe it was from the hospital. Was she healing from the wounds she received? Would she be able to walk again? Was she still alive? Was she reaching out to him again? He took a deep breath and tore open the letter abruptly. It wasn't from the hospital. It was from St. Benedict Joseph Labre, the school Chico and his seven-year-old sister were attending. He breathed a sigh of relief.

He recalled the young boy whose parents were murdered in Mompas because his father had dared to publish an exposé about a new drug being produced in the town by a mysterious man known only as El Apredido.

Fr. Bennis smiled as he pictured Chico devouring a meal of pata guisado and marinated duck meat in Cartagena before he left for the States. Monsignor Passeri, the pastor of St. Peter Claver Church in Cartagena, planned to make arrangements for Chico and his sister to go to school and live with a family. Young Chico followed his own code. He had taken care of his sister and chosen to survive on the streets of Mompas in the hope of avenging his parents' deaths. Chico reminded Bennis of a poem he had read many years before by William Ernest Henley called "Invictus." In the fell clutch of circumstances, Chico had not winced nor cried aloud. Under the bludgeonings of life, his head may have been bloodied, but never unbowed. Chico was a survivor. As much as any little twelve-year old could hope to be, Chico was convinced he was the master of his fate, "the captain of his soul."

Monsignor Passeri was a good man. He promised Father Bennis he would find a good home for Chico and his sister, enroll them in school and find a place for Chico's pet spider monkey and the bejeweled Muisca spear Chico did not want to part with. Monsignor assured Father Bennis he would take care of all the "loose ends."

Bennis' relief, however, proved temporary. The letter was from Sister Gracelyn Sánchez, the principal of the school.

> *Dear Rev. Fr. Bennis, S. J.:*
> *You entrusted two children to us, twelve-*
> *year-old Chico and his eight-year-old*
> *sister Maria. I need to inform you that*
> *things have not worked out well since*
> *they arrived at our orphanage and school.*
> *While Maria has adjusted very well and*
> *has excellent reports from her teachers,*
> *Chico has been a disruptive influence.*
> *He has been causing trouble with both*
> *his teachers and the other students. I*
> *have been forced to suspend him from*
> *school a number of times.*
> *On the last occasion, he placed a snake*
> *in Sister Magdalena Albatross' desk drawer,*
> *insulted Sister, and was sent to my office.*
> *I regret to inform you that Chico never came to*
> *my office and has disappeared. Somehow*
> *he left the orphanage and is no longer in*
> *our protection. The police have been informed,*
> *but we have not been able to locate him....*

How did this happen? Monsignor was supposed to find a home for the children, not put them in an orphanage. Chico had been through so much. He saw his parents murdered in cold blood. He had taken care of his sister. Bennis pictured the small, skinny boy with a large sombrero and no shirt squatting beside an assortment of fruit. He remembered Chico's pet spider monkey, Sergio, sitting on the street-wise boy's shoulder. Chico had saved his life. He never should have left him there. Chico had survived on the streets and in the jungles of Mompas. He wasn't accustomed to the rigid rules of a parochial school and a big city. But there was nothing else Father Bennis could have done at the time. He needed to get back to the States to save his brother's life. Yet, Chico was his responsibility, and he felt he had let him down.

He pounded his desk. I have to go back to Cartagena, he thought. I need to find Chico. I have to go back to Colombia.

He checked his watch. It was almost midnight. He needed to make flight arrangements. It was too late to call the school. Then he remembered he still had to lock the church doors.

Walking back to the church, Bennis made mental preparations for returning to Colombia. The church was mostly dark when he got there. As he was about to turn off the altar lights, he saw a figure in a pew on the left side of the church. He hadn't expected this.

"Excuse me," he called out. "I need to lock up the church. I am afraid you will have to leave."

The figure did not move.

Bennis held his hand on the light switch and called out again. "I'm sorry, but I have to lock up the church. You are going to have to leave."

The figure did not move.

He hated asking people to leave the church. But there had been a number of robberies and some vandalism in the neighborhood. Locking places of religious worship, he hated to admit, was a sign of the times.

6

Maybe the person had fallen asleep, he thought. The priest genuflected in front of the tabernacle and walked toward the figure in the shadows.

As he came closer, he saw the figure was a man. He was sitting back in the pew in front of him. The man was big, well-dressed in a dark blue suit and shirt and tie.

"Excuse me, sir," Father Bennis said touching the man's shoulder, "but I'm afraid...."

At his touch, the figure slowly toppled over like a dead tree.

Bennis reached down to grab him. "Are you all right?"

Then he saw his face. The eyes had been carved out and a long wooden skewer protruded from his neck. Attached to the skewer was a 3 x 5 index card with the number two written in bold red.

* * * *

The phone woke Tom Cavanaugh up from a deep sleep. He fumbled for the phone knocking over a glass of water on his night table. He cursed to himself and grabbed the phone. He glanced at the alarm clock. It was 3:04 in the morning. What was someone calling him at this hour for?

"Thomas, is that you?" the voice on the phone asked.

"Jack? Who the hell do you think it is? And why are you calling me at this Godforsaken time of the night? If you wake up the baby, I swear I'll kill you!"

"I had to call you."

"What couldn't wait until a decent hour of the morning?"

"The police were here. They are still in the church."

"The police? What the hell have you gotten yourself into now?"

"Someone was murdered in the church. I found him

when I was locking up the church."

Cavanaugh swung his legs out of the bed and sat up. "Murdered? How do you know he was murdered? Who was he?"

"I don't know. I never saw him before. He was a big man, well-dressed in a suit and tie. But ...."

"But what?"

"His eyes...."

Cavanaugh stood up and walked to the bathroom. "What about his eyes?"

Bennis paused.

"What about his eyes, Jack?"

"He had none. They were gouged out."

* * * *

Cavanaugh dressed quickly. He left a note on the bathroom mirror for his wife. No need to wake her. On a normal day it would take him well over a half-hour to get from the south of Staten Island to the north shore. He made the trip to St. Peter's Church in twenty-four minutes. The flashing lights of a half dozen patrol cars greeted him as he pulled into the church's parking lot.

Police and detectives swarmed over the church. A light rain began to fall. A tall, heavy-set patrolman motioned for him to stop. He knew the routine. He'd been through it too many times. Keep everyone away from the scene. Let the police do their work. Curious bystanders contaminated the crime scene.

Cavanaugh ignored the patrolman. He skirted between patrol cars and headed for the rectory.

"Hey," the patrolman shouted, "I told you to stop!"

Cavanaugh stepped in a puddle and cursed. He left his house without putting on socks. Suddenly, a hand grabbed his shoulder and spun him around.

"What part of 'stop' don't you understand, buster?" the cop asked.

Cavanaugh reacted instantly grasping the hand on his shoulder and pulling back on the patrolman's thumb while kicking his assailant's leg out from under him. The patrolman reached for his gun as he fell, but Cavanaugh's other hand stopped him. He stared into the cop's face. "Oh, for crying out loud," he said releasing his grip on his thumb and helping him up. "It's you, Shanley. I didn't recognize you."

Shanley stood. "Is that you, Cavanaugh? What are you doing here? I heard you retired."

"I did, but my brother called me. He's a priest here. He found the body. I came to see him."

"Well, why the hell didn't you say that?"

"I just did."

"I'm not supposed to let anyone in."

"I know the routine, but he's my brother and you and I go back a long time. I remember when we worked that case in Brooklyn where somebody was knocking off mob bosses."

"I don't know, Cavanaugh. We got a new boss. She's a real stickler for rules."

"Since when did you start worrying about breaking a few rules? He's my brother and one way or the other I'm going into the rectory to see him."

Shanley adjusted his bulletproof vest. "Well, as long as you're not going into the church, I guess it's all right."

"Thanks, Shanley. What can you tell me about the victim?"

Shanley scanned the parking lot. "I don't know much, but from what I overheard, the dead guy was a private eye."

"My brother told me his eyes were gouged out. Sounds

like the killer is keeping trophies or sending a message."

Shanley shook his head. "He's not keeping trophies. We found the eyes in his suit jacket."

Cavanaugh frowned. "Then he's sending some kind of message."

* * * *

At the door to his brother's room stood two uniform policemen. Cavanaugh recognized the older one. John Rhatigan had put on a few pounds since they worked together with Shanley in Brooklyn. His face was weathered but his blue eyes still sparkled when he saw Cavanaugh.

"Rhatigan," Cavanaugh said extending his hand, "I haven't seen you in a dog's age. I thought you'd be retired by now."

Rhatigan smiled. "I've got nowhere else to go. How have you been?"

"I'm here to see my brother, Father Bennis."

"You haven't changed much. You still cut to the chase."

Cavanaugh patted Rhatigan on the arm and moved past him. Suddenly, the other cop stepped in front of him. He was shorter than Cavanaugh and looked like a musclebound teenager. "You can't go in there, sir," he announced with the passion of a prerecorded message.

"Listen kid," Cavanaugh said. "I used to be on the job. I came to see my brother."

"We have our orders. No one goes in there."

Cavanaugh glanced at Rhatigan who shrugged his shoulders. "That is what Detective Perez said."

Cavanaugh turned back to the young cop blocking his way. He read his name plate: Jefferson. "Listen, kid. I know how this works. My brother is the priest who found the body.... He's entitled to a representative. I'm going in there!"

"I said you can't go in there, sir."

"And I said I am." Cavanaugh said and started to push the young cop aside.

"Don't make this difficult, sir. We have our orders."

"And what are you going to do? Shoot me?"

Officer Jefferson took out his taser.

"Hey, kid, you really don't want to do that. Rhatigan, talk to him."

Rhatigan held up his hands. "He's the new breed, Cavanaugh. I'm a short timer. Perez was adamant about this. No visitors while she is questioning your brother." He shrugged his shoulders again. "She emphasized *you* were not to interrupt her."

Cavanaugh looked at the bright yellow taser in Jefferson's hand. A taser wasn't going to stop him. He was within reaching distance. A quick move and he could disarm the kid.

He had never used a taser himself. He was from the old school. He preferred using his fists or his nightstick. They were more reliable. He knew the probes of the taser spread out as they move toward the target. When they hit their target, electricity pulses between the probes disrupting the neuron communications between the target's muscles and brain. In most cases, neuromuscular incapacitation occurs and the target's muscles tense and he becomes temporarily incapable of using his muscles. In most cases, but not all.

But it was the name Perez that concerned Cavanaugh more than the taser. Detective Perez had tried to get at Cavanagh through his brother before. She still held Cavanaugh responsible for her sister's death. He and her sister had once been an item. They had a stormy, sordid

11

relationship. He ended up embarrassing her by telling bedroom stories to the wrong people. Merry Perez became known as "Bubbles" Perez and was the victim of the sadistic killer known as the Maple Syrup Murderer. The fact that the killer was also another cop with a vendetta against Cavanaugh made him doubly responsible in Detective Perez's eyes for her sister's gruesome death.

Cavanaugh looked at the taser and then at Patrolman Jefferson's eyes. He wanted to twist the arrogant kid's wrist and smack his elbow into his head. In the past, he would have, but now he had a son and a wife. Assaulting a cop would bring him a bundle of hurt.

Rhatigan broke the tension. "She's been in there a long time, Tom. She should be out soon."

Cavanaugh took a deep breath. His muscles tensed. He wasn't accustomed to backing down. It wasn't in his nature.

Patrolman Jefferson stepped back. His hand was steady on the taser.

Then the door to Fr. Bennis' room flew open and Detective Perez stood there smiling. She brushed her long purple hair back and looked like she was sitting in the catbird seat. She laughed, "Well, look what the wind blew in. If it isn't Thomas Cavanaugh. I hear you're a private dick now. But that's not much of a change, is it? You always were a dick."

Cavanaugh's hands were shaking. He shoved them into his jacket and nodded. "May I see my brother now, Detective Perez?"

"Father Bennis is your brother? Fancy that. If I had known that I would have invited you in." Behind her another detective towered over her. He looked like a defensive tackle on the Chicago Bears.

"Cut the crap, Perez. You knew it. Now will you tell this young stud here to put his yellow toy gun away and let me see my brother?"

Perez gestured for him to enter like a matador baiting the bull. The massive detective behind her stepped aside. Cavanaugh looked into the room and saw his brother sitting on his bed alongside an older man in a red bathrobe.

*　*　*　*

Cavanaugh recognized the older man in the red bathrobe from stories his brother told him. Monsignor Liam O'Brien was in his late eighties. His brother told him how Monsignor had worked in Nigeria as a missionary. After thirty years on the Dark Continent, he returned to the United States and served as the pastor of a poor church in Harlem. When he reached the age of retirement, he breathed a sigh of relief and moved into a small condo in Boca Raton, Florida. But boredom swept in quickly. Watching "The View," "The Young and the Restless," "Judge Judy," "Dr. Phil," "Dancing with the Stars," and reruns of "Bonanza" and "Wagon Train" left him empty, and he came back to New York to serve as a parochial vicar at St. Peter's Church.

Monsignor O'Brien was full of stories and though he acknowledged his memory was slipping, he was one of the few priests who remembered saying Mass in Latin. He witnessed changes in the Catholic Church. Some of the changes he liked, some he had trouble with. He lamented that today few of the seminarians understood or even studied Latin. He believed saying the Mass in Latin lent it a degree of mysticism and mystery. But, he had to admit, saying Mass in the vernacular facing the congregation was better for all.

Cavanaugh never experienced a Latin Mass. He had a hard time keeping his eyes open and not falling asleep when

13

he did go to church and the priest spoke in English. He never understood why his brother decided to become a priest. Father Bennis claimed it was a calling he felt. The only calling Cavanaugh had ever heard was when his mother called him to get out of bed, get dressed, and go to school. He wanted to ask his brother if he really believed that, before the church changed its rules about eating meat on Fridays, if the kid who ate a hot dog at a Friday night Yankee game was really going to Hell. There were so many questions he wanted to ask him, but he didn't. Maybe it was because he respected his choice, maybe it was because he didn't want to poke holes in his faith, maybe it was he was afraid of his answers. Sometimes, his mother would say, it is better to keep one's mouth shut. Too often, he had found his mother's advice was right on.

When Monsignor O'Brien saw Cavanaugh, he slowly started to rise. His knees cracked, and he yawned. "I think it best I leave you two together now. It is past my bedtime." He patted Fr. Bennis on the shoulder and whispered, *"Adjutorium nostrum in nomine Domini."* Bennis made the sign of the cross and answered, *"Qui fecit caelum et terram."*

After the monsignor left, Cavanaugh pulled up a chair and asked his brother. "Was that some sort of Swahili prayer he said?"

Bennis smiled. "No. It was Latin. He just said, 'Our help is in the name of the Lord.' Sometimes he prefers to pray in Latin."

"I don't get it, but more important what the hell happened here tonight?"

Bennis recounted how he went to lock up the church and how he found the dead man in the pew on the side of the church.

"Who's the dead guy? Did you ever see him before?"

Cavanaugh asked.

"I've been through all these questions with Detective Perez. I have no idea who he is or how he got there."

"I met Shanley outside. He tells me the guy was some kind of private eye. For what it's worth, he tells me they found his eyeballs in his pocket."

"Why would anyone do this, Thomas? And do it in a church?"

"I doubt he was killed in the church, Jack. I think he was brought here for some reason."

Cavanaugh held his head in his hands. "I think we've got to work together on this. I'll find out who he was, and you can start asking around if anyone knows him."

Jack Bennis stood and walked to his desk. "I can't do that, Thomas."

"What are you talking about? Between the two of us we can find out more than purple-headed Detective Perez and her pumped-up steroid driven abominable snowman of a partner can."

The priest reached into his desk drawer and showed Cavanaugh the typed letter from Sister Gracelyn Sánchez. I'm leaving tomorrow for Colombia."

"Excuse me. What are you talking about? You're a material witness. Perez will have a shit fit. You can't go."

"I have to go." He held out the typewritten letter to Cavanaugh. "Chico is missing. I have to find him. He left school and disappeared. I have to find him. He's my responsibility."

Cavanaugh rose and grabbed his brother by his arms. "You have got to be kidding me! You can't leave now. You are a witness to a crime. Perez will think you did it, and she'll have every cop in the tristate area looking for you. There has to be a better way."

"I didn't do it, Thomas. Chico is my responsibility. I didn't see anything. I just found the body. I should not have left him in Cartagena."

"Be sensible, Jack. If Chico has been missing for months and the police haven't found him, what chance do you have of finding him?"

Father Bennis shook his head and walked to the door. "My mind is made up, Thomas. It's something I have to do. Remember that old Charlie Chan movie where he says when searching for a needle in a haystack; the haystack is the only sensible location to start." He opened the door and added, "Thanks for coming. You do your thing, and I'll do mine. Keep me in your prayers. Now go home and get some rest. I will be fine."

* * * *

A heavier rain had begun to fall as Cavanaugh left the rectory. Police and forensic teams were scattered around the church and the adjacent parking lot. He saw Rhatigan and Shanley talking in the portico by the main entrance. Life seemed simpler back when he was a part of the NYPD. He recalled the camaraderie, the excitement, the enjoyment he felt on the job. Maybe he could come back. He had read in the paper how his old partner, Morty Goldberg, had become Chief of Detectives. But then he remembered the young cop with the taser, his nemesis Detective Perez, and all the bridges he had burned while on the job. The times had changed, and so had he. Thomas Wolfe was right. You can't go home again.

His head ached more than the morning after he drank too much Champagne at his friend's wedding at the New Rochelle Country Club. He had tried to get his brother to change his mind about traveling to Colombia, but it was like trying to talk sense to a deaf mule. The brothers were so different, and yet so similar. They were both stubborn. If Father Bennis were going to leave the country, Cavanaugh knew he would become Detective Perez's chief suspect. If Jack was not going to help him, Cavanaugh decided he would have to find the killer himself. He didn't trust purple-headed Detective Perez, her steroid driven abominable snowman partner, or quick draw taser Officer Jefferson.

He wiped the rain from his face and heard a voice call out from the police barrier across the street. He turned to see a woman in a slick yellow raincoat and a huge umbrella. "Over here," she called waving with her umbrella. "It's me. I need to talk to you."

He didn't recognize the voice and couldn't see the face. "Do I know you?" he said walking across the street.

"I'm Lucy Bauer. I'm a reporter. We worked together tracking down the Staten Island Butcher. Do you remember me?"

"Yeah. I remember you now. But, lady, we never worked together. You were an obnoxious, persistent reporter who we couldn't get rid of."

"Well, thanks to my reporting of that case, I was nominated for an Emmy award in Crime News and I'm now working with the *New York Times*."

"Doesn't sound like much of an improvement, but what do you want from me?"

Lucy Bauer pulled her umbrella closer to Cavanaugh. "Watch that thing, will you?" he shouted stepping back. "You can poke someone's eye out with it."

Ms. Bauer lowered her voice. "Your brother found the body. I thought we might be able to work together on this."

The rain increased. Cavanaugh felt the rain rolling down his back. He didn't like working with reporters. They were unreliable. They printed what they wanted and some twisted the facts to meet their own or their editors' goals. He remembered she had studied law in graduate school. He looked straight into her eyes. He had nothing to go on. Sometimes hope, he thought, is as scarce as a midnight rainbow. Maybe he could work with her.

"Okay," he said, "you first. What can you tell me?"

"No, Cavanaugh, it's not going to work like that. You first."

She was shrewd, persistent, and knowledgeable. But what could he tell her? He didn't know much. He reached out and grabbed the umbrella and ducked under it. "Okay. The guy my brother found was well-dressed. Jack never saw him before. One of the cops told me he thought he was a private detective."

"His name is Dave Melrose. He was a mediocre lawyer who used to be an ambulance chaser until he got in trouble with drugs and alcohol. Recently he concentrated on divorces."

"Divorces?" Cavanaugh paused. "That might explain the eyes. Maybe he saw something he shouldn't have."

"What about his eyes?"

"My brother told me his eyes were cut out."

Lucy Bauer moved closer to Cavanaugh. "Maybe the killer is keeping them as some sort of sick trophy."

Cavanaugh shook his head. "One of my sources tells me, they found the eyes in the dead guy's pocket."

"I didn't know that," Bauer said. "They are probably keeping that secret. I may be able to use this to get more information.

Cavanaugh reached into his pocket and gave her his business card. "If you hear anything else, Ms. Bauer, give me a call. I'm getting soaked here. I'm going home." He had given her enough. There was no need to tell her about the note through the victim's throat or the fact that his brother was going to Colombia in the morning.

As he turned to go, she slipped him her business card. "It goes both ways, big guy. If you hear anything else, please give me a call."

"Count on it," he lied jogging through the rain to his car.

* * * *

Chapter 2

Staten Island, New York

After making arrangements to catch the 8:20 a.m. flight from Newark, New Jersey, to Cartagena, Colombia, Jack Bennis packed a few essentials and then woke the pastor to explain why he was abruptly leaving. Father Eugene Vivaldi was a meticulous, strongminded individual who had been captain of his high school basketball and football teams and magna cum laude in college. He worked two successful years on Wall Street before deciding to become a priest. His sermons were frequently long and boring, but he had been handpicked to study in Rome and rumors were he was on a fast-track to become a bishop one day.

The conversation with Father Bennis did not go well. The volatile and hot-tempered exchange of ideas, which included a number of words not usually associated with the clergy, woke up Monsignor O'Brien and possibly a few neighbors in the apartments near the rectory.

Fr. Vivaldi ultimately said, "I forbid you to go to Colombia."

"I'm telling you this," Bennis said, "so you can make arrangements for someone to cover my duties when I am gone."

"Didn't you hear what I just said? I forbid you to leave and go to Colombia!"

Jack Bennis wore his black suit and Roman collar. He stood an inch or two taller than Fr. Vivaldi whose arms were folded about his blue-plaid flannel pajamas.

"I didn't come to your room to ask permission. I came to tell you I was leaving. I have an Uber outside now waiting for me. You do what you have to do, Father. I am doing what I have to do. May God bless both of us."

As the door closed behind Bennis, Fr. Vivaldi whispered to himself, "That arrogant, insolent bastard! Who does he think he is? Nobody talks to me like that!"

* * * *

When Cavanaugh arrived home, he found his wife Fran sitting with a cup of coffee at the computer. "What are you doing up?" he asked.

"I couldn't get back to sleep after you left, so I came down here and started checking news I may have missed when I went to visit my sister two weeks ago."

Cavanaugh shook the rain off and poured himself a cup of black coffee.

"Do you remember," Fran asked, "that bar we used to go to on Forest Avenue?"

"Sure I do. I hear now it's become a hangout for kids, a lot of college kids, but underage kids as well."

Fran pointed to the computer. "It says here two seventeen-year-old boys died there of heroin overdoses."

"That was a couple of weeks ago. I remember reading about it. Apparently the kids were given heroin laced with fentanyl, a powerful opiate 100 times more powerful than morphine. When mixed together with heroin, it becomes a dangerous concoction which has killed too many people."

"I don't understand. Why would young people endanger their lives by taking this drug? They have a whole lifetime ahead of them."

"There are a million reasons why people take drugs. For some it numbs their emotions and lowers their inhibitions. The tragic part is many of these kids don't even know the drug they are taking contains fentanyl. The drug dealers cut fentanyl into drugs like heroin because it's cheap and available, and easy to make. The kid who takes the laced drug doesn't realize what he or she is taking can kill them. I have heard of individuals who had fatal overdoses after even one heroin-fentanyl combination."

"I don't understand why these people take the chance. It doesn't make sense to me."

"The drugs are very addictive. In 2016, over two million people ages 12 and older had an opioid use disorder. Today it's probably even higher and with fentanyl even more dangerous."

Fran turned to Cavanaugh. There were tears in her eyes. Her hands were shaking. "What's the matter, Fran?" he said hugging her.

"It's Stephen. What kind of a world have we brought our son into?"

He held her tightly. He thought of the man with no eyes, his brother leaving for South America, little Chico missing somewhere in Colombia, and dead teenagers and their parents. For the second time in two hours, he lied. "Don't worry, Fran," he whispered. "Everything will be all right."

* * * *

Chapter 3

Liberty International Airport, Newark, New Jersey

The flight to Cartagena, Colombia, did not depart on time. Rumors spread around the departure lounge like sparks from a bonfire. It was another technical outage affecting all airlines. It was another computer issue like a previous one that delayed over one hundred flights at Newark Liberty International Airport a month ago. It was some kind of maintenance issue with the aircraft. No one knew for sure, but tempers began to rise as minutes turned into hours.

Amid the complaints of passengers and the cries of infants, Father Bennis sat quietly clutching his overnight bag in his lap while his mind raced like a mouse on amphetamines. Where had Chico gone? How would he find him? What had prompted him to leave school and disappear? Had something happened to him?

Fr. Bennis overheard a young couple behind him discussing their pending adoption of a Colombian baby. "Mary, are you sure this is the right thing?" the man asked. "Carlos told me at work that a lot of these babies come from drug addicted mothers. Sometimes the mother's addiction affects the baby's brain. What if we get a child who has special needs? Can we turn him back?" The woman whispered sharply, "We discussed this before, Joseph. How many times do we have to go over this? It's not like we are picking up a puppy at the pound. The doctor said I can't have babies. We agreed that we want a family. We are adopting a human being, not a puppy. We will take care of him and give him all the love we can, no matter what. God will provide."

Bennis closed his eyes and pictured little Chico with his large sombrero warning him about the assassin hiding behind the barn. He saw the killer fire at María Isabelle a moment before he was able to reach him and snap his neck. Chico had saved their lives.

A soccer ball bounced off his leg. The priest opened his eyes. Four small boys raced down the aisle oblivious of the priest. Across from him a mother nursed her child and three older men discussed the greatest soccer players in Colombian history. The shortest one's belly looked like he had swallowed a watermelon. He munched on an unlighted cigar as he definitively advocated for striker Arnold Iguaran, from Riohacha, who retired from professional soccer at the age of 40 having scored a record-breaking 25 goals in 68 games for Colombia.

The tallest of the three proudly twirled his moustache and insisted the young midfielder James Rodríguez, from Cúcuta, had the potential to be even better based on his scoring six goals to earn the top-scorer spot at the 2014 World Cup in Brazil.

The oldest of the three shook his head and insisted there was no Colombian player who could compare with Pelé. He waved his finger at the other two and shouted how Pelé was voted World Player of the Century and was the most successful league goal-scorer in soccer history scoring 650 goals in 694 league games.

Fr. Bennis closed his eyes again. He wanted to block out the noise around him. He felt the two letters in his breast pocket. The typed one was from Chico's school. That was why he was here. The other one was handwritten. It looked like it was written by a woman. He still had not opened it. He recognized the writing from a previous letter he received. He feared it was from María Isabelle. Was she reaching out to him again? Why was he drawn to her? He shook his head like a wet dog and tried to block out all thoughts of María Isabelle. "Lead us not into temptation," his whispered to himself.

*　*　*　*

Staten Island, New York

After a quick shower, Cavanaugh peeked into his son Stephen's room. He smiled at how peaceful Stephen looked in his crib. Fran was right. What kind of a world would he be growing up in? Wherever one looked there seemed to be chaos, hostility, turmoil, discord. His brother, the priest, would claim it was the Devil at work. Cavanaugh wasn't so sure. He thought it was the self-centered, pleasure-seeking attitude of man at work. It really didn't make much difference to him. He was convinced the world was going to hell in a handbasket.

It may be a losing battle, he thought, but for his son and all the other innocent people he had to fight the good fight. He had to do whatever he could to rid the world of people who would mutilate and kill others. As he was wondering where he would start, the phone rang again.

The Caller ID indicated it was from the NYPD. He

tentatively picked the phone up and recognized the voice on the other end. "Cavanaugh, is this you? This is Detective Goldberg."

"Morty? I hear it's Chief Detective Goldberg now. Congratulations. To what do I owe the pleasure of your call?"

"This isn't a pleasure call, Cavanaugh. This is business. I just got a call from a Father Vivaldi, the pastor of St. Peter's. He tells me your brother has skipped town and he suspects he may be involved in the murder in his church."

Cavanaugh was silent.

"I'm calling you to give you a heads-up. We both know Detective Perez would like to crucify you if she has the chance. What's the story?"

"Jack didn't kill that guy. He just found the body when he was closing up the church. You know him. You know he wouldn't do this."

"I don't think he would, but where is he and why did he suddenly leave? It doesn't look good."

Cavanaugh took a deep breath and then told Goldberg in detail how his brother received a letter from Chico's school in Colombia stating the boy had disappeared. He told him that the school and the police had been unable to find him. Jack Bennis felt responsible for the young boy and left to find him.

"That's *meshugge*! That's crazy!" Goldberg stated. "How is he going to find the kid after all this time when the school and the police haven't found him?"

"You know my brother, Morty. You know how he is."

"This is more serious than you know. I think we have a very sick serial killer on our hands."

"I figured when I heard he left a card with the number 2 on it that might be the case. But why the church and why the eyes?"

Goldberg hesitated. "What I am about to tell you is confidential. I don't want to go reading about it in the papers. A couple of months ago there was a fire in a small Pentecostal store-front church on Bay Street. There was a body found in the ruins that we initially thought was some homeless guy who wandered into the church and accidentally knocked over a candle or something. The body was burned pretty badly. It took forensics a while to identify the body."

"Who was he?"

"As I said, the body was almost completely burned. We didn't have dental records, so we had to go by DNA, and that took some time."

"Come on, Morty, cut to the chase. How is this guy connected to the body my brother found in St. Peter's?"

Cavanaugh heard Goldberg clicking his ballpoint pen. He remembered how annoyed he got listening to the pen go click, click, click, click when they were partners and he was trying to concentrate on completing incident reports.

"You remember, Jimmy Monreale from the lab?" Goldberg asked. "He's very conscientious. He wouldn't let the death of the burn victim go. He analyzed everything. He found some human DNA in one of the vic's pockets. It wasn't much, but it had traces of what appeared to be granular material around it."

"Do you think this might have been his eyes that were burned in the fire?"

"It might well have been, but what was in what was left of the other pocket was most significant. He found traces of what looked like toast but could have once been a roll or a bagel. The bread had traces of beer and salt on it."

Cavanaugh shook his head. "So what does this have to do with Dave Melrose? What's so unusual for a homeless guy to wander into a church looking for a place to sleep after having a few beers? Maybe he swiped the bread planning to eat it later."

"I won't ask you how you found out the name of the latest victim or how you found out we found his eyes in one of his pockets. But what you don't know is that when we checked the name of the vic in the Pentecostal church, we found he wasn't just a homeless guy. He had a record. He was arrested last year for exposing himself to a third grade class of girls at the Staten Island Ferry Terminal."

Cavanaugh took a deep breath. "What else don't I know?"

"In Melrose's other pocket," Goldberg began slowly and deliberately, "we found a half-eaten roll that had been soaked in beer and had traces of salt on it."

Cavanaugh remained silent for a while and then said, "So your thinking is the pervert in the fire might have had his eyes gouged out too, and the eyes and the index card indicating this was the first of his killings might have been destroyed in the fire?"

"I'm convinced we have a very sick serial killer on our hands who is playing with us."

"I don't know, Morty. It's pretty flimsy if you ask me. No District Attorney would pursue this."

"I'm telling you, Tom. This is serious. The killer is smart and deliberate. He or she is leaving clues and taunting us. I called you to give you a head's up about your brother. But I also called you to ask your help. You always were a good detective. Sometimes I may not have approved of your methods, but you were effective and got the job done. You can do things as a private citizen that we can't. It's as simple as that."

"I want to help you, Morty, but I'm not convinced you

have a serial killer on your hands. Aside from the number 2 on Melrose and that both bodies were found in a church, there is no proof. It could all be a coincidence."

Goldberg laughed, "I thought you and your hero Charlie Chan didn't believe in coincidences."

"I don't, but your theory is pretty far out there."

"I didn't tell you what the granular material adhering to Melrose's eyes was. It turned out to be the same as what we found in the Pentecostal vic's pocket. It took us a while, but Jimmy Monreale is persistent. He finally identified it."

"What was it?"

"Corn flakes."

"Corn flakes?"

"That's what I said. I think our killer has a sick sense of humor and is letting us know there is more to come and he or she is a 'cereal' killer."

* * * *

Chapter 4

Cartagena, Colombia

Because of the departure delay, it was close to 5:00 p.m. when Fr. Bennis' plane touched down at Rafael Nuñez International Airport in Cartagena. It was too late to go to the school, so he took a taxi the short ride to St. Peter Claver Church. In some ways, St. Peter Claver Church reminded him of his assignment at the Cathedral of the Immaculate Virgin Mary in Havana, Cuba. They were both located on a plaza, had two large bell towers, and were popular tourist stops. St. Peter Claver Church, however, had a clock in the middle of the bell towers and the bones of St. Peter Claver displayed in a gold glass encasement in the main altar.

Like Jack Bennis, Peter Claver was a Jesuit priest. Claver's god-father was Christopher Colombus. In the seventeenth century, because of its position in the Caribbean Sea, Cartagena became the chief slave-market of the New World. The Spaniards needed workers to cultivate the land they had conquered and to work in the gold mines. They decided to import Negroes from the coasts of Guinea, the Congo, and Angola as slaves.

A thousand slaves arrived in Cartagena each month.

And although half the human cargo might die on the voyage from Africa, the profit was large and no censures from the Church could stop the booming slave trade. In Africa slaves were bought for 6 francos, and when shipped to Cartagena, they were resold for an average 100 francos. Since he could not stop the human trafficking of slaves, Peter Claver did all he could to alleviate it.

Claver declared himself "the slave of the Negroes forever," and every month he went out to meet the slaves. They were chained, thin, naked, often sick and afraid. Many thought they would be killed when they arrived in Cartagena. Claver would battle the nauseating smells and the depressing sights, to bring food and to teach them about his faith. In spite of the criticism he received from slave merchants and others who regarded the slaves as somehow less than human, he persisted in his efforts for over forty years and is estimated to have brought the Christian faith to more than 300,000 slaves.

As his taxi pulled up to St. Peter Claver Church, Fr. Bennis recalled how Pope Leo XIII said that no life, except the life of Christ, moved him so deeply as that of Peter Claver. Claver was a simple man with a strong will and complete dedication and selflessness to his mission. It is said that Claver kissed wounds of the slaves and even licked the dirt from their sores.

Jack Bennis, too, had a mission. It was to find Chico. Walking into the church and looking down the long aisle to the illuminated bones of Peter Claver in the high altar, he knew he was prepared to do whatever it took to find the missing boy.

Upon entering the church, Bennis saw an elderly man with white hair and moustache and dark, brooding eyebrows. His shoulders were hunched over as he slowly mopped the church vestibule. "*Cuidado,*" he shouted in a cigarette cultivated voice.

"Good evening, Juan," Fr. Bennis said. "I see you are still working hard."

"Padre Bennis," Juan said straightening up and pulling his trousers up. "Where have you been? I was wondering about you, but no one would say. Things have been difficult here."

Bennis avoided the newly mopped tile and gave Juan a big hug. "It is good to see you. I had to go to the States. I came back because I heard the young boy I left with Monsignor Passeri has disappeared. I wanted to ask him what happened. He said he would arrange for the boy and his sister to stay with a family, but I heard they were placed in an orphanage. Now the boy has run away."

"You haven't heard? Monsignor had a stroke soon after you left. Father Mealey is in charge now. He has made a lot of changes around here. Some think he wants to be bishop or maybe even the pope. Not only am I the sacristan, but now I responsible for cleaning the church."

Bennis remembered Miguel Mealey. He was energetic, earnest, enterprising, and most of all ambitious. He would volunteer to visit the children's hospital, but be sure to notify the media when he would be there. He oozed piety like a festering wound. While his homilies frequently spoke about the need for penance and alms giving, his clothes were always the finest and his taste for fine wines rivaled that of the sommelier at the finest restaurant. He walked with the air of royalty and never failed to wear his black three peaked biretta with a distinctive tuft on top when in public. Jack Bennis sighed at the news Fr. Mealey had replaced Monsignor Passeri.

"Where can I visit Monsignor?" Bennis asked. "I need

to speak with him."

Juan lowered his head and made a quick the sign of the cross. "*Lo siento mucho.* Monsignor died a month ago."

"I am sorry to hear that. May his soul and the souls of all the faithful departed rest in peace. He was a good man." Jack Bennis hesitated a moment and then asked, "Where can I find Father Mealey?"

Juan pulled his suspenders up over his protruding belly. "He has gone to visit Cardinal Ricardo Guastella in Bogotá. He said he would be gone for the week."

A blanket of fatigue suddenly enveloped Fr. Bennis. "I won't be staying long, Juan. Do you think you might have a room available for me for the night."

"You deserve the best, Padre Bennis. Why don't you take Fr. Mealey's room? It is by far the nicest and its bed is quite comfortable. He left early this morning and won't be back for the week."

Bennis started to protest, but then thought he might be able to find something in Mealey's room to explain why he sent Chico and his sister to the orphanage. It would be good to visit the school tomorrow with more information than he had. He would follow the trail to find Chico.

"Thank you, Juan. I would very much appreciate that. I am tired. I will only stay tonight. I have much to do, and tomorrow promises to be a long day."

* * * *

Jack Bennis did not go straight to bed. He wandered around Fr. Mealey's room in search of something – anything – that might give him a clue to Chico's whereabouts. The walls were painted cardinal red. The room was immaculate and lavishly decorated. Poverty was definitely not a vow Mealey coveted. A Queen sized four-posted bed replete with an elaborate red and gold canopy and matching bedspread stood in stark contrast to the single bed Bennis was accustomed to. On the opposite wall an intricately carved mahogany desk was surrounded by wall to wall book shelves. Fr. Mealey's degrees and photos of him with various political and social dignitaries and celebrities hung from a wall next to three large wooden filing cabinets.

Among various religious books Bennis observed were leather bound copies of Niccoló Machiavelli's *The Prince* and *Monita Secreta* allegedly written by Claudio Acquaviva. Bennis was familiar with *Monita Secreta* which dated back to the 17th century and claimed to be secret instructions of the Jesuits to gain power and wealth. It was long considered to be a forgery written to slander the Jesuits. The book claimed Jesuits were to use everything in their power to acquire wealth for the order. Looking around the room, Jack Bennis could see why it occupied a space in Fr. Mealey's library.

On the closet door, a wooden plaque proclaimed the Jesuit motto – *Ad majorem Dei gloriam* (For the glory of God). Bennis opened a closet door tentatively. He gazed in amazement at an assortment of what looked like custom made suits, cassocks, and vestments. He felt the material of the suits. They felt like silk. On the floor in carefully arranged files were dozens of shoes. In the right hand corner, a white sheet hung over a long slender object. Bennis lifted the sheet slowly. He gasped when he realized what Fr. Mealey had hidden beneath the sheet. It was the ancient Muisca spear young Chico rescued from the hidden tunnels in Mompas. He pictured little Chico clutching the spear with his pet spider monkey perched on his shoulder. What was the Muisca spear doing here in Fr. Mealey's closet? The ancient gold and silver spear would be worth a lot of money. As a historical artifact the spear was almost priceless. As Chico's personal treasure, the spear was priceless. What was it doing in Fr. Mealey's closet? Did the spear have something to do with Chico's disappearance? And more important, where was Chico?

* * * *

Chapter 5

Staten Island, New York

The following morning, Tom Cavanaugh sat at his kitchen sink staring out the window at the adjacent cemetery. He hadn't gotten much sleep the night before. The information Morty Goldberg had given him disturbed him. Why had Dave Melrose been murdered? Why had his body been left in St. Peter's Church? Was his murder in some way connected to the burnt body found in the Pentecostal church on Bay Street? Why were Melrose's eyes gouged out? Why leave the eyes in his pocket? Why the half-eaten beer-soaked bread in his other pocket? What was going to happen when his nemesis, Detective Perez, discovered his brother had left the country?

He got up and fixed himself another cup of black coffee and a peanut butter and jelly sandwich. Fran always complained about his eccentric eating habits, but Fran had taken little Stephen to her sister's and he felt like a peanut butter and jelly sandwich.

Cavanaugh took the coffee and sandwich back to the window and scanned the headstones in the abandoned cemetery. Weeds seemed to thrive amid the aged tombstones and scattered debris. Some of the headstones had fallen, some cracked with age. He wondered if anyone ever visited the graves. Did anyone miss Dave Melrose or the burned body? Did Melrose have any relatives? What kind of cases was he working on?

He watched a black bird swoop down through the trees and snatch a field mouse. Suddenly, his stomach tightened. What was he going to do when Detective Perez confronted him about his brother?

He jumped almost spilling his coffee when the phone rang. "Let it ring," a voice in his mind said. "It's probably another telemarketer." He looked at the number. He didn't recognize it. Something might have happened to Fran and Stephen. Maybe it was from his brother. His hand shook as he picked up the receiver.

It was Lucy Bauer, the reporter. "You didn't tell me your brother left the country," she began.

"How did you find out?"

"The pastor of the church, Father Vivaldi, called the editor to tell him. He thinks your brother might be involved in the murder of Melrose."

"That's ridiculous. You've met my brother. He would not do that."

Bauer's voice rose an octave. "I don't think so either so I did some research."

"What did you find?"

"You first."

"No way. I went first last night. It's your turn. What did you find?"

"There's another priest assigned to that parish. Everybody calls him Father Steve."

"Yeah. I heard about him. My brother told me he studied in Rome and sometimes says the Mass in Italian. The people seem to like him."

"Well, I did a little digging. Father Steve was born in Sicily. His last name is Impellizzieri. His grandfather was Giuseppe Impellizzieri, one of the most powerful notorious bosses of the Cosa Nostra. When Giuseppe died, his oldest son Mario became boss. From what I learned, Mario is a very, very dangerous man. He is reported to be into everything from protective racketeering, money laundering, drugs, smuggling, and human trafficking. Fr. Steve is Mario's only son."

Cavanaugh sipped his coffee and let her information sink in. Dave Melrose could very well have been investigating the Impellizzieri family and stumbled onto something that cost him his life. Maybe he saw something he shouldn't have and that was why his eyes were removed. Or maybe his murder had nothing to do with the Impellizzieri family.

"Well," Lucy Bauer said, "what do you think?"

"I think it's very interesting, but it doesn't prove anything except that you are one damn good reporter."

"Okay. Enough flattery. What do you have for me?"

Cavanaugh ran his fingers through his hair and rubbed the back of his neck. She was a good reporter. She had access to sources he didn't have. He had to give her something, but he had promised Goldberg he wouldn't give information to the press. He walked around the kitchen island, opened the refrigerator, then closed it.

"Well," Bauer said, "what do you have for me?"

"Okay. Listen. I'm not sure it means anything, but you might want to check on recent deaths in local churches. That's all I can tell you."

"Recent murders? There weren't any."

"I didn't say murders. I said 'deaths.' You're the reporter. It may be nothing, but it's all I have right now."

"You know you're a creep, Cavanaugh! You're holding out on me. We had a deal! You're a conniving fraud. You're nothing more than a dirty weasel and a liar. I hate your guts!"

Cavanaugh sighed, "Yeah, I seem to have heard that a few times before." But Lucy Bauer didn't hear him. She had already hung up.

* * * *

Cartagena, Colombia

Father Bennis looked at the large yellow brick building on a cobblestone road in one of the poorest sections of the city. It looked like an industrial complex with bars on the windows. The sign on the side of the building, however, said it was St. Benedict Joseph Labre School and Orphanage.

He walked up to the massive front door, rang the bell, and waited a few minutes. Finally, a nun in a white habit, a crucifix dangling from her neck, and rosary beads attached to a plain rope belt opened the large metal doors. The nun had beautiful unblemished, unwrinkled skin. Her brown eyes conveyed both physical and spiritual beauty. With one hand on the massive door and the other clutching her crucifix, she asked who he was.

The priest explained he had come to speak to the principal about a missing boy named Chico.

"I am Sister Gracelyn Sánchez, the principal. I sent you a letter months ago and you never responded."

"Yes. I know. Unfortunately, there was a delay. I came as soon as I read your letter. May I come in and discuss the matter with you?"

The nun moved back and pointed to the end of the corridor. ""My office is at the end of the hall. I will be with you as soon as I secure the door."

Fr. Bennis walked down the dark hall. The walls were painted the same yellow as the outside of the building. There were no bulletin boards or samples of students' work on the walls. On both sides there appeared to be classrooms, but the doors were windowless and closed. He heard his footsteps echoing in the hall, but no sign or sound of children.

Sister Gracelyn's office was painted bright white. There were five file cabinets by the window which had iron bars on it. Sister's desk was a simple wood table with a telephone and a number of open folders. There were three worn wooden ladder-back chairs in the room. One was the principal's, and the other two were for visitors. A large crucifix hung behind Sister's desk and a picture of the archbishop and the pope on the opposite wall.

He stood until Sister returned.

"Have a seat," she said.

"Gracelyn is a very beautiful name. I believe it means 'grace or blessing by the lake.' May I call you Gracelyn?"

"You may call me Sister."

"I came to see what happened to Chico," he said.

Sister's eyes seemed to say, 'It took you long enough," but she said nothing and swung toward the file cabinets, her rosary beads flying after her as she rifled through the files and extracted a manila envelope.

"What happened to cause him to leave, Sister?"

She sat down, opened the file and passed it to him. "We did everything we could to find him. We even notified the police."

Fr. Bennis read the file and then looked back at the nun. "What happened to cause him to leave?"

"It's all in the file, Father Bennis. The boy had an altercation with his teacher and was sent to my office. He never arrived. Apparently, he left the building and has not been seen since."

"What caused this altercation?"

"If you read his file, Father, you will see he has been in trouble since he arrived here. Because of this, he was placed in Sister Magdalena Albatross's class. She is a disciplinarian and one of our strongest teachers. The thought was if anyone could tame him, Sister Magdalena could. Apparently, we were wrong."

Father Bennis looked up from the file. "Chico is not an animal that needs to be tamed. He is a young boy who saw his parents killed in cold blood and his home burned down. If anything, he needs love."

"The boy was sent to us. This school and orphanage were named after St. Benedict Joseph Labre who met many failures in life. He was different from others as the children who are sent here are. Our job is to prepare them for the world outside. It is a rough world and they need discipline."

"As I recall, St. Benedict reacted against the banality and excesses of the world and preferred to live a simple, unrestrained life. He was never a great student, but he had a profound distrust of the world you speak of. Indeed, he used to say, 'Our comfort is not in this world.' But, Sister, I did not come here to argue or discuss your methods. I came to find Chico."

Sister Gracelyn folded her arms in her habit. "I told you, Father, we do not know where he went."

Bennis closed the folder and stared at the nun. "With your permission, Sister, I would like to speak with his teacher, Sister Magdalena."

"What good would that do? Sister Magdalena does not know where he is."

"I want to get a better picture of Chico. Perhaps, if I

find out what motivated him, I will be able to find him." He leaned forward and smiled. "After all, Sister, we are all trying to do the right thing, aren't we?"

* * * *

Staten Island, New York

Cavanaugh decided the first place he would start his investigation was the church where Dave Melrose's body was found. He wanted to look around. Maybe, if he were lucky, he would confront the priest who gave up his brother to the police and the press.

There was a funeral going on when he arrived at St. Peter's. A cordon of police tape marked off the place where his brother found Melrose's body. A lone police officer sat in a pew by the tape texting or playing a game on his cell phone. He seemed oblivious of the honor guard standing by the coffin in the center aisle or the deacon eulogizing the 96-year-old veteran who apparently loved pasta, the horses, homemade wine, and the Yankees.

There were few mourners in the church. Cavanaugh figured most of the 96-year old's friends were no longer around. He quietly moved behind the police officer and checked out the crime scene.

The killer or killers could have brought the body in from a side door. But why leave the body in a church? Cavanaugh looked around. Votive candles were on a side aisle. The Stations of the Cross hung from the concrete walls. Based on the crime scene tape, the body was positioned next to the first Station of the Cross – Jesus is condemned to die. The detailed painting of the Station depicted Jesus being led away by armed bodyguards as Pontius Pilate washes his hands in the background. Cavanaugh wondered. Was Melrose's body deliberately placed next to this Station for a reason? The killer could have positioned the body anywhere else in the church. Why here?

The pall bearers from Scalia's Funeral Home in their black suits quietly came down the main aisle to escort the 96 year-old to his final resting place. The few mourners that were present trailed behind the casket. The white linen covering was removed from the casket and replaced with an American flag. The priest who conducted the service greeted the mourners as they left.

Cavanaugh joined the line. He wanted to question the pastor who implicated his brother in Melrose's murder. But, as he approached the priest, he overheard a white haired woman dressed in black who was hunched over and walked with a cane address the priest. "Thank you so much, Father Steve," she said. "Mike would have appreciated your comments. He so loved the Yankees." She hugged the priest and added in a stage whisper, "Personally, I like the Mets, but I never told him that."

Fr. Steve Impellizzieri smiled and said, "We all have things it is sometimes better to keep to ourselves. May he rest in peace."

Cavanaugh stood back. So the handsome, young priest was Father Steve Impellizzieri. He wanted to ask him about his family, about the pastor, about his brother, but there is a time for everything, he thought, and this wasn't the time.

* * * *

Cartagena, Colombia

When Sister Magdalena waddled into the principal's office, Fr. Bennis was surprised. She was much older than

Sister Gracelyn. Unlike the slender, elegant figure of Sister Gracelyn, Sister Magdalena's habit looked more like a loose fitting tent. She had a little tuft of hair on her chin, her skin was the color and texture of leather, and her false teeth shifted as she spoke. But it was her eyes that struck Fr. Bennis first. There was a fierceness, a fire, and a lack of compassion in them.

Sister Gracelyn explained that Fr. Bennis came to inquire about Chico. "What has that miscreant gotten into now?" Sister Magdalena snapped.

"I came to find out where he is, Sister," the priest said.

"If you ask me he should be in Hell!"

Fr. Bennis felt his temper rising. "It is obvious you didn't get along with the boy, Sister. Can you tell me what he did to cause your rather strong reaction to him?"

Sister Magdalena sat down with a thud and pounded the desk. "I'll tell you what that little imp did. He placed a live boa constrictor snake in my desk drawer. And that wasn't the first time he caused a disturbance in my class. Once he let loose three field mice. Another time he filled my desk with bright orange assassin bugs. He was always causing trouble. One day I was teaching the class about the story of Jonah and the whale and explaining that some of the Old Testament stories in the Bible were symbolic. Jonah was a reluctant prophet. He did not want to do God's work. Chico stood up in the middle of the class and explained that the story was true and that Jonah did actually stay three days in the belly of the whale. The more I tried to explain that he could not have survived in the whale, the more he shouted that the story was true. Then he said, when he got to Heaven he would ask Jonah himself. When I asked what if Jonah wasn't in Heaven, he laughed and said, 'Then you can ask him when you go to Hell!'"

44

Bennis suppressed a smile at the old joke Sister had fallen for. "And did you punish him for his transgressions?" he asked.

"Of course I did! I do not tolerate impertinence in my classroom. Children need to be taught discipline." Her eyes seemed to glow with fire.

"May I ask, Sister," Fr. Bennis said, "how did you discipline Chico?"

"I did what I do to all the children who misbehave in my class. I use my ruler across their hands or their backsides. Boys and girls. It makes no difference. They all need to be taught the proper way to behave."

Bennis saw no sense arguing with Sister Magdalena. She was a dinosaur from another time. He had grown up with nuns like her. It was what they were taught. He didn't blame them. The times had changed, but Sister Magdalena had not. He left St. Benedict Joseph Labre Orphanage with sadness in his heart. But there was a glimmer of hope there, too. The only thing Chico had apparently taken with him was his large sombrero. The field mice, the non-poisonous boa, and the orange assassin bugs meant Chico had access to some kind of natural habitat. The assassin bugs usually hide under bark or between rocks, in or near flowers or certain plants waiting patiently for insects to land in their traps. Field mice are nocturnal animals and are found all over the place. They frequently burrow underground if they live in wild. The boa is found in many different areas but prefers to live in rainforests where they sometimes occupy the burrows of other animals and where they hide.

Jack Bennis smiled. Cartagena had a large park just outside the walled city. Parque del Centenario was fenced in and closed at night, but that would not stop Chico. Amid the trees, flowers, and pond, there were birds, iguanas, tamarins, sloths, and monkeys in the park. Chico was at home in the jungles of Mompas. He would feel at home in the park and it would make a suitable place for him to find bugs, mice, and snakes to torment Sister Magdalena.

But where would Chico be now? He couldn't hide in the park forever. Where did he go?

* * * *

Staten Island, New York

Cavanaugh's next stop was Dave Melrose's business address. It turned out to be a small rented office on the top floor of the old Paramount Theatre on Bay Street. He parked across the street at a McDonald's and ordered a double bacon smokehouse burger complete with cheddar cheese and fried onion strings. If Fran were with him she would have coaxed him to order a grilled chicken salad, but Fran wasn't with him and he was hungry.

He sat at a table by the window and watched the entrance to the long closed Paramount Theatre. At one time, he knew there were a number of theatres on Staten Island, but now there were few. The times had changed. As he watched the theatre, he recognized Detective Perez's car parked outside the theatre. She was doing what he expected her to do. She was checking on Dave Melrose's clients and business associates. Depending on how persuasive she and her partner were, they might need a court order to obtain the information she was looking for.

"Checking the old Paramount out, are you?" a heavy-set black man in a tattered, stained blue double-breasted peacoat said as he slid into the seat next to him. The man had long brown dreadlocks steaked with gray that cascaded over his shoulders. His eyes hid behind dark aviator sunglasses. "You know that place opened in 1930 before you were born. It was built on what was once Cornelius Vanderbilt's childhood farmhouse."

Cavanaugh glanced at him, but said nothing.

"They tried to restore it a lot of times, but nothing worked. They wanted to make it into a restaurant and use it for special events, but it all came to nothing. It was like they kept throwing money in the sewer. Now they use it occasionally to make movies."

Cavanaugh continued to eat his double bacon smokehouse burger while watching the Paramount building and Detective Perez's car.

"But you're not interested in any of that shit, are you? You're waiting for the cops to leave."

Cavanaugh stopped eating. "And who the hell are you?" he asked.

"Just a friend who could use a good meal in exchange for information about Dave Melrose."

"And just what do you know about Dave Melrose?"

"A lot more than Monica will tell you."

"And who's Monica?"

"She's Melrose's wife. She really runs the place. They hated each other's guts. She's probably pleased the creep's dead."

Cavanaugh saw out of the corner of his eye Perez and her Hulk partner leave the Paramount. They didn't look happy. Apparently, Monica wasn't that cooperative. He turned his attention to the overweight man next to him. He could smell his mucous-laden breath. "Okay. What do you know?"

"I know you're not a cop, but probably were at one time. For some reason you want information on Melrose and you want to avoid the police." He wiped his nose with his sleeve. "I also know I'm hungry and food costs money; the same as information."

Cavanaugh reached in his pocket and pulled out a twenty dollar bill. The man stared at it and said nothing. Cavanaugh pulled out another twenty and the man smiled. The fat man's hand swiped up the bills like a bullfrog snapping a fly over a lily pond. "Melrose was working on a missing person. A young woman came into his office about a month ago looking to find her brother. She was pretty and had a lot of dough. Her husband was some kind of financial guy. She claimed to be from Cincinnati and was concerned her brother didn't check in with her. Apparently, they spoke to each other every Sunday."

"What was this guy's name?"

"I think it was Brackmen or Bateman, or something like that. I'm not too good on names. I could check it out for you. I think he had gotten into some kind of trouble in Cincinnati and probably came to New York to avoid the cops."

"And why would she come to Melrose of all people?"

The big man was sweating. He held out his chubby fingers again. "You know, I'm real hungry, Mister. Talking builds up my appetite."

Cavanaugh threw another twenty on the table.

The fat man continued. "The last address she had for him was from a flop house down from the ferry on Slosson Terrace, not too far from that church that burnt down. She said she looked Melrose up on Google."

"And how do you supposedly know all this? If you're lying to me, I promise you, I'll find you, and you will be sorry you ever met me."

The man wiped his forehead. "Melrose's wife is my

sister. She told me he was stringing the Cincinnati chick along while he worked a divorce case involving some mob boss who was cheating on his wife."

Cavanaugh leaned forward. "And who was this mob boss?"

The big man slowly rose from his seat. "You don't have enough money to get me to tell you that." He reached over and grabbed a handful of Cavanaugh's French fries. "You know," he said, "McDonald's makes the best fries. Say hello to my sister." And then, as quickly as he had come, he disappeared into a noisy crowd of high school students returning from a class trip.

*   *   *   *

Cavanaugh crossed the street and entered the old Paramount building. Dave Melrose's office was on the third floor. Walking up the three flights, he recalled when he could have raced up the stairs two at a time. This time, however, he was out of breath by the time he reached the third floor. Fran was right. He needed to exercise more and maybe cut down on the cheeseburgers.

Age and lack of care had its effect on the building. Paint was peeling from the drab walls, the stairs creaked, and the smell of urine was everywhere. At the end of the third floor a stenciled sign on opaque glass read, "David Melrose, Lawyer, and Private Investigator." He opened the door and saw a buxom blonde with legs that never ended sitting behind a Costco folding table containing a single phone. There was a metal filing cabinet in the corner. The blonde wore a tight red dress as she filed her nails and chewed gum at the same time. She bore no resemblance to the overweight black man in the Navy peacoat he encountered in the

McDonald's across the street.

"Excuse me," Cavanaugh said, "I'm here to see Mr. Melrose."

The blonde continued her filing and chewing as she said, "He's dead, honey. What can I do for you? I'm Monica, his wife and partner."

"I don't understand. I was just talking to a man who said he was your brother."

The woman looked up for the first time. She scanned Cavanaugh like an MRI. "I ain't got no brother. You a cop?" she asked.

"No."

"Anyone ever tell you, you look like a cop?"

"Yeah. I get that a lot, but I'm not a cop. I'm looking for some information about a missing person's case Mr. Melrose was working. I think the man's name was Brackmen or Bateman."

"It was Robert Bateman. But how do you know about it?"

Cavanaugh told her the man who claimed to be her brother told him Melrose was stringing Bateman's sister along while he worked a divorce case.

"And what did this brother I never had look like?"

Cavanaugh described him.

"He definitely ain't my brother. He sounds like Rufus, the cleaning guy. He must have been sniffing around my office. I'm going to kill him when I find him."

Cavanaugh continued. "Listen, Mrs. Melrose. I'm a private investigator, too. I'm looking into the death of your husband for one of my clients who is a person of interest in his murder. What can you tell me about Bateman and the divorce case your husband was working on?"

Monica Melrose put her emery stick down and looked

straight at Cavanaugh. "I don't know what your story is, buster, but information doesn't grow on trees. It costs. You want info; you have to pay for it."

Cavanaugh explained that the man she called Rufus had depleted his wallet. "That's none of my business, honey. There's an ATM machine in the lobby of this dump. Bring me back five Benjamin Franklins and I'll give you all I've got." She smiled and added in a sensuous voice, "And maybe a little more."

"Five hundred bucks? Are you crazy?"

The door behind him opened and two large men appeared.

"That's the deal, honey. You know where the machine is. Now beat it. I've got real business to attend to."

Cavanaugh left. At the second floor landing, he heard loud noises coming from the third floor. He stopped. It sounded like furniture fell. Then he heard glass break and a woman's cry for help. He turned around and bounded back up the stairs. The disturbance came from Melrose's office. The opaque glass was shattered. He heard Monica Melrose sobbing as something thudded onto the floor. He opened what was left of the door and saw one of the men setting fire to papers he had thrown on the floor from the filing cabinet. The other man was pistol whipping Mrs. Melrose.

Cavanaugh caught the assailant's arm and dislodged his gun. It fell to the floor as Cavanaugh dislocated the man's shoulder and promptly gave him a karate chop to the neck. The man collapsed gasping and trying to clutch his throat and shoulder at the same time.

The arsonist in the corner turned suddenly and reached for his gun. Cavanaugh's foot met the man's chin first. The man fell back into the flaming fire he had set. His clothes went up in flames as he squirmed around and screamed in the fire. Cavanaugh stood there ready to suffocate the flames with his jacket when he felt a bullet whiz by his head. The woman-beater had retrieved his gun. Cavanaugh dove behind the flaming man and using him as protection rolled his body toward the man with the gun. He was shooting with his left hand and his aim was off. Bullets flew over Cavanaugh's head and thumped into the burning man in front of him. Cavanaugh pulled his Sig Sauer P365 pistol from his ankle holster and fired four shots into the shooter. They all hit their target forming a perfect cluster in the center of the man's chest.

Cavanaugh got up slowly, smothered the flaming man, and looked around. Both men were dead. The smoldering files on the floor were destroyed. Monica Melrose lay on the floor. Her face was bruised and cut. One of her eyes was swollen. She was sobbing. He retrieved the phone from behind the table and called Morty Goldberg. He explained the situation and asked for an ambulance for Melrose's widow and a police investigation team. "Oh, by the way, Morty," he added, "what was the name of that guy who was killed in the church fire on Bay Street."

"Robert Bateman. Why?"

"Just checking," Cavanaugh said and hung up. He turned to Monica Melrose and asked, "Now what can you tell me about Robert Bateman and that divorce case your husband was working on?"

She looked up at him with one eye and slowly opened her mouth. At least two of her front teeth were missing. She wiped the blood flowing from her broken nose. She glanced in the corner at the burnt files. "Nothing," she said. "I learned my lesson. You better be careful, too, honey, if you know what's good for you."

*   *   *   *

Cartagena, Colombia

The streets of Cartagena rang out with music and song. Street performers danced, gyrated, and threw their bodies through the air. Vendors hawked everything from lemonade and *papas criollas* to necklaces and baseball caps. Women wearing colorful dresses carried fruit baskets on top of their heads. Tourists mingled through the narrow streets admiring the yellow, white, and red homes with their painted wooden balconies decorated with rainbows of flowers as bronze statues of chess players, gigantic shoes, and a large naked fat lady stood silently by.

But Father Jack Bennis saw and heard nothing. The beauty of Cartagena with its seven mile fortress surrounding the city and the bicycles and horse drawn carriages that passed him went unheeded. His mind ran through various scenarios where Chico might be found. If he were wearing his favorite sombrero, he would be easier to find. But how was Chico providing for himself? Bennis had seen teenagers from the Midwest who escaped the "confines" of their homes come to New York City to "find themselves" only to fall prey to the pimps and chicken hawks who lay in wait for them. And what were these innocent, naïve children to do? They had little or no money, no food, no place to live. While some would condemn their ultimate choices, Bennis never did. Necessity poses hard choices. As Irvin Yalom, the American existential psychiatrist, once wrote, "Things change; alternatives exclude." For every yes, there must be a no. Each decision we make in life eliminates other choices. The lines between good and evil are often hazy.

As he left the walled city of Cartagena, he only hoped he was not too late.

* * * *

53

Jack Bennis stood at the entrance to Parque del Centenario. A few homeless slept on the park benches as tourists ogled at the monkeys, red squirrels, parrots, and iguanas in the trees. He wondered what happened to Chico's pet spider monkey. There were street vendors all around the park. An older white-haired, stout man with a white shirt and a Panama hat guided tourists to see a sloth high in the trees. But where was Chico?

The priest approached a young boy about the age of Chico who was selling fruit and asked him in Spanish if had seen a boy with the large sombrero. The boy stiffened and looked around. "No, señor," he said staring across the street. Bennis bought a banana and walked across the path toward the white-haired man. As he peeled the banana, he glanced across the street. A dark-haired man with a thick moustache leaned against a gold building with white columns. His arms were folded and he was looking directly at the boy selling fruit.

"Excuse me," Bennis said after the white-haired man with the Panama hat had shown his tourists a sloth feeding her newborn baby, "I'm looking for a young boy...."

The man frowned and said, "No, Padre. I am not into that sort of thing."

"You misunderstand," Bennis said. "The boy ran away from St. Benedict Joseph Labre Orphanage. I am trying to find him. He was small and could be wearing a large sombrero."

The white-haired man hesitated. "There was a boy here a while back. He had a large sombrero, but he disappeared. He was selling fruit to the tourists, but I don't think he had approval."

Bennis reached in his pocket and pulled out a crisp twenty dollar bill. "Show me where the monkeys hide and tell me more about the man who gives approval."

* * * *

54

Chapter 6

Staten Island, New York

Dave Melrose was hired to find Robert Bateman. Bateman is killed in a fire in a storefront church. Then Melrose is killed in a church. Was there a connection or was it just a coincidence? After hours of questioning by the police, Cavanaugh sat in his car and tried to figure out the connection between Bateman and Melrose. He didn't believe in coincidences. Goldberg had told Cavanaugh that the only way they could identify Bateman was by his DNA. They only had his DNA on file because of a prior arrest he had at the Staten Island Ferry for exposing himself to a third grade group of girls. Could the motive for his death be revenge? Could one of the parents have been so pissed off at Bateman that he killed him? But why kill Melrose? Could Melrose have come across something in his investigation that implicated Bateman's murderer? And what about Robert Bateman's supposedly rich stepsister? How did she fit into this?

Cavanaugh needed more information. He called Goldberg again. "Listen, Morty, I've got an idea. I'm beginning to think you might be on to something about this

Bateman's death. Can you send me a list of the girls he allegedly exposed himself to?"

"I've got it right here. I was just reviewing it. There were eleven girls involved. If you want, I'll fax them to you."

Cavanaugh opened the glovebox of his car and took out a pad and a pen. "I don't do fax, Morty. If you read them to me, I'll copy them down."

"What do you mean you don't do fax? Everybody faxes."

"I don't. Can you just read me the names like the good Jewish boy you are, and I will copy them the old fashioned way?"

After a string of Yiddish words from Goldberg that Cavanaugh had no idea what they meant or how to pronounce them, he copied down the girls' names and addresses. "You're lucky it was a small group," Goldberg commented.

The names of the girls were:

1. Carolyn Wilton
2. Clarissa Quilty
3. Sophia Gambella
4. Wilhelmina Sikes
5. Kim Malloy
6. Emma Pacchiano
7. Rhoda Penmark
8. Harper Higgins
9. Amelia Rivers
10. Charlotte O'Hanlon
11. Cathy Gallagher

Cavanaugh studied the names. He asked, "Did you check the parents out?"

"There wasn't any need to at the time. Bateman's death wasn't thought to be a murder. It was my hunch. There's still not enough to go to the D.A. with."

"Is there anything I should know about the girls' families?"

"It's like I said. I haven't had the time to investigate them fully. But I think you should know Sophia Gambella is the daughter of Lawrence Gambella."

"I never heard of him. Who is he?"

"He owns a travel agency in Rosebank. Has a clean record. No problems with the law. He's president of the Italian American Society of Staten Island. He's on a number of corporate boards, including the Board of Staten Island Hospital, and is a major contributor to the Garibaldi Museum."

"Sounds like a decent guy. What's his deal?"

Goldberg hesitated, "It may mean nothing, but his family is from Sicily, and he is the first cousin of Mario Impellizzieri, the mob boss, who also just happens to be Sophia Gambella's godfather."

* * * *

Cartagena, Colombia

The white-haired man with the Panama hat proved most informative. Not only did he direct Jack Bennis to a family of tamarin monkeys jumping through the trees not far from the pavilion where some small children splashed in the fountain, but he explained who controlled the vendors and the nefarious after-hours activities that took place around the park and the walls of the city. As Bennis suspected, it was the man with the dark moustache leaning against the building across the street. His name was Lopez.

Bennis sat at a bench and drank a cup of Colombian coffee and waited for the park to close. He watched as the sun began to sink into the Caribbean Sea and the women of the night began to appear. One by one each of the vendors approached the man with the dark moustache and handed him money. After the last vendor left, Bennis approached Lopez. "Excuse me," he said, "I am looking for a young boy."

Lopez smiled. He looked the priest over. "What makes you think I can help you?"

Bennis moved closer. "I was told you were the one who could help me."

Lopez smiled again. Beneath his thick moustache were crooked yellow teeth. "It will cost you, Padre."

"How much?"

"Fifty American bucks a half hour," Lopez said.

"I will give you one hundred dollars, but I want to see a small boy around twelve years old."

Lopez smirked, "You like them young. I think I can help you, but I have to make a call."

"Then make your call. I will pay you, but I don't have all night. Make it fast."

Señor Lopez made his call and then led Fr. Bennis to a blue two story house a few blocks away. The house was dark. Only one light glowed in an upstairs window. "Here we are," Lopez said. "Now let's see your money."

Bennis counted out five twenty dollar bills. He made sure to show him he had more money in his wallet. "Okay. Show me where I have to go. I will follow you." He followed Lopez up the dark stairs. Bennis felt the walls. The paint was peeling. The stairs creaked, and the place smelled of dirt, urine, and sex. The hall at the top was almost completely dark except for a light flickering from under the door at the end. Bennis thought he heard muffled sobs from behind the door.

Lopez opened the door. A shirtless boy sat at the edge of a bed. His head was down. He was sniffling. "I'll be out here to lead you out so you don't get hurt," Lopez said. "You have a half-hour. Have fun."

Jack Bennis closed the door behind him and looked at the boy. He squatted down to get a closer look in the dimly lit room. There were tears running down the boy's cheeks. Bennis lifted the boy's chin. Then he stepped back suddenly. The boy looked up. He wasn't Chico. He was the young boy he had seen selling fruit in the park.

* * * *

"Who are you?" Jack Bennis whispered.

"I am Angel. Please don't hurt me."

"I won't, son. Tell me how you ended up here."

The boy told how his father was an alcoholic and abusive to him and his mother. They lived in Minca, a small village high in the Sierra Nevada Mountains. His father blamed him for everything. He ran away to get away from the constant yelling and beatings by his father. He wanted to be free and not have to answer to anyone. He thought Cartagena would be the perfect place. But without money or friends, he realized quickly he was wrong. The man with the dark moustache promised him a better life. Angel started sobbing again.

Fr. Bennis sat next to the boy and tried to calm him. "I am not going to hurt you. I came to find a young boy who I am worried about. His name is Chico and he is about your age. He usually wears a big sombrero. He ran away from the school he was in and I am trying to find him. I owe it to him. He saved my life and my brother's."

59

Angel looked up at the priest. He wiped the tears from his eyes. "What did he look like?" he asked.

Bennis described Chico and told how he came from Mompas and how he had seen both his parents murdered.

"Did he have a pet monkey?"

"Yes," the priest said. "The monkey's name was Sergio and he had lost his tail to a jaguar. Do you know him? Do you know where I can find him?"

"Chico was my friend. The man who brought you here took the both of us from the park one day when we were selling fruit. He tried to force us to do things we didn't want to do. They were bad things. Sinful things. I didn't want to do them. Neither did Chico. But Chico was stronger than I was. He refused, and they beat him. He was braver than I was."

"Now, listen to me, Angel. This is important. Do you know where Chico is?"

The boy looked down. "They are keeping him in the basement of the building where they keep me. I hear them beating him each night. They tell me if I do not do what they want, they will beat me like they do to Chico. I am sorry. I am a coward. They let me come to the park to sell fruit because I do what they want. I am a coward. I am not like Chico."

Suddenly, there was a loud rap on the door. "Finish up in there, Padre. I'm hungry and want to go home for dinner."

Jack Bennis leaned closer to Angel. "Do you want to get safely out of here?"

The boy nodded yes.

"Do you know where they are keeping Chico?"

The boy's body stiffened. "Someplace in a red building beyond the wall."

"What I am going to ask you to do will take courage, Angel. It may be dangerous, but I want you to take me to Chico."

"They will kill us! You don't know them."

Jack Bennis smiled. "They don't know me. I will take care of you. I promise. I need you to help me rescue Chico. I will get you out of this situation whether you help me or not. It's up to you. Your help would make it a little easier. Are you with me or not? It's your decision. Whatever it is, remember you are not a coward."

Two more loud thumps on the door. "Time's up, Padre!" Lopez shouted.

Bennis looked at Angel. The boy nodded. "I am with you."

* * * *

When Bennis opened the door, Lopez stood in front of him in the dark hallway. In his hand, he held a gun. The priest recognized the gun. It was an Obregón .45 caliber pistol, the same as he used when he was a Black Ops officer before he became a priest. The Obregón looked like the traditional Colt 1911 .45, but it was designed and made in Mexico.

Bennis looked at Lopez. He was an amateur. He was standing much too close. "What do you mean by this?" he asked stepping in front of Angel.

"What does it look like? I saw that wad of money you have in your wallet. I want it all."

"This is ridiculous. I paid you already. We had a deal."

"The deal's over. I hate predators like you. You make my stomach sick. You're nothing but a pervert and a hypocrite. I should just shoot you here. Now give me that wallet of yours."

Bennis moved as if to get his wallet with one hand, but swung his body and grabbed the pistol with the other. He twisted Lopez's wrist back and smashed the palm of his free hand into Lopez's nose. Lopez fell back releasing the gun and reaching for his nose.

Bennis took the gun and raked it across Lopez's face. "That was for calling me a pervert and a hypocrite. I don't prey on people like you do."

Lopez slid against the wall. "What do you want?"

"First, your shoes."

"My shoes?"

Bennis pointed the pistol at Lopez's head. "Don't make me have to ask you again."

Lopez quickly removed his shoes. Blood streamed down his face.

"Now, give me my hundred and all the other money you collected from the park vendors today."

"I can't do that. They'll kill me if I don't bring that money back."

The priest moved the pistol closer and rested it between Lopez's eyebrows. "The wages of sin, Señor Lopez, are often most costly. Need I remind you it is said that he who lives by the sword, dies by the sword. Now, give me the money and get out of here before I change my mind."

Lopez struggled to get up. "What am I going to tell them? They are expecting the money when I bring the boy back."

Bennis stepped back. "They are going to be very disappointed then because I am taking the boy, the money, and your shoes with me."

Lopez stumbled back along the dark hallway, shoeless with one hand holding the wall, the other holding his face. "But what am I going to tell them?"

Bennis released the safety on the gun and fired a shot into the floor by Lopez's feet. He lost his balance and tumbled down the stairs. As he staggered quickly out the front door, Bennis said, "You can tell them you met your worst nightmare or perhaps your last chance at redemption. Your choice."

*   *   *   *

Staten Island, New York

When Cavanaugh arrived home, Fran was busy preparing something in the kitchen. There were pots, pans, bowls, vegetables, and canisters all over the place. He gave her a hug and asked, "What's for dinner?"

Fran rolled her eyes. "My sister gave me this great recipe this afternoon."

Cavanaugh peeked over Fran's shoulder tentatively. "What is it?"

"You are going to love it! It's called Mexican chicken quinoa salad. It's a great combination of avocado, onions, spinach, carrots, red and yellow bell pepper, cucumber and jalapeno peppers. You mix it all together and add chicken-quinoa and salsa. It is really delicious."

Cavanaugh felt nauseous. He suppressed a gag response and said, "I'm sorry, Fran, but I think I'm allergic to that quinoa thing."

"You are so full of it, Thomas Cavanaugh. You don't even know what quinoa is. It is very good for you. It's high in protein, fiber, B vitamins, and it's gluten free!"

"Actually, Fran, I had a late lunch, and I'm really not that hungry. Plus I have a lot of work to do on the murder in Jack's church."

Fran turned with her hands on her hips. She had that look that told him she knew he was lying. Before she could say anything, however, the phone rang. "I'll get it. It might be Goldberg."

"It also might be Detective Perez. She left five messages for you."

Cavanaugh picked up the phone in the living room. It wasn't Perez, and it wasn't Goldberg. It was Lucy Bauer. "Before you say anything," she said, "I'm calling to apologize."

"What for? Could it be for calling me a creep, a fraud, a dirty weasel, or a liar?"

"Okay. I get it. I overreacted maybe a little. I did some checking as you thought I would. There was a fire in a storefront church on Bay Street a couple of months ago. Apparently, some homeless guy wandered into the church and started a fire. He was burned beyond recognition."

Cavanaugh collapsed into his favorite lounge chair. If he were going to clear his brother, he was going to need more help. He decided Lucy Bauer could do a lot of the legwork for him. "Are you there, Cavanaugh?" she asked.

"Yeah, I'm here. I'm just deciding what I'm going to tell you. Everything I tell you is off the record, and you have to promise me you won't print any of it."

"Okay," she said. "You've got my attention."

"Do I have your word? None of what I am going to tell you goes to anyone else. I don't want to read about it in the paper or on Facebook or Twitter or see it on television. When we're finished I will give you an exclusive. Who knows? There might even be a book in it for you."

Lucy Bauer agreed, and Cavanaugh explained that the dead man was actually Robert Bateman and that he had a record for exposing himself to a class of third grade girls on a field trip to the Statue of Liberty. He had no proof that his death was related to the victim found in St. Peter's, but he thought motive might be the reason.

"But what does his death have to do with Dave Melrose's death?" she asked.

"That's a good question I don't know the answer to. But Melrose was hired by someone trying to find Bateman. Maybe he got too close to the truth. Whatever the case, I could use your help. Are you in?"

"What do you want me to do?"

Cavanaugh looked over the list of names of the girls Bateman encountered at the ferry. "Now let me get this straight and make it very clear. We may be dealing with a killer here. I don't want you getting yourself in danger. If I give you a list of some of the parents of the girls, could you follow up with a brief interview? You could say you were doing a human interest story about crime on Staten Island and its effects on people. You can promise them you won't use their names. I just want to get an idea of the temperament of the parents. Then you can tell me how they reacted and any gut feelings you had about them."

Bauer told him she didn't think they would talk to her.

"It's a long shot. I agree. There were eleven eight-year-old girls there. They didn't deserve this. Maybe Bateman deserved to be burned alive. And then maybe it was just an accident like the police think. I don't know. I just want to get a feeling about the parents. If I give you five names, could you make contact with them? I will check out the remaining six myself. You have to be careful. You may be talking to a killer."

Bauer didn't hesitate. "Give me the names, and I'll get started on it tomorrow."

Cavanaugh looked over the list carefully. Then he gave

Bauer the family addresses of Carolyn Wilton, Clarissa Quilty, Kim Malloy, Charlotte O'Hanlon, and Cathy Gallagher. That left him with Wilhelmina Sikes, Emma Pacchiano, Rhoda Penmark, Harper Higgins, Amelia Rivers, and last, but not least, Sophia Gambella.

*   *   *   *

Chapter 7

Cartagena, Columbia

Fr. Bennis felt his way down the stairs with Angel following closely behind. At the front door Bennis hesitated. He turned and looked down at the young boy carrying Lopez's shoes. In the dim light from the street, he saw bruises and scars on his face and chest he hadn't seen before. The boy's eyes were wide and dark. He clutched the shoes close to his heart.

"Why did you tell him to take off his shoes?" Angel asked.

Bennis smiled. "It will make it easier for us to follow him. I am sure along the way we will find someone in need of a good pair of shoes."

The boy froze. "Why would we need to follow him, Padre?"

"We are going to find Chico and rescue him."

Angel stepped back into the darkness of the hallway. "No. Please. They will kill us. They are bad people."

Bennis turned and grabbed the boy by his arms. "You told me they made you do bad things. If we don't stop them, they will do bad things to others. They must be stopped, and

I must find Chico." He felt the boy shaking. "I need you to understand just because they made you do bad things doesn't mean you are bad. God forgives us all if we are sorry for what we have done. All we need to do is ask Him. You are not a coward, Angel. You are loveable and capable of many good things."

"Must I go with you?"

"I will not lie to you. It may be dangerous, but I have Lopez's gun, and he has no shoes and no money. We can follow him safely. But if you choose, you do not need to come with me. But where will you go? We need to clear this matter up or it will follow the both of us like a dark shadow all the days of our lives."

Angel frowned, "Are you really a priest?"

Bennis grinned. "I get asked that question a lot of times, but yes, I am a priest, and I have the power to forgive sins. Do you want me to hear your confession?"

"No. Not now!" Angel said. "We need to follow the man. Maybe later." He took a deep breath and pointed toward the walls surrounding the old city of Cartagena. "He went this way, Padre. Follow me."

* * * *

Some say that New York never sleeps. But this is not quite true. New York is composed of five separate boroughs. While Manhattan with Broadway and its bright lights, restaurants, theatres, fancy night clubs and bars may be seen like a pulsating, vibrant, constantly moving location, the rest of the city quiets down somewhat at night. Cartagena is similar. Named by UNESCO as a world heritage site, Cartagena has become a popular place to visit. When cruise ships arrive, the streets take on a life of their own. Tourists, residents, and lovers come to places high on the stone walls that peer out over the Caribbean. People of all ages stroll the walls of Castillo San Felipe de Barajas. Taxis and horse drawn carriages travel some of the narrow streets deep into the night. Afro-Latin-Cuban rhythms float out of active social clubs and fill the warm night as people dance and sing in the streets.

It wasn't difficult to Fr. Bennis and Angel to follow the limping Señor Lopez. They walked through a section of Cartagena known as Getsemani. They passed multicolored buildings covered with street art and graffiti. Detailed portraits of native Colombian women seemed to stare at the man and the boy as if wondering why they were trailing the staggering shoeless man. As they walked deeper into the city, the lights, the crowds, and the sounds diminished. They dropped back a bit. Lopez slowed down.

"Does this area look familiar, Angel?" the priest whispered ducking into a dark alley.

"I am not sure, Padre. All I know is the building is painted red."

Ahead of them, they saw Lopez stop and knock on a door. He waited a few moments and then the door opened "Where the hell were you? We've been waiting for you. You're the last one to report," an angry male voice called out. Lopez froze in the doorway. Suddenly, a hand reached out and pulled him violently into the house.

Bennis turned to the young boy. "I think we're here. I want you to stay here."

"No! They will kill you. You can't go in there."

The priest took out Lopez's gun and checked it. "Don't worry. Say a prayer for me, and I will be fine."

Bennis left Angel and moved toward the building. He stopped at the door and listened. Inside he heard noises and loud talk. It was a scene he had lived through a lifetime ago. His hands started to sweat. How many times had he crept into a house or apartment as the leader of a Black Ops group to assassinate someone for his government? It seemed so long ago and, then again, just like yesterday. He was never told the country or the reason. He looked at the Mexican made pistol he held in his hand. None of his weapons or clothing he had then could be traced back to the United States.

He tried the door. It was open. He moved stealthily into the house. He had killed eleven people for his government. He remembered each of them. They visited him frequently in his dreams. He never questioned his orders. It was on the twelfth assignment that their cover was blown, and he almost shot a young girl about the same age as Chico and Angel. He was wounded and left to die, but somehow he escaped and met a missionary priest who changed his life. That last assignment, he remembered clearly, had been in Colombia.

He inched forward, back against the wall, toward the room at the end with the light and the talking. There would be no killing this time. His mission was to rescue Chico and stop their preying on innocent children. He would turn them over to the police.

"Where's the money, Lopez?

"I told you some priest took it, the boy, and my shoes. Why won't you believe me? Look at my feet and my face. I tell you he took the money!"

"You're no good to me if I can't trust you, Lopez."

Bennis peeked into the room. A heavy-set man with a full black beard in a flowered yellow and red short-sleeve shirt sat at a long table. In addition to a number of hand guns, there were drugs and money grouped in neat piles all along the table."

"It's not that I don't believe you, Lopez, but I answer to the cartel. My reputation is on the line. I have to give them a reason for the shortfall."

"What do you mean?"

"I think you know. It's strictly business, but I'm going to have to kill you."

Bennis stepped into the room as Lopez was pleading for his life and the man with the beard was reaching for a gun on the table. "I don't think that is necessary," he said and pointed the Obregón at the seated man. "Put your hands in the air. Both of you."

"And who the hell are you?" the beard asked.

"It's that priest I told you about!" Lopez shouted.

"My name is Father Jack Bennis, and I've come to shut down your operation and rescue the boy you are keeping in the cellar."

The man with the beard raised his hands slowly and smiled. "And my name is Juan Carlos Montañez, but people call me 'Graso.' Is it true you took Lopez's shoes and money? I like your nerve. I could use men like you. I will make a deal with you. Give me the money and the boy and I will allow you to leave here alive."

Bennis aimed the gun at Graso's head. "You are in no position to make deals, Señor Montañez."

Graso placed his hands behind his head and started laughing. "But you are wrong, Padre." And at that moment Bennis felt the tip of a knife in the small of his back and a deep voice whisper in his ear, "Drop the gun or die."

* * * *

Jack Bennis' eyes assessed the scene like a high speed camera, but everything seemed to go in slow motion. Lopez stood like a terracotta statue with bloody face and feet. Graso was grinning through his thick beard as he slowly lowered his hands and started to reach for one of the guns on the table. Bennis felt the tip of the knife from the man with the deep voice sticking into his spine. It was now or never.

His attacker was an amateur like Lopez. Bennis' advanced combat training from years ago kicked in. He remembered in advanced infantry training how Staff Sergeant Gianvito demonstrated how to disarm a person with a knife to your back. In order to stab you, the attacker will have to pull the knife back first. The Staff Sergeant picked Bennis to illustrate various techniques.

He dropped the gun flipping it behind him and then lunged forward twisting his body left and hooking his left arm under the arm with the knife. He smashed his right elbow into his attacker's throat and brought his right knee rapidly into his groin twice.

A bullet whizzed by his head. And then another. Bennis pulled his attacker's body in front of him like a shield. He felt bullets striking his attacker. Bullets seemed to whizz by him from all directions. Then there was silence.

He peered around the limp body of the knife assailant. Graso lay back in his chair. Blood streamed from his head and chest. Lopez still stood like a store mannequin, his eyes staring behind Bennis. "No! Please, no!" he stammered raising his arms. And then three more shots came from behind the priest. Lopez fell back and slowly crumbled to the floor.

Bennis turned to the doorway behind him. Angel stood there with the gun Bennis had dropped. He lowered the pistol and said, "Now, Padre, I think I need to go to confession."

* * * *

Chapter 8

Staten Island, New York

Cavanaugh spent a restless night, tossing and turning. The realization he was almost killed at Dave Melrose's office in the abandoned Paramount Theatre slowly dawned on him. He sat up and looked over at Fran. She slept on her side. Her breathing was heavy. The truth was she was doing what she swore she never did. She was snoring.

In the dim light from the moon, he thought she looked like an angel. He bit his lip and sighed. When she asked him how his day went, he said fine. He didn't tell her about Rufus, Mrs. Melrose, or the two thugs who ended up dead on Melrose's office floor. He didn't tell her about the questions he had to answer to the police. He didn't tell her he had killed a man.

He walked into the bathroom and looked into the mirror. Who was the face staring back at him? Why was he lying to people? Why was he lying to his wife?

He gripped the porcelain sink. "I don't want her to worry," he whispered to the mirror.

The face in the mirror seemed to talk back to him. "Why did you involve yourself in this investigation in the first place?"

"My brother asked me for help, and then Goldberg asked me to help," he murmured to the mirror.

The sad, tired eyes in the mirror seemed to say, "This is not your fight. You need to walk away."

He closed his eyes and shook his head. "I can't let them pin the murder on my brother." He turned away from the face in the mirror and walked quietly into his son Stephen's room. He leaned over the crib. Stephen was sucking his thumb. He seemed to glow with beauty, peacefulness, and innocence. What kind of a world would he be growing up in? The world seemed to be growing crazier and crazier each day. How could he expect to change things? He felt a little like Don Quixote chasing windmills. But Don Quixote was crazy.

He walked into his living room. The house was eerily quiet. He sat in his favorite lounge chair. He thought about his brother, a suspect in a murder, now in a country over 2,000 miles away, looking for a twelve-year-old boy who had been missing for months. Who was crazier?

He leaned back and closed his eyes again. Then he heard it. It was low, slow, and steady. It sounded like a distant motorcycle. He sat up and looked around. It seemed to be coming from the front door. He walked to the door. Who would be riding a motorcycle to his house at this time of night? He checked his watch. It was 3:46 in the morning. He opened the door and peered into the darkness. No one was there, only the silent tombstones in the adjacent cemetery. He shut the door, but he continued to hear the motorcycle. He locked the door and cursed to himself that they had bought a house next to a cemetery.

Then he looked at the table by the door where he kept his keys, wallet, and cell phone. "Of course," he said to himself when he realized the sound was coming from his cell phone. It was his brother's unique ring tone.

He lunged for the phone almost knocking the table lamp to the floor. "Jack, is that you?"

"Who else would call you at this time of the morning?"

"Are you all right?"

"Yes, Thomas. I just wanted to give you an update and to ask your advice."

Cavanaugh waited.

"I seem to have stumbled upon some drug distributors and human traffickers. How do I get rid of the drugs? It looks like cocaine and there's a lot of it. I counted fifteen bricks of it and fifty-six plastic bags ready for distribution."

"That's a lot of crack, Jack. Why don't you just turn it over to the police?"

"I can't leave it here and I can't turn it over to the police. I don't know if I can trust them. I don't know if I should flush it down the toilet or put it in the trash. If I put it in the trash or flush it down the toilet, I'm afraid it might leach into the groundwater and aquifers."

"Your best bet is to turn it over to the police."

Bennis hesitated. "It's a little more complicated."

"What's complicated about it? That's a lot of cocaine. Let them sort it out."

"Like I said I'm not sure I can trust them. But there is the matter of the drug dealers."

"What about them?"

"They're all dead."

"Jack! Don't tell me you killed them!"

"No. No. Things happen. I came here to find Chico. They were keeping him in the basement. A boy named Angel helped me find the house. Actually, it turned out there were four boys tied up in the cellar."

"Okay, if you can't take it to the police, break it up, mix it with dirt and drop it along the road or in the trash. It's no big deal. Just don't put it all in the same garbage can."

"You think that will work?"

"I know it will work, Jack. Now tell me about Chico. How is he?"

There was silence on the phone for a moment. Then Bennis spoke. "I can break up the cocaine mix it with dirt and scatter it around the trash in the street. The kids can help me. Thanks, Thomas."

"Jack, I asked you a question. How is Chico? Is he hurt? Is he okay?"

Cavanaugh heard his brother take a deep breath. Then he said, "I don't know, Thomas. He wasn't one of the kids in the cellar."

* * * *

When Fran woke up, she found her husband on the phone with his brother. She fixed coffee for both of them and warmed a bottle for Stephen.

"Who are you talking to?" she mouthed to Cavanaugh.

He held up his index finger and spoke into the phone. "Okay, Jack, but keep in touch. Let me know if you need anything.... Thanks.... Take care of yourself and good luck."

He took the coffee cup from Fran and said, "Thanks. That was my brother. He ran into a little problem in Cartagena, but he says he's fine." Cavanaugh went on to explain how his brother busted up a cocaine dealership and rescued four young boys who were being held captive in the basement. He left out the fact that the dealers had been shot and killed by twelve-year-old Angel. There was no need to worry her needlessly, he thought.

76

He told her how his brother told him he planned to start a home and school for the four boys and Angel. His plan was to use the largely empty cloister behind St. Peter Claver Church as the starting place for the school. When Cavanaugh pointed out that while it was a noble idea, it would take money, a lot money, to get it started, he told Fran that Bennis said, "I don't think we'll have to worry about that. The dealers were kind enough to leave us some money to start the school. They didn't realize it, but sometimes good comes from bad. God sometimes works in mysterious ways."

"Don't you need approval from the pastor or the bishop, or, I don't know, the pope to get approval for starting a school like this?" Fran asked.

Cavanaugh explained to Fran that his brother's plan was to gain the approval from Fr. Mealey, the ambitious pastor of St Peter Claver Church by suggesting the school be named after him. "Mealey loves publicity. He would milk this for all the press coverage he could get. If he gets an anonymous donation to start a school for displaced children, who knows?" he told Cavanaugh, "I think Mealey could easily be convinced if he started the school, there was a good chance he might be rewarded with being selected as the diocesan bishop of Cartagena. He would love the physical trappings of the miter, the purple skull cap, and the ecclesiastic ring. I can picture him prancing around in a purple cassock, holding a gold plated crosier in one hand and fingering the pectoral cross dangling from his neck."

"Why would they make him a bishop? Why not a monsignor? Isn't that the normal promotion for a priest?" Fran asked.

Cavanaugh blew on his coffee. He shook his head. "I thought so, too, but Jack told me Pope Francis pretty much suspended granting the title of monsignor to most priests."

Fran shrugged her shoulders. "I don't understand that church stuff. I'm just glad he found Chico. When will he be coming home?"

Cavanaugh took a sip of coffee. "He still has a few loose ends to tie up."

They both heard Stephen start to cry. Fran rushed into the kitchen to get his bottle while Cavanaugh sat in his chair wondering why he didn't tell Fran the truth. Why didn't he tell her his brother had not found Chico? Chico was still missing. He could be anywhere. He could even be dead. For some reason, he recalled reading *The Catcher in the Rye* back in high school. Was he acting like Holden Caulfield? He remembered how Holden tried to rub off the curse words he saw written on the wall. Some couldn't come off. Could he really protect Fran by shielding her from the truth? Or was he actually in some way protecting himself? Was he what Holden would call just another phony?

He hated lying to his wife, but he saw no reason to worry her. He wondered if the time would ever come when he would have to tell her the whole truth. He stood up and stretched. He watched Fran holding Stephen in her arms in the kitchen. She was feeding him his bottle. They looked so innocent and pure. The time may come, he thought, but it was not today. He remembered his mother sitting across the kitchen table telling him, "The secrets we keep, Thomas, tend to control our lives. It pays to be honest and truthful." He wondered if and when the time did come if she would forgive him.

* * * *

Chapter 9

Staten Island, New York

Two weeks went by with no news from Jack Bennis about Chico. Detective Perez, however, kept Cavanaugh busy. She seemed to have made no progress on gathering any additional suspects and concentrated her investigation on Fr. Bennis. She repeatedly questioned Cavanaugh. She knew Jack Bennis flew out of Newark the morning after the murder of Dave Melrose and traveled to Cartagena, Colombia. She threatened to arrest Cavanaugh as an accessory or an accomplice to Melrose's murder.

Perez attempted to accuse Cavanaugh of going to Melrose's office and deliberately destroying his files. Monica Melrose refused to cooperate. The two dead thugs who attempted to intimidate Mrs. Melrose were successful. She testified that Cavanaugh came to her rescue, but she claimed to have no information about any cases her husband was working on. Perez knew she was lying because she was scared, but there was nothing she could do.

Meanwhile, Cavanaugh and Lucy Bauer's investigations of the parents of the girls Robert Bateman accosted at the Staten Island Ferry yielded some interesting facts. Although most of the parents didn't want to talk about Bateman and the incident, both Cavanaugh and Bauer were able to gather potentially important information.

The parents of Carolyn Wilton were Dr. Vito and Nancy Wilton. Vito was an oral and maxillofacial surgeon. His wife was head nurse in a geriatric nursing home. Vito reacted strongly to Bateman's actions and expressed the opinion that people like him should be castrated and given life imprisonment or the death penalty. Nancy didn't want to talk about it. Carolyn was the youngest of five children.

The parents of Clarissa Quilty were Aidan and Alice Quilty. Aidan owned two dry cleaning stores in Brooklyn. It was the second marriage for Alice. She had one child from her first marriage and two from Aidan. She worked as a bank teller at Chase.

The parents of Kim Malloy were Tom and Kathleen Malloy. Tom was a decorated New York City fire lieutenant and Kathleen was a school librarian. Tom was a deacon at the United Methodist Church. Kim was their only child.

The parents of Charlotte O'Hanlon were Roberta and Jack O'Hanlon. Jack was a physical education teacher at Susan Wagner High School and the coach of the varsity baseball team. He was known for his hot temper. His wife Roberta was a human relations coordinator at Staten Island University Hospital and a Eucharistic minister at St. Peter's Church. She worried about the long term effect of the ferry incident on her daughter and expressed concern for a couple of their elderly neighbors. Charlotte was the oldest of their two young children.

The parents of Cathy Gallagher were Brian and Gwen Gallagher. Brian was a bartender at a bar on Bay Street called appropriately "The Bucket of Blood." His wife Gwen was a cosmetic salesperson at Macy's. They both expressed the feeling that Bateman should be locked up and the key thrown away. Cathy was their only child.

The parents of Wilhelmina Sikes were Wolfgang and Mary Sikes. Wolfgang was the vice president of Yalumba Wines, Australia's oldest family-owned wine brand. He stood six feet five and weighed more than 250 lbs. His wife Mary worked part-time as a special education aide in P.S. 23. They both said they wanted to put the incident away and refused to talk about it. Wilhelmina was their third child.

The parents of Emma Pacchiano were Dr. Mark and Laura Pacchiano. Mark was a certified physical therapist and former defensive end for the Miami Dolphins. Laura was an oncology nurse at NYU/Langone. They said they had put the matter out of their minds. Emma was the younger of their two children.

The parents of Rhoda Penmark were Richard and Althea Penmark. Richard was a professor of creative writing at Wagner College. His wife Althea was a licensed pharmacist at CVS. Rhoda was their only child. She was adopted. They said they believed sexual predators should be hospitalized and rehabilitated, not imprisoned.

The parents of Harper Higgins were Charlie Johnson and Greta Higgins. Charlie was a waiter at the Staaten Restaurant on Forest Avenue. Greta was a court stenographer. Harper was her only child. Charlie and Greta were domestic partners. They refused to talk about the ferry incident.

The parents of Sophia Gambella were Lawrence and Cinderella Gambella. Lawrence owned a travel agency and was a well-respected member of the community. His first cousin, however, was Mario Impellizzieri, a notorious mob boss and the godfather of Sophia. Cinderella Gambella was a struggling actress and a member of the Staten Island

Shakespeare Playhouse. They claimed to have put the ferry incident out of their minds.

Cavanaugh was reviewing the list of parents when the telephone rang. He hoped it was his brother, but it was Chief of Detectives Morty Goldberg. "How are you doing on your investigations?" Goldberg asked.

"I went through all the parents of the girls Bateman exposed himself to. There are some possibilities, but nothing definite. Sometimes I feel like I'm punching at ghosts."

"I'm calling you to tell you we may have a lead. There was another murder sometime last night. The body of Fernando Mondego was found this morning by the custodian at the United Methodist Church in New Brighton. His eyes were removed, the number 3 pinned through his neck on a 3 X 5 index card, and a half-eaten bagel soaked in beer and salt was found in one of his pockets."

"What about the eyes?" Cavanaugh asked.

"They were in his other pocket caked with what looks like corn flakes just like Melrose's."

"Who was this guy Fernando Mondego? I never heard of him."

"He doesn't have a record. He owns, or used to own, two bars on Staten Island. One was on Bay Street and the other on Forest Avenue."

Cavanaugh scanned the list of parents from the ferry incident. He recalled an old Charlie Chan movie in which he points out that the innocent grass may conceal a snake. "Looks like you were right, Morty. I think Bateman might have been the killer's first victim."

"I'm not happy about being right, Tom. I'm afraid this isn't this killer's last murder."

* * * *

Cavanaugh stared at the phone for a few minutes after he hung up. Then he got up and walked to the kitchen window. He gazed out at the worn gravestones in the abandoned cemetery next to his house. Some of the stones were crumbling and collapsing. He watched a robin perched on top of a lopsided Celtic cross. Buds were starting to appear on the trees. A few crocuses poked their heads between the headstones. The sun was trying to peer through the trees. He thought of T. S. Eliot's "The Wasteland," and its opening lines came to mind. "April is the cruelest month, breeding / Lilacs out of the dead land, mixing / Memory and desire...."

What did Robert Bateman, Dave Melrose, and Fernando Mondego have in common? Bateman was a sex offender; Melrose was a lawyer and private investigator; Mondego was a bar owner. Did the murder victims have something in common or were they random murders? What was the killer's motive? Why leave the bodies in churches? Why cut out their eyes? What significance did the beer-soaked bread have?

He went back to the list he and the reporter Lucy Bauer had compiled:

Dr. Vito Wilton was a surgeon with rigid belief in harsh punishment for sex offenders. Tom Malloy was a fire lieutenant and his wife Kathleen was a deacon in the United Methodist Church where Fernando Mondego's body was found.

Jack O'Hanlon was known to have a violent temper, and his wife was a Eucharistic minister in the church where Dave Melrose was found.

Brian Gallagher was a bartender in a rough bar on Bay Street that was not far from where Bateman's burnt body was found.

Wolfgang Sikes was a huge, wealthy man capable of moving bodies or paying someone to move the bodies.

Dr. Mark Pacchiano was a strong man knowledgeable in the human anatomy.

Charlie Johnson was a waiter at the Staaten Restaurant on Forest Avenue.

Lawrence Gambella was a first cousin of Mario Impellizzieri, a man known for his ruthless dealings with his enemies and anyone who crossed his family.

And then there was Father Steve Impellizzieri, the only son of the Cosa Nostra chieftain, who was a priest at St. Peter's Church where Dave Melrose's body was found.

Cavanaugh scratched his head. "Too many suspects," he thought. "And the snake may still be hiding in plain sight in there or somewhere else in apparent innocence." He looked at the clock above the refrigerator. It wasn't noon yet, but he opened the refrigerator and took out a bottle of beer. He took it to his favorite chair and thought about his brother. He wished he would check in. He was worried about him. Dealing with the drug cartel could be fatal. One good point was that Detective Perez could not accuse Bennis of the murder of Mondego. Now was the time when he could step away from his investigation and leave it to the police. He looked at the green bottle in his hand and realized he couldn't do that. He was in too far already. He had been shot at, and he had killed a man. One name kept coming up – Mario Impellizzieri. He took a long gulp of beer. It was cold and tasted good. He knew where his next step would be. It was dangerous, but he was going to question the notoriously treacherous and vindictive Mario Impellizzieri.

* * * *

Chapter 10

Cartagena, Colombia

Things didn't go as Father Bennis had planned. As he knelt in front of the gilded casket containing the body of St. Peter Claver under the main altar of the church, he prayed for direction. When the pope visited Colombia, he used his visit to the shrine to highlight the perils of modern-day slavery including human trafficking. While he knew all lives matter, Peter Claver lived at a time when it was most important to show the world that black lives mattered.

It wasn't a unique idea that Bennis had. He knew Covenant House in New York provided food, clothing, and a safe place to sleep for homeless young people in crisis. To Jack Bennis, it was logical and important that there be a refuge in Cartagena for young, desperate, homeless boys and girls who ran away from home only to be caught up in a new form of slavery.

It made sense to him, but not to Father Mealey. Bennis promised to find funding for the project and subtly expressed his thoughts that naming the school after Mealey would be appropriate and gain the priest favor with the bishop. But Father Mealey was adamant. He would not be turning his church over to be a sanctuary for homeless gutter snipes and drug addicts. Appearances were important. The four boys and Angel could stay in the cloister, but only on a temporary basis until Bennis found another place for them. Bennis looked at the skeletal remains of Peter Claver and thought how the Scottish poet Robert Burns was right. The best-laid plans of mice and men often go astray.

But Peter Claver did not cave in to hostile reactions. Jack Bennis would not do so either. His primary mission was to find Chico, but if he could not find him at least he could help children who found themselves slaves to unscrupulous people. He stood up and genuflected before the altar. If Father Mealey would not help, Bennis decided he would travel to Bogotá to plead his case to Cardinal Guastella.

*   *   *   *

Jack Bennis gave Juan, the sacristan, a portion of the drug money he had confiscated equivalent to more than a year of Juan's salary to make sure the five boys were properly taken care of in his absence. Then he traveled by bus to Bogotá with two heavy suitcases to visit Cardinal Guastella.

He had heard Cardinal Guastella was kind, hospitable, intelligent, and receptive to helping the poor and needy. When he was introduced to the cardinal, Cardinal Guastella was dressed in a simple red cassock and was working on a pile of papers on the desk in his office. Cardinal Guastella rose and came around the desk. "Father Bennis," he said, "I have heard much about you. The rumors of your exploits have traveled wide. It is good to finally meet you."

Bennis bowed and moved to kiss the cardinal's episcopal ring, "Your Eminence," he said, "thank you for taking the time to see me. I know you are a busy man."

"Nonsense," the cardinal said and pulled his hand away giving Bennis a bear hug and then pointing to a chair. "Sit, please. You are my guest. Formality is socially required for me at times, but I honestly detest the pomp and circumstance that go along with my title. What brings you all the way to Bogotá?"

Bennis sat and proceeded to tell the cardinal that he had come into a substantial amount of money recently and wished to start a home for displaced, homeless youths. The cardinal returned to his desk and sat listening intently. He clasped his hands in front of his lips. His deep brown eyes peered over his glasses and never wavered from looking at Bennis.

Finally, the cardinal spoke. "I have heard about a drug war of some sort in Cartagena. Three dealers were recently shot and killed. Rumors were they were also involved in human trafficking and were using young boys as sex slaves. The police found evidence of drugs, but were unable to locate any on the premises. They theorized whoever took the drugs absconded with a lot of drug money. They found evidence that children had been held captive there, but no children were found." He leaned back in his chair and asked, "Have you heard about the incident, Father?"

Bennis said, "I read about it in the paper, your Eminence, but I have learned from experience you can't believe everything you read in the paper."

The cardinal smiled. "Fake news? I have been hearing a lot about that recently."

"I came to you today because I know you have been an outspoken advocate for a peaceful resolution to Colombia's long-running armed conflicts. I come here on behalf of displaced children who are in crisis themselves and need peace and safety. They have no place to go. I propose to give them a place where they can be provided food, shelter, clothing, and the hope for a better future. I feel as a church it is our responsibility to help homeless and runaway children in their times of need, but I need your compassionate help."

"Me? What can I do?"

"I have found five young boys in need of help. I would like to establish a place where they can be safe and given support so that they can lead independent lives."

"Where would you establish this place?"

"The cloister at St. Peter Claver has available rooms. At present I have the five young boys staying there. The money I am prepared to turn over to you would be more than enough to initiate the project for these children and others."

Cardinal Guastella leaned forward. "And what is preventing you from starting this project yourself?"

Father Bennis looked down and rubbed the scar over his eye. After thirty seconds, he looked back at the cardinal and said simply, "Father Mealey."

The cardinal took a deep breath. "Father Mealey is a good man. He is conscientious and obviously ambitious. Like all of us, he has his virtues and his shortcomings. I must confess I worry about him at times. I know he is very rigid. But make no mistake about it, he means well. His methods may not agree with others, but his motives are sincere."

"I mean no disrespect, your Eminence. I hoped I could give you the money and you could speak with Father Mealey."

The cardinal's eyes narrowed. "And where would this money come from? We cannot accept ill-gotten gains."

"The money comes from an anonymous donor, your Eminence." Jack Bennis tapped the two suitcases he brought with him. "Sometimes God works in miraculous ways. Who are we to question God? God is good all the time...."

The cardinal looked at the two heavy bags and answered, "And all the time God is good." He smiled again and said, "I will speak with Father Mealey. We need to help children in need. Go in peace, my child, and be careful. We live in a dangerous world."

Father Bennis stood, bowed, and said, "Thank you, your Eminence." Then he turned and left leaving the two heavy suitcases by his chair.

* * * *

There was a large crowd milling around St. Peter Claver Church and the plaza in front of it when Jack Bennis arrived back from Bogotá. One of the cruise boats had arrived. Men and women in shorts and sunscreen wandered about taking pictures with expensive cameras, camcorders, and cell phones. Juan, the sacristan, stood at the main door directing tourists to the museum next door and asking for their respect when visiting the church. He wore a white long sleeve shirt and a tight blue vest. When he saw Fr. Bennis approaching, he left his post and pushed through the crowd to get to him. "Padre, what have you done? Father Mealey is angry and demanding that you see him immediately. I have never seen him so mad. If looks could kill, you would be dead! And then there were men from the Cali Cartel who were looking for you and asking questions. They looked mean, and they had guns."

"Thank you, Juan. I will see Fr. Mealey now. Did you tell the others about the boys in the cloister?"

"No. I told them nothing about the boys. You must be careful, Padre. They are dangerous people. Men like them kill people."

"I appreciate your concern, Juan. You have been a good friend. If I do not see you before I leave, please take

89

care of the children and keep them safe. People will be coming after me to help them soon." The priest gave the sacristan a warm embrace and then moved through the crowd to meet with Fr. Mealey. There were tears in Juan's eyes as he watched Father Bennis disappear in a group of boisterous tourists.

Bennis found Father Mealey preening at a full-length mirror in the rectory and adjusting his cassock. "You look gorgeous, Miguel. A blind man would be glad to see you."

Mealey swung around. His face was red. "How dare you go to the cardinal without my permission? You are nothing more than a trouble-maker! I want you out of this church immediately!"

"Before I go, Miguel, I think you should know the cardinal thinks you are a good man. He is more charitable than I am."

"The Cali cartel is looking for you, Bennis. You are a dead man walking. Get out of my church before I call the police!"

"No need to get your bowels in an uproar. I'm going, but before I go I'm taking Chico's spear with me."

"What are you talking about? Who is this Chico and what is this spear you mention?'

"He's the boy I left here with his sister when I had to leave. Monsignor Passeri promised to place him and his sister with a caring family."

"I know nothing about this boy and his sister. And I never heard of this spear you speak about."

Jack Bennis sprang forward like a cat. He grabbed Mealey's cassock, pushed him back against the wall ripping the buttons off his previously meticulous cassock.

Mealey looked down. "Look what you've done! I'll have your head for this!"

Bennis moved closer. He could smell the fragrant ingredients of paella valenciana on Mealey's breath. "Listen closely, Miguel. When Monsignor got sick you sent the kids to St. Benedict Joseph Labre Orphanage. The boy ran away. I came back here to find him."

Father Mealey started stammering. Sweat dripped down his forehead. "I ... I seem to remember something. But it is very vague. It was some time ago. Things were chaotic when Monsignor became ill. I ... I placed the children there on a temporary basis until I could find suitable placement with a willing family. I didn't know about the promise Monsignor made to you."

Bennis's eyes narrowed in on Mealey's eyes. "You can lie to me and yourself all you want. What about the boy's spear? It was an ancient Muisca spear he discovered in Mompas. I found it in the back of your sumptuous wardrobe closet."

"What were you doing in my closet? You had no right!"

Jack Bennis slapped the priest across the face. "One more time, Mealey. What are you doing with Chico's property?"

Father Mealey started shaking. The stories and rumors of Jack Bennis' prior service as a combat veteran were well-known. "I ... I was holding it for him. I was trying to keep it safe. I ... I guess I forgot about it."

Bennis slapped him one more time. Mealey covered his face with his arms and crouched down. He was crying.

"You make me sick, Mealey. I don't know what the cardinal sees in you, but I will take his word. He says you're a good man. I think you can be better. To be truthful, I guess we all can be better. Loosen up a little. Try thinking more about others and not your precious self. It will do you good. I am going up to your room now, and I'm going to take Chico's Muisca spear with me. You will never hear from me again unless I hear you have done something to harm the boys in the cloister or that you have done something to sabotage the program to help homeless youths. If that happens, you can count on seeing me again and, in a phrase we used to use in Brooklyn, I will shove that spear up where the sun don't shine."

* * * *

Chapter 11

Staten Island, New York

Tom Cavanaugh sat in his car staring at the graves in the cemetery next to his house. He didn't have a definite motive for the murders. Impellizzieri's name kept coming up. Was the motive revenge? Was Impellizzieri getting back at Bateman for exposing himself to his godchild? Was Melrose blackmailing him about something he discovered? But how did the murder of Fernando Mondego fit in? Mondego owned two bars on Staten Island. Was Impellizzieri involved in some way with his businesses? Could Mondego have refused to follow Impellizzieri's demands which could be anything from laundering money to dealing drugs to installing cigarette or gaming machines? Was the motive revenge or power?

He watched a chipmunk scurry behind a lopsided tombstone. Cavanaugh still lacked a definite motive. Impellizzieri could easily have ordered a hit on the victims. But why cut out their eyes? Why leave their bodies in churches? And why place beer-soaked bread in their pockets? It didn't make sense. He was missing something.

He fumbled for his cell phone in his back pocket and called Morty Goldberg. There was a question he needed to ask him. "Morty," he said, "I'm trying to figure this thing out. I can't put my finger on a definite motive yet. How exactly did the victims die?

Goldberg took his time as he examined the medical examiner's reports. "Well," he finally said, "we can't be quite sure of the first victim. There wasn't much left of Bateman's body, but Melrose and Mondego had high doses of fentanyl and heroin in their blood. The fentanyl alone was enough to kill an elephant. Death would have been quick. It's really scary, Tom. People are buying this stuff online from China."

Cavanaugh thanked Goldberg and went over his list of possible suspects in Bateman's murder. He looked for people, in addition to the doctors, who might have access to drugs. He noted that Roberta O'Hanlon worked at Staten Island University Hospital; Laura Pacchiano was a nurse at NYU/Langone; and Althea Penmark was a licensed pharmacist at CVS. Instead of getting shorter, his list was growing.

He started the car and headed toward St. Peter's Rectory. One can't just go up to a mob boss like Mario Impellizzieri and ask him questions. Maybe his son, Father Steve, would give him some information about his father and arrange for a meeting. He needed to know more about this popular parish priest. He hoped he might also get to see Father Vivaldi, the pastor. He wanted to know why he turned on his brother and went out of his way to implicate Bennis in Melrose's death. His hands gripped the steering wheel a little harder. He saw his knuckles turn white. He smiled and imagined giving Vivaldi a "knuckle sandwich."

"You don't mess with family," he said to himself as he turned onto the West Shore Expressway.

* * * *

Cavanaugh was driving along Victory Boulevard when his cell phone went off again. It was Lucy Bauer. "There's been another murder in a church, Cavanaugh. What can you tell me about it?"

"You're kidding me. Who got killed now?"

"Fernando Mondego. Don't tell me you know nothing about it."

"I'm not God, Ms. Bauer. Believe it or not, I don't know everything. Who is this Fernando Mondego? I never heard of him."

"He owns a couple of bars on Staten Island. One's called the Bucket of Blood. It's on Bay Street."

Cavanaugh remembered the name. Brian Gallagher was a bartender at the Bucket of Blood. "I think I did hear something about that bar," he said.

"It was all over the papers awhile back. A couple of teenagers died there from apparent drug overdoses."

"If it's the same place I'm thinking about, my wife and I used to go there years ago. I think it was called the Crystal Lounge back then. They made great cheeseburgers."

"That's the same place," Lucy Bauer said. "It changed hands a couple of times since then, but Mondego owns it now, and it's become a real hangout for under-aged kids."

Cavanaugh turned left onto Westervelt Avenue. "And what makes you think his death may be connected to the Melrose murder?"

"You're lying to me again, Cavanaugh. I can feel it. You know something. Melrose and Mondego were both killed in a church. I think it's the work of a serial killer. This could be his third murder!"

Cavanaugh stopped at a red light at Crescent Avenue. "When did I ever lie to you? I've given you information."

"That may be true, but you have also been holding out on me."

"Listen, Lucy, I'm in the car right now, and I'm on my way to the 120 Precinct to ask some questions. If I hear anything, I'll call you back."

"Promise?"

"Of course," he said and clicked off. Then he leaned over and looked at his eyes in the rearview mirror. He could have told her about the index card pinned to Mondego's neck. He could have told her about his eyes being cut out. He could have told her he was actually going to St. Peter's Church to question Fr. Steve and not to the 120 Precinct. But he didn't. He began to worry. It was becoming easier and easier to lie to people.

* * * *

Cavanaugh rang the bell at the rectory of St. Peter's Church. An androgynous woman with long white hair answered the door. She wore a faded navy-blue mumu that flowed over her bulky body like a loose fitting tent and a frown etched into her face that reminded him of a cross between the matron with the flashlight at the movie theater when he was a kid and a reincarnation of Madame Defarge.

She led him into the parlor, a dark room with English chestnut paneling, a thick mahogany table with three violet velvet cushioned chairs, a scarlet sofa, and a large crucifix dangling from the wall. She seemed to slither out of the room without a sound.

A few minutes later, Father Steve came into the room like a breath of fresh air. He smiled and shook Cavanaugh's hand. It was a firm, strong handshake, not like the dead fish handshakes Cavanaugh detested. "So you're Father Bennis' brother. I've heard a lot about you. Your brother's very proud of you. What can I do for you today?"

Cavanaugh explained he was investigating the murder of Dave Melrose in an attempt to clear his brother's name. The smile on Fr. Steve's face melted. "I'm not sure I can help you, Mr. Cavanaugh," he said. "I don't believe for a second that your brother was involved with Mr. Melrose's death, but I wasn't here that day."

"Do you mind me asking where you were?"

"Yes, I do."

Cavanaugh caught his breath, smiled, and said, "I'm sorry, Father. The old detective thing kicks in every once in a while. What I'm really interested in his learning why your pastor, Father Vivaldi, seemed to go out of his way to accuse my brother of Melrose's murder. He called the police and the press and said he suspected him of the murder."

"I can't speak for Fr. Vivaldi, but I think he was angry that your brother left so abruptly. I understand he also called the Chancery's Office and left a message for the cardinal."

"The man seems to have anger issues or power issues."

"We all have our problems, Mr. Cavanaugh."

Cavanaugh casually said, "I understand your father is alleged to have some problems of his own."

Fr. Steve gave Cavanaugh an icy stare. "I don't speak with my father, Mr. Cavanaugh. I pray for him."

"I'll be honest, Father. Your father's name keeps coming up in my investigation. I wonder if you could arrange for me to meet with him to ask him a few questions."

Fr. Steve smiled. "Maybe you didn't hear me, Mr. Cavanaugh. I don't speak with my father. You would have better luck talking with my brother."

"Your brother? I didn't know you had a brother."

"Most people don't. He grew up in Sicily and only came here a few years ago."

"When can I meet your brother? Maybe he could tell me more about your father."

"I am sure he could. He owns a barber shop in New Dorp. His name is Stephen. Yes, it's my name, too. We are twins. My father liked the fact that George Forman named all five of his sons George. Being that my brother and I are identical twins, my father thought it amusing as well as appropriate to give us the same names. I personally never found it amusing. My brother and I are very different people."

Cavanaugh nodded. "I can identify with that. May I ask if your brother works for your father?"

"That you will have to ask him yourself, Mr. Cavanaugh. But I advise you to be careful. My grandfather's motto was, '*L'ascia dimentica ma l'albero si ricorda.*' (The axe forgets, but the tree remembers.)"

"And is this your motto, too, Father?"

Fr. Steve looked up at the crucifix on the wall. "No. No matter how many times as a young boy I heard my father preach, '*Nessuna caratteristica è più giustificato della vendetta nel momento e nel luogo giusto* (No trait is more justified than revenge in the right time and place), I have always felt it is important to forgive our enemies. Perhaps that's why I became a priest. I believe revenge is like eating rat poison and waiting for the rat to die."

Fr. Steve turned back to Cavanaugh. "I would be very careful, if I were you, if you do talk to my brother. His loyalty to family could be very dangerous for you." He reached out and shook Cavanaugh's hand again and added, "May God be with you," and left Cavanaugh suddenly standing alone in the dark room.

*   *   *   *

Chapter 12

Cartagena, Colombia

Father Jack Bennis walked through the Church of St. Peter Claver. In his hand he held Chico's Muisca spear. He had coated it with black shoe polish found in Father Mealey's closet in hopes of disguising it as a walking stick. At the door of the church, he turned and looked once more at the glass encased body of St. Peter Claver. He doubted he would ever return.

Walking through the doors, he saw the crowds of tourists had thickened. Perhaps another cruise ship arrived. He scanned the sea of bodies. Some were taking pictures of the church, the museum, and the various metal sculptors in the plaza. There was laughter mixed with the smell of suntan lotion and sweat. He noticed two men on opposite sides of the plaza that did not look like tourists. Just then, a hand reached out and touched his shoulder. He spun around and saw Juan, the sacristan. He looked worried and afraid. "The men from Cali who were looking for you," he whispered. "They are back."

Suddenly, Bennis felt like the bull's eye of a target. He was still dressed in his clerical black suit and Roman collar.

Surely people had seen a priest walking through the streets of Cartagena leading five youths from the drug dealers' house to St. Peter Claver Church. The Cali Cartel wanted the drugs and the money back. They also wanted to eliminate the troublesome priest who had disrupted their drug and sex trafficking business.

"Juan," he said, "I have another favor to ask of you."

"Anything, Padre."

"Do you have any old clothes I might be able to borrow?"

"There are some old clothes people have donated to the poor. They are in the vestibule of the church. But they are worn and dirty. Why would you want them?"

"I am a sitting duck in my clerical uniform. Those men from the cartel are looking for me. I need to change into civilian clothes."

Juan asked no more questions. He led Bennis to the closet where the used clothes were kept and disappeared. Bennis changed into a red and yellow plaid shirt and a pair of filthy, torn dungarees. He found a New York Yankee blue cap probably dropped by a tourist. The trousers were too big for him so he stuffed his clerical shirt and pants in them and pulled the shirt over his now protruding belly. He took a deep breath, pulled the cap over his eyes, and ventured into the crowd of tourists.

Using the spear as a cane, he limped through the sea of sightseers. They moved cautiously out of his way as if he had leprosy. He felt a little like Moses crossing the Red Sea. The man leaning against the museum did not notice him. The man on the other side of the plaza took an interest in this unfamiliar figure. He started to follow him.

Bennis moved closer to the buildings as he moved away from the crowd. He turned a corner. He heard steps quickening behind him. Then he heard the click of a pistol. He turned quickly. The man of Cali was pointing a .45 ACP Springfield Armory XDM model with a suppressor at him. "We've been looking for you," he said. "Where's the money, the drugs, and the boys?"

Bennis calculated the distance between them. The man could fire off five shots before he could reach him. "The money and the drugs are gone, and the boys are safe."

"Then you're a dead man," the man said and aimed at the center of Bennis' loose fitting red and yellow plaid shirt. Suddenly, the man stiffened. His eyes widened. He dropped the gun and toppled forward. There was a knife sticking in his back.

Bennis looked up. Juan, the sacristan, stood at the corner about thirty feet away. He was staring at the body on the cobblestone pathway. "I am sorry, Padre. I didn't know what to do. He was going to kill you."

The priest reached down and pulled the knife out of the man's back and picked up his gun. He wiped the bloody knife on the man's back and shoved the gun beneath his red and yellow plaid shirt. The knife had a one piece stainless steel blade with a cord wrapped handle and looked to be about nine inches long. Bennis handed the knife back to Juan. "Where did you get this thing, and how did you learn to throw like that?" he asked.

"I use the knife to cut packages at the church, Padre. I am old, but I used to pitch for the Cartagena Tigers. They used to say I was pretty good." He stared at the dead man on the ground.

"You're still pretty good as far as I'm concerned. Thank you."

"I am sorry, Padre. I didn't mean to kill him. God forgive me."

Bennis gave Juan a blessing and said, "Give thanks to the Lord, for He is good. His mercy endures forever. Go in peace. You are forgiven. Now take your knife and get the hell out of here. Your penance is to say nothing of this to anybody. God forgives you, and so do I."

When Juan left, Bennis lifted the Cali Cartel man onto a nearby bench and propped him up so he appeared to be sleeping. Then he walked toward the bus station.

*   *   *   *

The bus ride to Bogotá was bumpy, hot, crowded, and smelly. Somewhere along the ride, the bus driver explained because some of the roads were washed away from recent flooding, they would be altering their route and following detour signs. The ride would be longer and at times uncomfortable, but in the end much safer. His announcement was met with jeers, curses, and complaints from most of the passengers and some of the chickens.

Jack Bennis sat by a cracked half-opened window in the back. Conversations swirled around him like rapid gunfire, children cried, someone strummed an out-of-tune guitar, and chickens ran up and down the aisle. The black shoe polish on his "walking stick" stained his hands and rubbed off on his face. He pulled his Yankee cap down farther on his face, leaned against the window, and closed his eyes. He had stopped a drug ring, saved some boys from sex traffickers, and gotten a commitment from the cardinal to establish a place for homeless children. He had also been involved in the death of four men, and alienated the pastors of St. Peter Claver Church in Cartagena and St. Peter's Church on Staten Island, as well as the Cali Cartel. But he was no closer to finding Chico than he was before.

The four boys he rescued told him Chico had escaped earlier that day. He managed to open a small vent in the basement and crawled through. He pleaded with the other boys to join him, but they were too big and could not fit through the vent. Chico promised them he would get help. But where could Chico get help? He wouldn't go to the police. The boys all knew the local police were being paid by the cartel to mind their own business.

Bennis reached beneath his shirt and fumbled until he found the handwritten letter he still hadn't opened. It was tucked into the pocket of his black clerical shirt. He looked at the crumpled letter as if it were an IED, an improvised explosive device. He hesitated opening it. His hands trembled. He recognized the writing. He knew it from the beginning. It was María Isabelle's handwriting. Why hadn't he opened the letter? She was the woman he loved. He wanted so much to hold her in his arms, to tell her he loved her. But the words of scripture rang out in his mind, "No man can serve two masters: for either he will hate the one, and love the other, or else he will hold to the one, and despise the other." He had taken vows of poverty, chastity, and obedience when he became a priest. He told her that, but she said she loved him. Did he really love her? He thought he did, but did he love her enough to renounce his vows?

Was he going crazy? What is love? How does anyone know he or she is in love? What's the difference between infatuation and true love? How does one know? How does one know love will last? Is it like a candle that burns hot for a while and then goes out? Was Oscar Wilde right when he wrote that each man kills the thing he loves?

He continued to stare at the crumpled, unopened letter. When one weighs temporal pleasures against eternity, which one wins? Thoughts bounced around his mind like an out of control pinball machine. He didn't want to hurt her again.

Why did María write him the letter? Could the letter be about Chico? Chico did save María's life. He met her in the Mompas hospital. He knew her brother took her by helicopter to a bigger hospital in Bogotá. Holding Chico's spear between his legs, he looked around the bus. There was conversation, movement, and noise everywhere except for two people. One was a woman with a red scarf near the front of the bus. She stared straight ahead most of the time, but turned toward the back of the bus every few minutes. Was she watching Bennis? The other was the man two seats in front of him. They both had gotten on a few stops after the bus left Cartagena. He was young and fit. He wore a loose fitting jacket despite the heat. When he got on the bus, he seemed to glance around, checking each passenger, until his eyes locked on Bennis. Then he turned abruptly and found a seat next to a brawny elderly woman with a hacking cough who was holding two squawking chickens in a wooden cage.

Bennis felt for the pistol under his shirt. The voice of his former combat instructor Staff Sergeant Gianvito rang in his ears. "Forewarned is forearmed." He took a deep breath and tore the envelope open.

* * * *

His hand shook as he read the first lines.

My dearest Jack,

I am in Santo Jose Gabriel del Rosario Brochero Hospital in Cali. My brother thought this was the best hospital for me and moved me from Bogotá. It is a small private hospital that specializes in a multidisciplinary team of doctors who deal specifically with traumatic injuries. The doctors here have been great.

"Cali?" Fr. Bennis whispered to himself. He looked up in time to see the woman in the front quickly turn her head back to the front of the bus. He thought María Isabelle was in Bogotá. The Cali Cartel was after him. Was he going from the heat of the kitchen into the frying pan? He continued reading.

The good news is they say I am going to live. If it hadn't been for you and my brother, I probably would be dead. I can't forget little Chico with his big sombrero. He called me the other day from Cartagena. I don't know how he got my number or even found out where I was. But, as you well know, Chico is a unique young man. He said he was having trouble in school and hated his teacher who is a nun. He said he wanted to reach you, but was unable to. He hoped I would be able to get in touch with you so I sent this letter to your brother's address. Chico sounded desperate on the phone.

Bennis checked the postmark on the letter again. It was sent over three months ago. He remembered his mother telling me, "The worse feeling is regretting not having done something when you had a chance. Don't regret the things you've done. Regret the things you didn't do when you had a chance." Chico had reached out for help, and he was not there for him.

I tried calling him back, but could not reach him. He said he would check back with me to see if I could reach you. But he never did. He seems to think you are a savior of some kind. I know what he means.

Jack, I really miss you. I wish I could see you again. I know what you said, but I don't understand why we can't be together.

Fr. Bennis looked up. It seemed that time had stopped. He didn't hear the noise of the bus or the conversations among the passengers. He brushed a tear from his cheek.

I guess I need to tell you it all has not been good news. My brother was arrested and is in La Modelo prison in Bogotá. It's a rough place, but my brother tells me not to worry. His people are taking good care of him.

I'm sorry to have to tell you Aunt Jo died a few days before Santiago was arrested. I'm glad Aunt Jo didn't see my brother being arrested. She died peacefully in her sleep after a brief illness. My brother was at her side. She really loved him so much. He was the son she never had. I miss her, too. She would often bring me flowers and keep me company for a few hours. She was ninety-five-years-old, and it's still hard to believe she's gone. She was truly an amazing lady.

Bennis closed his eyes. He remembered Aunt Jo and Santiago in the Mompas hospital where they originally took María Isabelle after she had been shot. He took a deep breath and continued reading the letter.

It's lonely in the hospital. I miss you. I wish I could see you. I don't know how long I'm going to be here, but it could be a long time. The bullets did a lot of damage. I should have listened to you, but it's too late now. The doctors say I will live, but I may never be able to walk again.

If you can't come to visit, please pray for me, Aunt Jo, and my brother. Maybe your God will have pity on me.

All my love,
María Isabelle

The priest folded the crumpled letter carefully. He felt a tear rolling down his cheek. He also felt eyes from the front of the bus looking his way again.

* * * *

Chapter 13

Staten Island, New York

The weather, like life, has a way of changing quickly. As Cavanaugh walked out of the rectory, a steady light rain began to fall. He looked up at the huge stone church. Father Steve gave him a lot to think about. He wished his brother Jack was here. He had not heard from him in a few weeks. He thought his brother was probably enjoying the beautiful weather in Colombia while he was dodging rain drops and nasty people on Staten Island. Why was it, he thought, that his brother always seemed to luck out?

He saw a priest walking up the steps to the church. He stopped at his car. If that was the pastor, now was his chance to confront him. Fr. Steve was right about family and as much as he and his brother disagreed, Jack Bennis was his brother and he would defend him till his dying breath.

Cavanaugh raced across the street and bounded up the church steps. As he opened the doors, he stood face to face with Lucy Bauer.

"What the hell are you doing here?" he asked.

She stood there with her hands on her hips. "You lied to me again," she said. "I went to the precinct, but guess what? No Cavanaugh. I was coming back this way when I saw your car."

Cavanaugh looked over her shoulder. The priest he had seen seemed to disappear. "I ... er, I stopped to check out the murder scene."

"You're lying again, Cavanaugh. But coming here, I learned something. Did you realize Melrose's body was found next to the first Station of the Cross?"

"What are you talking about?"

"Melrose's body was in the pew next to the first Station of the Cross where Pilot condemns Jesus to death."

"So what?"

"Don't you get it? The killer is sending a message. He is condemning people to death. First Bateman, then Melrose, now Mondego."

"Lucy, I think you're reading into this things that aren't there. The Stations of the Cross are a Catholic thing. Not all churches have the Stations of the Cross."

"I don't care. It makes good copy. I'm going to write about the Stations of the Cross Murderer. It will sell papers."

"You can't do that! That's irresponsible."

"I figured it out. While you have been fidgeting with your fingers, I figured that the killer is cutting out his victims' eyes because they saw something they shouldn't have."

"You don't know about Bateman. His body was burned too badly. And you don't know about Mondego."

She folded her arms and stared at Cavanaugh. "You're not my only source. I know Mondego's eyes were cut out, too."

Cavanaugh realized she didn't know about the beer-soaked bread. "Listen, Lucy, there's a lot you don't know. I would hold off on this 'Stations of the Cross' thing. It could screw up the whole police investigation and create a panic at the same time. It could also put you in danger. This killer is smart and crafty. I think he or she is playing with the police."

"You don't scare me, Cavanaugh. I have nothing to fear. The killer's not after me."

"He might think you are putting the puzzle together too quickly. He might be afraid you'll discover who he is. Maybe he'll think you've seen too much."

"It's a free press. Maybe the killer will even write to me. The public loves stuff like this. If we can attach a name to the killer, they'll eat it up. Think about it. There was the Son of Sam, the Zodiac Killer, Lex Talionis, The Mad Bomber, BTK, the Beast of Birkenshaw, the Staten Island Butcher, the Angel of Death, and even Billy the Kid and Jack the Ripper. The list goes on and on. My editor will love the 'Stations of the Cross Murderer.' Nicknames sell papers, Cavanaugh. If I play this right I just may have found my ticket to a Pulitzer Prize. If he's as smart and crafty as you say, he might write a letter to me at the paper like George Metesky, The Mad Bomber, or Ted Kaczynski, The Unabomber, or The Zodiac Killer, or the Golden State Killer, or the Axeman of New Orleans did."

Cavanaugh shook his head. "I don't like it. I think you're putting yourself in harm's way. No Pulitzer Prize is worth dying for. This killer is intelligent, devious, and very dangerous. He or she is not after power or control. I don't think he's doing it for pleasure either. I fear he's on a mission. You don't want to become part of his mission."

"You can read about it in the paper," Bauer said and pushed past Cavanaugh into a heavier rain as a bolt of lightning suddenly lit up St. Mark's Place.

"Don't say I didn't warn you!" Cavanaugh shouted after her, but his words were drowned out by a loud clap of thunder.

* * * *

Cartagena, Colombia

Jack Bennis looked down the crowded aisle of the bus as it bounced along the rough road. The Cali Cartel was after him. They wanted their money, their drugs, and revenge for the deaths of four of their men. They had come looking for him. He was headed for Bogotá, but now he learned María Isabelle was in a hospital in Cali. He glanced up and saw the woman in the front of the bus turn again and nod her head. The man two seats in front of him nodded back. The word had spread fast. They knew the priest they were looking for was on the bus headed toward Bogotá.

The man and the woman had gotten on the bus three stops after he had. The man was carrying a gun. Why else would he be wearing a loose fitting jacket in the hot, humid weather? They were probably waiting for him to get off the bus in Bogotá where they would have opportunity to stop, question, and kill him. He was about to jump from the frying pan into the fire.

María Isabelle might have information about where Chico was. But the realization that she was all alone in a hospital in Cali sunk in like a fishing hook and dragged him to a different place. Aunt Jo was dead. Her brother was in prison. She wrote that the doctors thought she might never walk again. The woman he loved was lonesome and scared. She must have felt isolated and abandoned. Chico had reached out to her, but now he had disappeared. Bennis had not anticipated going to Cali, the home of one of the biggest and most dangerous drug cartels in the world, but here he was! María Isabelle needed him again.

He needed to get off the bus with as little damage as possible. There were children and innocent men and women on the bus, not to mention what seemed like a brood of chickens. His first step was to get past Scylla, the woman in front of the bus, and her accomplice, Charybdis, the man two rows in front of him. He knew the man in front of him had a gun. The woman may not have looked like the mythological twelve foot tall, six headed monster with three rows of shark-like teeth that Odysseus had to deal with, but Bennis knew she was dangerous.

The bus began to slow down. The road became narrower and muddier. They were approaching the small town of El Valle. It was a relatively isolated beach town. It was unusual for buses to travel to El Valle, but the recent floods had washed out many of the normal roads.

His mother's often repeated adage came to mind. "He who hesitates is lost." Bennis got up, grabbed Chico's spear, and pushed his way past a heavy-set man with a handlebar moustache who reeked of garlic and was busy eating a choripán sandwich. Pieces of sausage, parsley and chopped yellow onion clung to his moustache and belly like Velcro. As Bennis moved past Charybdis, he noticed the wooden grip of a revolver sticking out from his loose fitting jacket. The man appeared to be asleep.

Bennis moved quickly through the chickens in the aisle toward the front of the bus. At the woman with the red scarf he paused and shook his head slowly from side to side. She looked younger than he originally thought. He motioned toward his hand buried beneath his shirt and the outline of the pistol he was concealing. She froze long enough for him to reach the driver and request to be dropped off immediately. The driver was about to protest when he saw the gun Bennis had. The door opened and Bennis jumped off the bus as it was still moving. The bus skidded slightly on the muddy road as the driver wasted no time in driving away.

Jack Bennis watched the bus disappear down the

road. No one else got off. He looked around. Through the trees, he could hear in the distance the rolling waves of the Pacific Ocean. He didn't know where he was, but he was safe – for the moment at least.

* * * *

Chapter 14

Staten Island, New York

It was raining pretty heavily when Cavanaugh started driving toward Fr. Steve's brother's barber shop off New Dorp Lane. He didn't know what Stephen Impellizzieri could tell him about Mario Impellizzieri, but he was grasping at straws. Traffic was heavy so he decided to get to the New Dorp section of Staten Island by going over Emerson Hill.

Most people thought Emerson Hill was named after Ralph Waldo Emerson, but Cavanaugh knew from his love of trivia that the hilly, winding exclusively affluent community was actually named for Emerson's brother, Judge William Emerson. Cavanaugh had once tried to find information about Judge William Emerson, but all he came up with was that the judge was said to be a boring, unexciting individual. Cavanaugh thought the hill would have been more appropriately named Thoreau Hill because Henry David Thoreau, the author of *Walden* and one of the prime forces in the nineteenth century American Transcendentalist movement, once lived in "The Snuggery," the long, brown shingle house of Judge William Emerson on Douglas Road. Although Thoreau only lived there for six or seven months while tutoring Judge Emerson's children, Haven and Charles, and seeking publishing contacts in Manhattan, Cavanaugh thought Thoreau Hill would have been more appropriate. Thoreau was a much more significant historical figure than the stodgy Judge Emerson. In fact, Thoreau's brief stay on Staten Island was the only time in his adult time that he lived outside of Concord, Massachusetts.

Cavanaugh thought about his own brother and wondered how William and Ralph Waldo got along with each other as he maneuvered up and around the intertwining, meandering roads on Emerson Hill. Suddenly, he spotted a huge three story white brick building with thick white concrete columns and a tremendous paved driveway big enough to be a parking lot. The trees and shrubs were strategically located between statues of what looked like naked Greek goddesses. The building was situated on more than an acre of land. At first glance, except for the naked female statues, he thought the building looked like it could have been a cathedral in some cities. The architect designed a building that reeked of the *nouveau riche* or what Cavanaugh thought was the *nouveau ugly*.

In the midst of elegant, older homes, the building stood out like a brown mole on the lip of a model. He couldn't have missed it if he tried. But the flashing lights of police cars and emergency vehicles brought him to a stop. At the driveway entrance three police officers were taping off what could have been a crime scene or a scene from "Blue Bloods."

Cavanaugh recognized the police. Shanley and Rhatigan were holding the tape while Jefferson, the taser cop, was busy attaching the tape. Cavanaugh rolled down the window. "Hey, Shanley, what's up?"

Shanley handed the tape to Rhatigan and came over

to the car. "You're like a bad penny, Cavanaugh, you keep turning up. What are you doing here?"

"I was just taking a shortcut. I'm going to a barber in New Dorp. What's going on? Are they making a movie or something?"

"I wish. I always wanted to be in one of those Dirty Harry movies."

"What happened?"

"We're not sure yet. We got a report of a disturbance and when we got here we found a lot of blood, but no body."

"Who lives here?"

Shanley looked over his shoulder like he was revealing state secrets. "The owner of the house is listed as Mr. and Mrs. David Melrose."

"Melrose? The guy that was found in St. Peter's?"

"Same one. But the blood's not his. This blood is fresh. We think it might be his wife's."

* * * *

Cavanaugh slowly drove down Douglas Road to Richmond Road. The rain continued to fall sending small rivulets along the narrow road. A barrage of thoughts bombarded his brain. Was Monica Melrose dead? Did Mario Impellizzieri finish the job he sent his two goons to accomplish? What was it that Melrose knew or had uncovered that would motivate him to kill Melrose's wife?

He stopped at a red light at Four Corners Road. This whole thing didn't make sense. The police knew the thugs Cavanaugh encountered in Melrose's office worked for him. All Melrose's records had been destroyed. Mrs. Melrose was so scared she refused to talk to the police. Was Impellizzieri just making sure she wouldn't talk?

But something was wrong. Something didn't fit. Killing Monica Melrose would make him the prime suspect and put Impellizzieri under intense police scrutiny. Why would he risk this? Cars behind him started honking. The light was green. He felt the back of his neck. He decided he didn't need a haircut today after all. He turned onto Richmond Road and made a few turns. When he hit Garretson Avenue, he headed straight to Lee's Tavern. He needed a cold beer, one of Lee's famous thin-crusted clam pizzas, and time to think.

What was an ambulance chasing disgraced lawyer and part-time detective with a shabby office in an almost abandoned building doing in a sumptuous mansion fit for an NBA player or a Rap star? Where did he get the money?

At Lee's Tavern, Cavanaugh called Goldberg while waiting for his pizza. "What's the story with Monica Melrose?" he asked.

"I see you heard. That was fast."

"I happened to be going over Emerson Hill when I saw the police cars."

"What were you doing on Emerson Hill? I think it unlikely you were looking to sell your house and move there."

"No. I don't think I'm their cup of tea. I was headed to New Dorp for a haircut."

"You weren't headed to Impellizzieri's barbershop, I hope."

"Why?"

"We've had young Stephen's shop under surveillance for months. The FBI, DEA, and we are building a case against him and his father. All we need is you walking in there and blowing the whole operation."

"I was only trying to help, Morty."

"Do us all a favor, Tom. Stay away from the Impellizzieri family. They're a dangerous, treacherous bunch."

"Okay. I get it. What can you tell me about Melrose and his ugly house?"

"Beauty is in the eye of the beholder, Tom."

"Where did they get the money to buy that place? It looks like a cross between a Greek temple and a Nazi fortification."

Goldberg laughed. "You definitely have a way with words. It seems Mr. and Mrs. Melrose were involved in another lucrative business we were unaware of."

"Drugs?"

"No. They produced porno movies. They had a complete studio set up in the house equipped with multiple cameras, a sophisticated sound system, all sorts of sexual paraphernalia, and, of course, a heart-shaped bed."

Cavanaugh realigned the facts in his head. After a few seconds, he asked, "Morty, do you think her disappearance has anything to do with the other murders?"

"We don't know. We hoped the home security system would tell us something, but it was disabled. There was a lot of fresh blood in the house. It could be hers. Right now we don't know. Somebody called it in as a disturbance. We don't know who. It came from one of those prepaid cell phones you can buy almost anywhere. We have no way of tracing who sent it. It could be from our killer who is playing with us again. Right now the official copy is we are treating Monica Melrose as a missing person, but we have assigned additional police to patrol the churches just in case."

"There must be over a hundred different churches on Staten Island. You can't possibly monitor all of them."

"You're right. We can only hope the killer makes a

mistake. Meanwhile we will do our best and pray."

Cavanaugh sighed and said, "I'm afraid my brother's better at that praying business than I am. We could really use him."

* * * *

El Valle, Colombia

Using Chico's Muisca spear as a walking stick, Jack Bennis began his trek through the dense forest toward the sound of the water. He realized he must be somewhere in the rain forest. Everything was moist and green. Soon he came upon a waterfall. He followed the stream from the waterfall toward the sea. He was cut, bruised, and exhausted by the time he reached the dark, pounding sea along a rocky beach of black sand.

On an outcropping of black rocks sat a woman in a two-piece bikini. In her hands she held a drawing pad as she stared at the waves crashing against the rocks. He walked toward her. Her hair was black and pinned back like a pony-tail. Her skin was paler than the native Colombians. Her concentration was on the sea and on the pad she was drawing on.

He stood back and watched her drawing. She was an artist. He waited, not wanting to destroy her absorption in her subject. As the tide started to change, she stood and turned. Then she saw him. "Who are you?" she demanded.

"You're American," he said.

"Who are you and how did you get here?"

Bennis raised his hands. "I mean no harm. I came through the forest. I'm lost. Can you tell me where I am?"

She folded her drawing pad and slowly climbed down the rocks. "I didn't hear you. I was ...."

"I could see. I didn't want to disturb your concentration. I see you are an artist."

She looked him over. His clothes were torn, his face and hands were smeared with black shoe polish, and he carried what looked like a large spear. She backed up slightly. "Get away from me," she said. "I have no money."

"Please, Miss, try to understand. I am an American priest. I mean you no harm."

"You don't look very much like a priest," she said. There was fear in her eyes and voice.

"I seem to get that a lot lately." Bennis reached beneath his shirt to show her his clerical shirt and collar. As he did so, however, the gun he was carrying fell unto the black sand.

"Get away from me," she repeated. She turned and realized she had no place to run. The rocks were behind her. The crashing waves to her right, and the dense rain forest to her left.

Jack Bennis bent down slowly and picked up the gun. He placed it under his shirt again. "I'm not here to hurt you in any way. Some people are after me, and I need to find some shelter and get to Cali. Just tell me which way to go and I will leave you."

"Cali? That's a long way away from here."

"I know. The bus I was on got diverted and when I had a chance, I got off. There were some people on the bus planning to kill me. I am trying to find a twelve-year-old boy who ran away from school. There is a woman in a hospital in Cali I think can help me find him."

"I may be crazy, but I believe you. Maybe it's your eyes or your voice. No one could make up a story like that." She pointed over her shoulder. "I am staying at the Humpback Turtle Hostel. It's about five miles from here. From there, it is about a fifteen minute walk into the town of El Valle. There's not much in the town to be honest. It's mostly plain wooden buildings and dirt roads. In a couple of months there will be some tourists here to watch the whales and the turtles, but right now the place is boringly dead unless you're a fan of fish and coconuts."

"I'm Jack Bennis," he said extending his hand to the woman.

"It's nice to meet you, Father Jack," she said shaking his hand. It was a firm handshake, the kind he liked. He looked out at the sea and saw the sun was going down.

"I'd better get on my way. Five miles is a long way, and it will be dark soon."

"Follow me. I'll give you a ride."

Beyond the next outcropping of rocks, he saw a tuk-tuk. It was a motorized three wheeled rickshaw. He had seen them in Bangkok, Sri Lanka, Bolivia, and a few in Cartagena. "Where did you get this?" he asked.

"I came here to get away from it all and do some drawings. The only way to get to this place is by boat or plane. From the plane, you can hire a tuk-tuk to take you here. I decided to rent a tuk-tuk while I was here so I could do some exploring of my own. I like adventure, but not at the expense of pleasure. Hop aboard."

"But wait! I don't even know your name."

"Perhaps, it's better that way. But if it makes you feel better, you can call me Dianna."

* * * *

On the ride to the hostel, Bennis asked Dianna, "Why are you helping me?"

"Let's put it this way, Father Jack, I don't buy that

stuff about you being a priest for one minute. It's a good story, but I never saw a priest carrying a gun under his shirt."

"All the more reason to ask, 'Why are you helping me?'"

Dianna looked at him. "Here I am, all alone in a bikini, on a deserted beach, and you come out of the rain forest. There are no people within us for miles. I work on my body. I know I'm in good shape. Yet you don't make a move on me. You could have raped me or killed me. But you didn't."

"So what does that prove?"

Dianna smiled. "Maybe nothing."

They rode the next mile in silence. Then Bennis said, "I thank you for the ride, but what I told you back there was all true. There are people after me. I don't want you getting involved in this. Being with me could be dangerous."

"Let me put it this way," Dianna said as they bounced over some rocks, "I came here to get away from the pressures back home. I've been here a week, but it's felt like a month in solitary confinement. If I didn't have my art work, I'd go crazy watching the palm trees grow. A little excitement in my life is a good thing."

"You don't understand. I inadvertently stumbled on some drug dealers who were involved with trafficking young boys for sex. In the course of my encounter with them, I disrupted their organization somewhat, and now the Cali Cartel is after me."

"Hold on, Father Jack. If the Cali gang is after you, why are you planning on going to Cali? Are you on some suicidal mission or does Father Jack intend to be a martyr?"

"It's a long story, Dianna. I think it will only bore you. Right now I have to figure out how to get from here to Cali as soon as possible."

"Well, you won't be able to go anywhere tonight. It

gets real dark around here at night. Why don't we get you settled at the hostel and then we can sit at the tiki bar and have a drink while you bore the artist with your tale of woe?"

Bennis looked at the darkening sky. Ahead of them a huge bonfire blazed in front of the Humpback Turtle Hostel. A drink, some food, and a shower sounded great. "I think I'd like that," he said. "First, I'll get room and then take you up on that drink. My treat."

As they pulled up to the Humpback Turtle Hostel, they saw a swarm of people gathered around the bonfire with drinks in their hands. Loud music and laughter filled the air. "I thought you said this place was empty," he said.

Dianna looked at him with a surprised face. "Let me put it this way, it was when I left. I don't know where all these people came from." She stopped the tuk-tuk next to a tall, muscular black man carrying a stack of towels. "Hey, Esteban," she called, "where did all these people come from?"

Esteban bowed slightly, "*Buena noches*, Miss Dianna. This place is going loco. I don't ever remember these many people here in the off season. Two large groups of backpackers arrived today, one from Germany and one from Australia. We are booked solid. There are no rooms available, even the dorm is full."

Jack Bennis felt his stomach drop.

Dianna looked at him and smiled. "No sweat, Father Jack, I have a thatch roof cabin rented for another week." She reached over and patted his leg. "You can stay with me. I have a nice, big, comfortable bed."

Bennis felt his stomach drop a little more.

* * * *

Staten Island, New York

The beer was good. The pizza was even better. Cavanaugh sat at a table in the back corner of Lee's Tavern. Monica Melrose's disappearance put things in a different light. If Bateman was the first killing and he was killed because he exposed himself to a group of young girls, his death could be related to his sex crime or to revenge or to something entirely different. Cavanaugh's initial theory had been Dave Melrose's death was a result of his divorce investigation. If he worked in pornography, however, the reason might have something to do with his sex business or something else entirely different. Mondego owned bars where drugs were prevalent and two teenagers recently died from drug overdoses in one of his bars. His death might be a direct result of his drug involvement or something else entirely. Cavanaugh wasn't getting anywhere, but somehow he felt he was getting closer.

Now Monica Melrose turns up missing. The amount of blood left at the scene suggested she was attacked in the house. Was she already dead? Would her body turn up in some church with her eyes torn out and beer-soaked bread in her pocket or purse?

Cavanaugh stared at his glass of beer. Why waste good beer on murder victims? Why cut out their eyes? Why leave their bodies in churches? The killer was sending a message. But what was the message?

He heard chairs being pulled over and two people abruptly sat down at his table. "Well look who's here! If it isn't former Detective Cavanaugh, the brother of our chief murder suspect, Father Jack Bennis!"

Cavanaugh looked up to see Detective Perez and her enormous partner. "What are you doing here, Perez? Why don't you take your purple hair and the Hulk, go somewhere else, and stop harassing me?"

"Where's your brother?"

"I think we have been over this before and you know the answer. I don't know."

"We know he flew out of Newark to go to Cartagena, Colombia, but when and how did he get back?"

"You've got a bug up your rear end, Perez. Why don't you ask Godzilla next to you to scratch it and leave us alone? My brother is innocent."

Perez reached over and took a piece of Cavanaugh's clam pie. "I don't give a rat's ass about your brother. It's you I want, Cavanaugh, for what you did to my sister. If I have to get to you through your brother, I will."

Perez's partner reached over for another piece of Cavanaugh's pizza. Cavanaugh grabbed his hand and twisted back on his thumb and kicked his chair. The big man screamed and lost his balance. "Touch that pie, buster, and you'll have nine fingers."

Cavanaugh stood, still twisting Perez's partner's thumb, "Now get out of here the both of you before I report you the police for harassment and petty theft!"

The purple-haired detective stood. She threw the half-eaten piece of pizza she had taken on the table. Cavanaugh released his hold on her partner's thumb. All eyes in the tavern looked at them. Perez and her massive partner slowly backed away. "You'll be hearing from us, Cavanaugh," she said.

When they left, the waitress came over to his table. "Are you all right, sir?"

Cavanaugh sat down and said, "To tell you the truth, I could use another beer."

He wrapped the half-eaten piece Perez had taken in a napkin and finished his beer. He looked up expecting to see the waitress bringing him another beer, but instead saw an attractive woman in a blue business suit standing at his table. "I overheard that woman with the purple hair call you Cavanaugh. Are you really Father Bennis' brother?"

Cavanaugh frowned. "Do I know you?"

She smoothed the front of her suit and looked down. "My name is Roberta O'Hanlon. My husband and I met with your brother the night of that man's murder."

He remembered the name. Lucy Bauer had interviewed her about the ferry incident with Robert Bateman. Her husband was a physical education teacher and she worked at Staten Island University in human relations. They had two young children.

"I was wondering how Father Bennis is. He spent a lot of time with us that night."

"Please sit down," Cavanaugh said. "My brother left to find a young boy who went missing in Colombia. I hope he will be home soon. May I ask what you and your husband were discussing with my brother?"

"We were concerned about a neighbor. He used to be outgoing and friendly, but now he is reclusive and seems to avoid us."

Cavanaugh offered Roberta a piece of his pie. "No thank you. I'm waiting for two pies to bring home. It's been a long day dealing with layoffs at the hospital. I just don't feel like cooking tonight."

"What did my brother say about your neighbor?"

"He wanted to know if anything changed in his life recently, and it did. Mr. Wallowmire lost his wife in a hit and run accident about a year and a half ago. He and his wife were very close. They had two sons, Gerard, who attended M.I.T., and Gerald, who was a student at the College of Staten Island."

Cavanaugh noticed her eyes were watering. She looked down and said softly, "Gerard killed himself at school shortly after his mother's death. They found him hanging from a ceiling fan in his dorm room."

Cavanaugh shook his head. "I'm sorry to hear that. That must have been a great shock to Mr. Wallowmire."

"It was," she said as she wiped a tear from her cheek, "but when his other son, Gerald, died, he withdrew from everybody. I hoped your brother could come to speak with him. We tried everything."

"I take it Gerald's death was sudden."

"Yes. I think it literally broke his heart. He died of a drug overdose at a party somewhere. He was a bright boy. He was only seventeen and in college."

The waitress came back with Cavanaugh's beer. "Your pies are ready, Mrs. O'Hanlon."

"Thank you. I'm sorry, Mr. Cavanaugh, but I must be going. Please tell your brother when you speak to him that we appreciate his help and look forward to seeing him soon."

Cavanaugh stood and shook her hand. "I will do that, Mrs. O'Hanlon. My mother used to say we receive a special blessing if we help others. I can see both you and your husband are very special and very blessed people. It has been a pleasure meeting you."

As he watched Roberta O'Hanlon pick up her two pizzas and walk out of Lee's Tavern, he thought how different she was from purple-headed Detective Perez. He thought how sensitive to the plight of others she was as compared to Perez whose idea of comedy would be when you fall into an open sewer and die."

He finished his beer and looked at his watch. He needed to go home. He called the waitress over and ordered a black coffee and a meatball sausage pie to go for Fran. It was her favorite.

* * * *

Chapter 15

Staten Island, New York

Cavanaugh woke up the next morning to the aroma of coffee brewing and his wife's shaking him and asking, "Did you read the paper?"

"Fran, you woke me up. I'm still in bed!"

"Well, *The Times* has a big story in it about what they are calling the Stations of the Cross Murders."

Cavanaugh sat up like a Jack-in-the-box. "I can't believe she did it. I warned her not to do it!"

"It says there is a serial killer running around, and he's already killed three people. It says he cuts their eyes out and leaves their bodies in churches."

Cavanaugh rubbed his eyes. He threw his legs over the edge of the bed. "I can't believe she went ahead and did it."

"Look at what the article says about you."

"Oh no! She didn't mention me, did she?"

"Yes. It says, 'Former homicide detective Thomas Cavanaugh pointed out that all three murder victims were deliberately positioned next to the first Station of the Cross – Pontius Pilate's condemning Jesus to death.'"

Cavanaugh jumped up and grabbed the newspaper. "I

never said that! She's lying!"

"Oh, Tom, what are you so upset about? You always say you can't believe everything you read in the papers."

"This is different, Fran. She used my name and I never said that. In trying to make a name for herself, Lucy Bauer has put all of us in the killer's sights!"

Fran stepped back.

Cavanaugh read the news article aloud:

"According to Mr. Cavanaugh, Robert
Bateman was the killer's first victim. His
body was found in a Pentecostal Church
on Bay Street. The second victim was
David Melrose, a private investigator. His
body was found in St. Peter's Church on
St. Mark's Place. The third victim,
Fernando Mondego, a prominent
business owner, was discovered by
Jerry Lipton, the custodian at the
United Methodist Church on Scribner
Avenue. All three victims had their eyes
removed. Mr. Cavanaugh theorizes the
removal of the victims' eyes may have
to do with something they saw. The police
were unavailable for comment...."

"Oh, this is not good," Cavanaugh said. "My brother is off enjoying the warm weather in Colombia, and here I am dealing with this crap!"

Fran shook her head. "I don't know what you are moaning about. The publicity will be good for your private investigation business. Didn't P. T. Barnum say there's no such thing as bad publicity?"

Cavanaugh sat back down on the bed. "Barnum didn't know what he was talking about. We are dealing with a murderer here."

The telephone rang on the night stand next to him. Cavanaugh looked at the caller I.D. It was Morty Goldberg.

"Oh no!" he said. "This is so not good!"

* * * *

El Valle, Colombia

Father Bennis and Dianna sat on the porch of her thatch roof cabin sipping coffee and looking out at the rolling waves of the Pacific Ocean. Down on the black sand beach, the remnants of last night's bonfire smoldered in the slight breeze. "So you really are a priest?" she said wrapping her beach blanket tighter around herself.

"You don't make it any easier," he said.

She looked at him intently. "I never met anyone like you before."

He smiled. "I'm just a man who answered a call and took some vows that I try to adhere to. It's hard sometimes because like most people I have feet of clay."

"You are one of the most honorable men I have ever met."

He smiled again. "You haven't known me long enough."

They sat in silence for a while watching the sun rise above the pounding surf. Finally, she turned to him and asked, "How do you plan to get to Cali?"

"I haven't thought that out yet." His eyes drifted from the ocean to the sands. In the distance he saw two figures walking along the sands. One was a woman; the other a man.

As they came closer he saw the woman was wearing a red scarf and the man a loose fitting jacket. It was Scylla and Charybdis. They were looking for him.

Bennis stood up suddenly. "Thank you for everything, but I have to go now."

"Why?" Then she looked down the beach. She saw the man and the woman. "It's them, isn't it? It's the people you told me about on the bus. What are you going to do?"

"I'm going to get away from here as fast as possible. I don't want to involve you in any of this. They are dangerous people."

"Listen, Father Jack, like it or not, I am involved in this. Hop in my tuk-tuk and we'll get you out of here."

They both saw the woman speaking to Esteban, the friendly man with the towels they had met last night. Esteban pointed to Dianna's cabin. "No time to discuss this, they are on their way. I will take you as far as I can in the tuk-tuk. It's not very fast, but it beats walking. "

"But what about you?"

"You think I'm crazy? Those guys are headed up here. I'm driving you as far away from here as possible. The town of Tadó is about fifty miles away. The tuk-tuk should make it there with no problem. You can rent a car from there. We can discuss things later. Now if you will excuse the language, Father Jack, let's get the hell out of here!"

* * * *

Staten Island, New York

Cavanaugh picked the phone up and started talking. "Listen, Morty, I swear I didn't say all that stuff to the reporter. I met her at St. Peter's and she told me she was going to run with the Stations of the Cross thing. I told her not to. I warned her not to write that. She claimed it would sell papers."

"Take a breath, Tom," Goldberg said. "The cat's out of the bag, but she obviously doesn't know about Monica Melrose's disappearance and the bread. At least not yet. That's a good thing."

"What am I supposed to do, Morty? She expects the killer to write to her, but I'm afraid he or she is liable to come after her or my family."

Cavanaugh heard Goldberg's pen clicking, then Goldberg cleared his throat and said, "Be prepared for the other media to reach out to you."

"I hate those people! I didn't say those things she wrote. She put her own thoughts in my mouth! It's not fair. It's irresponsible!"

"Get over it, Tom. It's what they do. Their business is selling papers. Ours is catching the bad guys."

"You should know she claims to have sources in the P.D. Somebody told her about the eyes."

"It's my job to shut that source down, and I will. You can imagine how pissed off the Commissioner is. Trust me. Ms. Bauer will be *persona non grata* around here. If she wants any information, she will have to speak to me personally."

Cavanaugh looked out his bedroom window. "The press is here already. An Eyewitness News truck and a CBS TV truck just pulled up in front of my house. I should have never asked her to help."

"What did you ask her to do?"

Cavanaugh explained how he asked Lucy Bauer to interview some of the parents of the girls Bateman accosted in the ferry terminal.

"That was your first mistake, Tom. It sounds like you made a deal with the devil."

"She's not a bad person, Morty. She's smart and thorough. Her biggest problem is she's ambitious."

"But why would she mention you in her article. Usually reporters quote unnamed sources. Why put you in the crosshairs?"

"I swear, Morty, I never said those things she said I said. I think she's getting back at me because I lied to her a couple of times. I did it to get her off my back."

"That may have been your second mistake. Lying to a reporter is never a good thing. Lying to a woman reporter is a terrible thing. It sounds to me that she feels turn-around is fair play."

Cavanaugh reached out and grabbed his wife's hand. "But she's put all of us in harm's way. We don't know how the killer will react."

"I've got to go now, Tom. There have been some new developments I have to follow up on. Stay cool. Try to avoid putting your foot in your mouth in dealing with the reporters. I'll try to send a patrol car around your house to watch Fran and the baby. Meanwhile, watch your back."

Cavanaugh felt Fran tightening her grip on his hand as he heard Goldberg hang up.

* * * *

Tadó, Colombia

The road from El Valle to Tadó was rough and bumpy. It wound through the Rain Forest and dense vegetation. The tuk-tuk didn't go very fast, but it produced a slight breeze through the dense, humid air of the forest, and it was much better than walking. When the priest and the artist reached Tadó, they were both tired. Along the way, Father Bennis explained in greater detail the events that occurred since he arrived in Colombia. Dianna was interested in the mysterious woman in the Cali hospital, but Bennis evaded specifics. He said he hoped she would be able to help him track down Chico.

"He's been missing a long time," she said. "Do you really think you will be able to find him?"

"All I can do is try. I feel responsible for the boy."

"You're risking your life for a missing boy. I don't know many people who would do that. In fact, I don't know anyone else who would do that."

Tadó proved to be an even smaller town than El Valle. There were no rental cars, but they managed to convince a grocery store owner to sell them a rusted, dented 2006 Kia Picanto with a busted axle, balding tires, and poor brakes. "It's an accident waiting to happen, but it should be able to get me to Pereira. It's only about a four hour ride," Bennis said.

"I don't think you should go alone," Dianna said.

"I will be all right. I'm worried about you. What will happen to you when you get back to the hostel? What if those people are waiting for you?"

"They're looking for you, not me. Don't worry about me. If they are there, they won't get any information from me. Your plans are safe with me. Like Winston Churchill once said, life is filled with opportunities to keep one's mouth shut. Believe it or not, I'm one woman who knows how to keep a secret."

When he offered to give her a blessing before she left, Dianna replied, "I'm not Catholic, Father Jack. It's not that I don't believe in God. It's more like I don't believe in organized religions. Sometimes I feel they are responsible for more problems than solutions. I don't know why people can't just get along with one another."

"I understand where you are coming from, but I'm giving you a blessing anyway. I think we are all born with a belief in God. It's part of our nature. We may not see it as God, but it's there in the rising of the sun, the clashing of the waves against the rocks, the floating of the clouds overhead, the chirping of the early morning birds. Maybe if more people helped and loved one another instead of following their own selfish, worldly pursuits things would be a lot better. I believe there are many paths we can take in life. Our job is not to judge the paths of others, but to find the path that will lead us closer to spiritual happiness. That's where, I believe, religion comes into play. Religion offers a path, but it's not the only path. Sometimes we need people to show us or remind us of the path we need to follow."

Dianna hopped back in her tuk-tuk and smiled. "You are truly a remarkable man, Father Jack. I wish I had met you years ago. Maybe life would have been different." She turned the tuk-tuk around and headed back to El Valle. "Take care, Father Jack. It's been a blast!" she said. As he watched her disappear in a cloud of dust, Bennis said a quiet prayer for her safety.

* * * *

Staten Island, New York

There was a woman waiting outside Cavanaugh's office when he got there. She could have been a model. She had long black hair that cascaded in waves over her shoulders. She wore a tight black dress with a string of pearls around her neck. Her skin was the color of a caffè latte. Her smile and her sparkling green eyes lit up the dreary morning. Cavanaugh thought if he could describe her in one word it would be "exquisitely beautiful" – but that would be two words.

"Mr. Cavanaugh?" she said.

"I have no comment," he replied. "I'm sorry, but no comment!"

"I'm not a reporter, Mr. Cavanaugh. My name is Katherine Ames. Bob Bateman was my brother. I read in the paper you believed my brother was killed by the Stations of the Cross Murderer."

Cavanaugh raised his hands in surrender. "Hold on, lady! I never said those things they said I said in the paper."

"May I come in?" she asked. "I would like to hire you to find something my brother had."

Cavanaugh opened the door to his office which still smelled like the donut shop it once had been just as an NBC News van pulled up to the curb. He pointed to a chair for Ms. Ames and then closed and locked the door.

"I know my brother had his problems. I can't excuse him. He used to be a professional photographer back in Cincinnati before he got into trouble with pictures of young boys and girls he was taking and sharing. To be honest, it made me sick, but he was my brother."

"I'm not sure I can help you, Ms. Ames."

"Call me Kathy," she said crossing her long shapely

legs. "My brother told me he had taken some pictures recently that he thought would prove very profitable. I want to hire you to find those pictures."

"I'm sorry, Ms. Ames, but you've come to the wrong person. I don't deal with pornography. You're going to have to find someone else."

She leaned forward and rubbed the string of pearls around her neck. "I know the kind of pictures he took, but the pictures I am referring to involved adults engaging in some kind of illicit activity."

"And what do you plan on doing with these photos? I don't get involved in blackmailing schemes either."

Katherine Ames lowered her head and brushed a tear away. "I plan on destroying the pictures. I asked another man to find my brother, but instead he tried to blackmail me into making prurient movies. I think he may have found the pictures himself and was using them to blackmail someone else. He was a despicable person who deserved to die."

"By any chance, was this man's name Dave Melrose?"

"Yes. He and his wife were bad people. The world would be a better place without people like them."

"Well, someone seems to have taken care of that."

Katherine Ames stared at Cavanaugh, but said nothing. An NBC reporter started knocking on the door. Cavanaugh ignored him. "I'm not the man for this job, Ms. Ames. If I did find the photos, which I don't know that I could, and they showed illegal transactions, I would have to turn them over to the police."

"I did a little research on you, Mr. Cavanaugh, and I believe you are an honorable man. If you find the pictures, all I ask is that you show them to me and then you can do what you want with them."

"I don't know how honorable I am, but I do try to be

honest. And to be completely honest, I don't know where to start. The police had a difficult time identifying your brother's body because it was burned so badly, and there is no record of where he was living."

Katherine Ames took a piece of paper from her purse and handed it to Cavanaugh. "This is his address. He lived in a third floor one room apartment on Slosson Terrace. I know because I pay the rent. The apartment is in the name of Karl Trask."

Cavanaugh looked at the address. It was only a few blocks from the Ferry Terminal. "If you know where he lived," he asked, "why don't you go and look for the pictures there yourself?"

Ms. Ames stood up. "I don't have the key. I figured you would be able to circumvent that obstacle." She opened her purse and took out an envelope.

"Wait! I didn't say I would take the job, Ms. Ames."

"You will," she said and handed him the envelope which was filled with cash. "This is a down payment. There will be a bonus when I see the pictures." She turned and started walking toward the door.

Cavanaugh looked at the money. There was over a thousand dollars in the envelope. "And how am I going to get in touch with you? I don't have your address or phone number."

Katherine Ames paused at the door. There were reporters outside. She turned. "Don't worry, Mr. Cavanaugh. I will be in touch with you." And then she lowered her head and pushed her way through the reporters on the street.

* * * *

Chapter 16

Pereira, Colombia

The ailing 2006 Kia Picanto never made it to Pereira. Three hours into the ride, it died after a frightful fit of coughing. Jack Bennis pushed it to the side of the road and managed to hitchhike on a red jeep loaded with coffee beans and bananas the rest of the way. The driver wore a lightweight straw hat with a wide brim. His skin was wrinkled from the sun and was the color of maple sugar. He had a long Grecian nose and a thick black unibrow and full beard that reminded Bennis somewhat of Ulysses Grant. When he smiled two of his front teeth were missing. The driver's name was Maximillian Ortiz. "No relation to King Maximillian or that Boston baseball player," he laughed.

To say Max was loquacious would be an understatement. He talked most of the way to Pereira as he drove through the foothills of the Andes. He told Bennis about the rigors of his job and his life. He told him where he could best rent a car and rent a room. He explained how Pereira is the center of the coffee growing axis of Colombia. He told him how Pereira is a vibrant city filled with highways, skyscrapers, coffee shops, nightclubs, bars, casinos, street vendors, cable cars, the largest theme park in South America, and a cable bridge known as the César Gaviria Trujillo Viaduct. He even told him to check out the famous naked statue of Simon Bolívar riding a horse in the middle of the Plaza de Bolívar.

When they arrived in Pereira, Max dropped Bennis off at a decent looking hotel. "Ask for John Fumando. He's a gringo, but you can trust him. The rumors are he made a lot of money on Wall Street and came down here to relax in retirement, but he saw how Pereira was growing and started investing. I hear he now owns a few hotels, a rental car business, laundromats, a travel agency, and a couple of car washes. Tell him Max sent you."

Bennis did as he was told. Fumando was able to cut through a lot of red tape and before long the priest had rented a car and bought some new clothes. It was still a seven hour trip to Cali and Bennis was tired and not looking forward to a long drive on unfamiliar roads in the night, so he secured a room for the night, ate a good meal in his room, and took a hot shower.

Before going to bed, he said a prayer for Dianna, Chico, and María Isabelle. Then he turned on the television to check the weather forecast for the next day. After a story about a local soccer player arrested in a nightclub brawl in Bogotá, the station switched to a breaking story of the death of an American at a resort in El Valle. Bennis turned the volume up.

The on-the-scene reporter explained how a famous international artist was found dead in her cabin at the Humpback Turtle Hostel. The police reported she was shot three times, twice in the chest and once in the back of the head. Unconfirmed reports were she was tortured prior to death and eight of her fingers were cut off. Police were not revealing her name until her family could be contacted.

Jack Bennis sat on the edge of his bed. They had tortured Dianna to find out where he was. Cutting her fingers was the ultimate torture for an artist. Had she told them where he was headed? Who could blame her if she did?

He uncovered the pistol he had hidden in his clerical clothes and carried with him from Cartagena. He had hoped he wouldn't have to use it. Looking at the television reporter in front of the thatch roofed cabin where he had coffee with Dianna that morning, he realized he might have to use the gun.

He turned the television off and lay back on the bed. "There is a time for everything," he said softly to himself, "a time to be born and a time to die; a time for peace and a time for war; a time to heal and a time to kill...."

* * * *

Staten Island, New York

Tom Cavanaugh sat in his office. Outside, a number of reporters milled around drinking coffee and chatting with each other. His office phone rang constantly. CBS, NBC, ABC, Fox, CNN, even Staten Island Live called. The constant ringing gave him a splitting headache. He thought about disconnecting his phone, but decided on a simpler approach. He checked the ID number, answered the phone quickly, said, "No comment," and then hung up. He had to give them credit. They were a persistent group.

Around noon, his cell phone rang. It was Goldberg. "Morty, these reporters are driving me nuts. They keep calling. Any news on Monica Melrose?"

"None yet. I'm calling you about a different matter. I just had a call from my friend in the Colombian National

Police, Marian Fraumeni. She's now a captain."

"I remember her. She was that girlfriend you were nailing at some conference you went to a few years ago. She was gorgeous, Morty. You definitely have good taste."

"You are a pig, Cavanaugh. There was never anything between us. She's a good person, and she helped you out when you went to Bogotá."

"What happened to '*meshuggener*'? I love it when you speak Jewish."

"*Meshuggener* is too good for you! And for the last time, it's Yiddish, not Jewish."

"Okay, okay. I was only breaking chops. It's been a tough day. Fraumeni was a real help. But what did she call you about and why are you telling me?"

Cavanaugh heard the pen clicking again. "It seems four members of the Cali Cartel have been killed recently."

"That sounds like a good thing to me. Why is she bothering you about it?"

"There are reports that a priest was involved in the killings and in the theft of a large quantity of Cali drugs and money. From the description she received, she thinks the priest may be your brother."

Cavanaugh looked out his window. The reporters and TV trucks were still there.

"Where is he, Tom?"

"I don't know, Morty. He called shortly after he arrived in Cartagena, but I haven't heard from him since. I tried calling him a couple of times, but either his phone is turned off or he's somewhere where there is no cell phone reception. That's the truth, Morty. I honestly don't know where he is, and I'm worried about him. You can tell Captain Fraumeni that as soon as I hear from him, I'll let you know."

After ending his call with Goldberg, Cavanaugh sat

motionless for a while staring at his phone. He tried calling his brother's cell phone again, but the call did not go through. He held his hands against his temples and tried to think. Then his desk phone rang again. He picked it up quickly and said, "No comment."

As he was about to hang up, a garbled voice said, "You've got it all wrong, Cavanaugh."

Cavanaugh hesitated. "Who is this?"

"You've got it all wrong, Cavanaugh," the voice repeated. "Stay out of my business. It could prove hazardous to your health and the health of your family."

* * * *

Chapter 17

Cali, Colombia

Jack Bennis set out early in the morning for the drive to Cali. Along the ride he had a lot of time to think. He couldn't get the picture of Dianna driving the tuk-tuk over the rugged rainforrest roads out of his mind. He remembered how she laughed when he complimented her on her art work, how concerned she was about Chico and María Isabelle, how she never worried that Scylla and Charybdis would bother with her. She worried about his safety, not hers. But they had come after her. Her voice echoed in his brain like nails hammered into his flesh. "You are truly a remarkable man, Father Jack. I wish I had met you years ago. Maybe life would have been different." She went out of her way to help him, and she paid dearly for it. They had tortured her to find out where he had gone. Had she told them? They cut off all but two of her fingers. Were the two remaining fingers the ones she held her pencil and brush in? Was that when she told them he was headed to Cali? Once they had their information they killed her.

He remembered her last words to him as she drove away. "Take care, Father Jack. It's been a blast!" He shook his head. He had let her down just as he had let Chico and María Isabelle down. Why was it everyone he came in contact with seemed to suffer? It wasn't supposed to be that way. He tried to help people, but innocent people always seemed to get hurt.

He prayed for Dianna, Chico, and María Isabelle. Would he ever find Chico? Maybe his brother was right. Was it an impetuous reaction to come to Colombia to locate a missing boy? Finding a needle in a haystack would be easier. Already five people were dead because of him. Would María Isabelle be able to help him find Chico? And what about María Isabelle? In trying to do the right thing, he had abandoned her. Now she was lying alone and despondent in a hospital for months because she was shot by bullets intended for him.

He pounded the steering wheel. "My God, my God, why have you forsaken me?" he shouted. "I cry by day, but you do not answer!" How often had he prayed that psalm? He knew it went on, "For he has not despised or abhorred the affliction of the afflicted, and he has not hidden his face from him, but has heard when he cried to him." He wanted so much to believe the psalm, but he felt like a lamb crying in the wilderness, but no one was answering.

He arrived in Cali around 1:00 p.m. His overnight stopover in Pereira had delayed him. Scylla and Charybdis had a head start on him. They could be waiting for him. But his mother ingrained in him never to give up. He knew the odds were against him, but as Aristotle once said the greatest quality of mind next to honor is courage. It allows one to keep going into the dark tunnel even if there is no light at the end of it.

Cali is a big, busy city of over 2,000,000 people. It is almost three times as large as Pereira. Nestled between mountains on the west and the Cauca River on the east, it is the only major Colombian city with access to the Pacific Ocean. It is a city of highways, skyscrapers, parks, sports arenas, and all kinds of street vendors.

Unfortunately, the drug cartels which operate on the outskirts of the city have given Cali a bad reputation. Jack Bennis knew they operated on intimidation and that was one of the major reasons they were after him. He couldn't be allowed to get away. Frequently, the threat of violence by the Cali Cartel was enough. At the height of their power, members of the cartel were a self-proclaimed vigilante group and went through the streets murdering prostitutes, homosexuals, petty thieves, homeless, and street children. They sometimes left their bodies with signs saying, "*Cali limpia, Cali linda*" (Clean Cali, beautiful Cali), or they simply dumped the corpses into the Cauca River causing it to be known as the River of Death.

Bennis needed to stop a few times to ask directions to Santo Jose Gabriel del Rosario Brochero Hospital. It wasn't a big hospital. Along a crowded strip of nightclubs and bars, he stopped to ask directions of a young woman with long black hair, silver hooped earrings, a black halter wrap around, six-inch high heels, ripped blue dungaree denim shorts and a silver belly button ring of an iguana. She gave him detailed instructions about how to get there. When he thanked her, she said. "No problem, *señor*. I have been there many times for cosmetic surgery. They are the best."

He smiled as he drove away. He felt like a caveman wandering into another world. He grew up being taught the importance of honor and loyalty, but in this new world materialistic things seemed more important.

Within ten minutes he found the hospital just as the young woman had said. It was a three-story, nondescript red brick building. The only indication it was a hospital was a small sign on the side of the main door that read, "Santo Jose Gabriel del Rosario Brochero Hospital." For better or for worse, he had arrived. The die was cast.

He drove around the block several times looking for anyone who might be waiting for him. He saw no one. He found a parking space and parked. He took a deep breath, patted the gun concealed beneath his shirt, got out of his car, and started walking toward the hospital.

* * * *

Staten Island, New York

Cavanaugh called Chief of Detectives Morty Goldberg immediately. A voice recording told him to leave a message. "Morty," he shouted into his cell phone, "where the hell are you? I think the killer just left me a message telling me I had it all wrong. He threatened my family. I want this guy bad. Check my incoming calls. Maybe we can learn where he called from. Where the hell are you anyway? I'm going home now to check on Fran and the baby. I want a police car there. It's that article that Bauer reporter wrote. I know it. I want to wring her neck!"

Cavanaugh continued to rant and rave, but the message machine clicked off. The voice was garbled on the phone. It could have been a man or a woman's voice, but he was sure it was from Mario Impellizzieri. Who else would have the nerve to call and threaten him? "You've got it all wrong, Cavanaugh," the voice said. "Stay out of my business. It could prove hazardous to your health and the health of your family."

The reporters outside his office attacked him as he left his office. He pushed his way through a bombardment of questions.

"What do you think the victims saw that led to their deaths?"

"How did you know Robert Bateman was the killer's first victim?"

"Is it true the police suspect your brother of being the killer?"

"Do you have any additional information about the killer?"

"Why is the killer leaving his victims in churches?"

"How did you come by your information?"

"What is the significance of the Stations of the Cross?"

Cavanaugh acted like he was called to testify before a Congressional Committee. He said nothing.

Driving home, Cavanaugh fantasized about what he would do to Mario Impellizzieri and Lucy Bauer if anything happened to his family. He drove through traffic lights, broke speed limits, and almost crashed three times. While cutting in and out of traffic on the West Shore Expressway, his cell phone rang again. It was Goldberg. "Where the hell have you been?" he barked at the Bluetooth in his car. "Mario Impellizzieri called me and threatened my family. I want that bastard arrested!"

"Hold on, Tom! What are you talking about?"

"He called me and told me to stay out of his business!"

"How do you know it was Impellizzieri?"

"It had to be him. Who else would say that?"

"Did he give his name?"

"No. His voice was garbled on the phone. It was like he was using one of those machines that distort his voice. You've got to check my incoming calls. You'll see he called me."

"If he's half as smart as he thinks he is, he wouldn't

call you on a line we can trace. But we will check it out. I've sent a patrol car over to your house just to make sure Fran and Stephen are okay."

Cavanaugh's shoulders relaxed when he saw the police car in front of his house and pulled into his driveway. "Thanks, Morty. I appreciate that. I wish I could get my hands on that Lucy Bauer. I've got the killer calling me to back off and reporters hounding me. Even Bateman's sister came by the office this morning. I didn't realize so many people read the paper!"

Goldberg's pen started clicking again. "Bateman's sister? What did she want?"

"Apparently, her brother was a professional photographer in addition to being a pervert. She said he took some pictures he said would be worth a lot of money. I think he was planning on blackmailing someone. She told me she thought Melrose may have found the pictures and decided to blackmail whoever Bateman caught in the act."

"But why did she contact you?"

"She wanted me to find the pictures."

"Tom, tell me you are not getting involved in this."

"Think about it, Morty. There's some kind of a connection between Bateman and Melrose. The pictures might be the reason the killer is cutting out the eyes of his victims. Maybe the pictures show something that implicates the killer. My bet is on Impellizzieri. This could be the way to finally get the guy!"

The pen clicking stopped. Cavanaugh heard Goldberg's breathing on the other end of the phone line. "And how does Fernando Mondego figure into this theory of yours?" Goldberg asked.

"Maybe he's in the pictures? Maybe they show Mondego double-crossing Impellizzieri."

"That's a lot of maybes, Tom. Let me give you a couple of facts. You are dealing with dangerous people. I was wrong to ask you to get involved, just as you were wrong in asking Lucy Bauer to help. It's time to step back from this investigation and let the police handle it."

"You don't understand, Morty. If I find those pictures...."

"No. You don't understand. Listen to me closely. Robert Bateman never had a sister. He was an only child. Whoever this woman who came to you was, it was not Bateman's sister."

* * * *

Chapter 18

Cali, Colombia

Santo Jose Gabriel del Rosario Brochero Hospital was unlike any hospital Jack Bennis had ever seen. Two armed security guards met him at the door. They asked him for identification and whom he was coming to see. When he told them he was coming to visit María Isabelle Rodriguez, one leveled an AR-15 at his chest while the other checked the computer. The one on the computer nodded to his companion and said, "He checks out. He's on the list." Then he motioned to the elevator where another armed security guard stood watch. "Follow Miguel, Padre Bennis. He will escort you to *señorita* Rodriguez's room."

They knew he was a priest. Security was tight, yet they hadn't patted him down for weapons. Somehow his name was on a list of approved visitors for María Isabelle, but he had never been here before. This was, indeed, a strange hospital. The walls were stark white, almost too white like the color of an actor's teeth. There was no signage to be seen anywhere. There were no doctors or nurses or patients walking the halls. Everything was eerily silent.

At the third floor, the elevator stopped and two more

armed security guards met them. "This way," the taller of the two said leading the way. The second guard walked behind Bennis with an AR-15 aimed at his back. The only sounds in the hall were their footsteps on the tile floor. Security cameras followed their every step as they passed unnumbered room after room.

They stopped at the end of the corridor where another armed guard stood watch. The tall security guard nodded to the man at the door and then punched a series of numbers into a keyless touchscreen deadbolt lock. Bennis heard the lock click open. Both security guards stepped back. "We will be here if you need us," the tall security guard said as the door swung open.

* * * *

Staten Island, New York

When Cavanaugh got out of his car at his house, he looked around. There was a police car across the street as Goldberg promised. He saw no sign of the battalion of news media he encountered at his office. Fran's car was in the driveway with a black Ford Fusion parked behind it. He felt his stomach drop when he thought for a moment the car might be Detective Perez and her Hulk-like partner's. He braced himself for the worst.

Opening the front door, he saw his wife chatting at the dining room table with another woman whose back was to him. He breathed a sigh of relief when he realized the other woman did not have purple hair. She wasn't Detective Perez.

Fran waved to him. She was smiling. "Tom, we have a guest. I think you two know each other."

The other woman turned. It was Lucy Bauer, the

Times reporter.

Cavanaugh snapped. "How dare you come into my house? Get out of here before I throw you out!"

Fran stood up. "What's gotten into you, Tom? Lucy is a guest in our house. She wrote that nice article about you in the paper."

Cavanaugh pounded his fist on the table. "That article is liable to get us all killed, Fran! She put words in my mouth that I never said. Now her Stations of the Cross Murderer is threatening to kill you, Stephen, and me!"

Fran's mouth dropped open. She stared at Lucy Bauer. The reporter backed up knocking over a dining room chair. "I'm sorry," she said. "I didn't realize ...."

"I warned you, but you didn't listen. Your good buddy killer called me at work today." He lunged at her. She threw the chair in front of him. "If anything happens to my family because of your article, I swear I'll kill you with my bare hands!"

Bauer held her hands in front of her. "Don't! Please! I was wrong. I apologize."

"Apologies don't cut it, lady!"

"Wait! Please! He called me today, too! That's why I came here!"

Cavanaugh lowered his hands as well as his voice. He looked down at the coffee that had spilled over the table. "What did he say?"

"He warned me not to write anything about him."

"Listen, Lucy. This is important. Exactly what did he say?"

"His voice was garbled. It was like he had a voice altering device of some sort. He said, 'You have it all wrong. If you print another word about me or go to the police, I will kill you, too. Stay out of my business.' That was all."

"Did you go to the police?"

"Of course not! He said he'd kill me. That's why I came here to you. What should I do?"

"Get out of town immediately. This guy is a dangerous nut case."

"You don't understand. This is the biggest story I ever had. The killer spoke to me! I have an exclusive!"

"No. You don't understand. You won't call the police. You're vulnerable. The killer is dangerous. For once, take my advice. Get out of town and lay low for a while."

"But I have an exclusive here ...."

"You are going to be exclusively dead if you don't watch your ass!"

"Tom!" Fran exclaimed. "Watch your language. Lucy is a guest in our house."

"Okay," he said and then turned to Lucy Bauer. "Listen. I realize I got you into this situation by asking you to help. That was my mistake. I shouldn't have done that. I'll make a deal with you. Tell your editor you have to do some undercover work on this, that you've got a good lead. Then lay low for a few days. A week at most. When we catch this guy – which we will – I'll give you an exclusive. There are a lot of details to this case I haven't told you."

"Like what?'

"Lucy, if I told you now, I'd have to kill you."

"Tom!" Fran exclaimed.

"Relax. I'm only kidding. But the less you know right now, the better things will be." He held out his hand. "Do we have a deal?"

Lucy Bauer hesitated for a moment staring at his hand. Then she shook his hand. Cavanaugh felt her hand. It was cold and wet. She was scared. He looked into her eyes. They were black and expressionless. He recalled Goldberg's comment that when he initially asked her to help. He had made a pact with the devil. Had he just made the same mistake again? He hoped not.

* * * *

Cali, Colombia

"Padre Bennis, long time no see!"

Jack Bennis recognized the voice immediately. It was Dr. Stevan Peters. They met in Mompas when María Isabelle was shot. "That's what the dead fish said, Doc," he said extending his hand. Peters was a little grayer and had put on a few pounds, but he was the same doctor who came with María Isabelle's brother and Aunt Jo by helicopter to take her from the small Mompas hospital to a better hospital in Bogotá.

Behind Dr. Peters, Bennis saw María Isabelle in a hospital bed. She looked thinner and paler. She appeared to be sleeping. "How is she, Doc?" he asked.

"We've done all we could for her here. We took a bullet out of her back, but there is another lodged close to her spine. We simply do not have the facilities or the expertise here to remove it."

Bennis moved to the bed. "Is she going to be okay? Will she be able to walk again?"

"If we don't remove that bullet, walking will be the least of her worries. She has developed an infection from the bullet and has been having chills. Her temperature spiked today. It was between 103 and 104. I am afraid if we don't get her to a hospital with a specialized neurological team, we are going to lose her. Unfortunately, it's not a pretty picture, Padre, but it is a fact. I contacted a Doctor Louis in New York. He is the foremost authority on injuries like María

Isabelle's. He agreed to try to help and I have made arrangements to move her to New York as soon as possible. I just hope we are not too late."

María Isabelle's eyes flickered open. "Is that you, Jack?"

He reached down and held her hand. It was cold. "Yes, María, it's me. How are you feeling?"

She tried to smile. "I've been better. I should have listened to you. I'm sorry."

"You have nothing to be sorry about. I should have come here sooner. We are going to get you out of here." He suddenly felt a tug on his leg. He looked down and a hand was reaching out from under the bed.

"Can I come, too, Padre?"

Bennis pulled back and looked down. A small head appeared from under the bed. "Chico? Is that you? I've been looking all over for you. The principal of your school wrote me you went missing. And where do I find you? Hiding under a bed in a hospital in Cali! How did you get here? Is that really you, Chico? I can't believe it. What are you doing here?"

"I have been staying with *señorita* María. I have to hide here at night so no one sees me. The doctor lets me stay, but the others want me to leave. The doctor is a good man. I like him very much."

"How did you get here?"

"It is a long story, Padre, but here I am. I have been watching *señorita* María and keeping her company. Doctor Peters says I am good for *señorita* María."

Bennis turned to the doctor. He shrugged his shoulders. "Security is pretty tight here. That is thanks to her brother. Those are his men in the halls. He left strict orders to protect her."

"We need to get her out of here," Bennis said. "When can she get the specialized care she needs?"

"As I said, I have already contacted Dr. Louis in New York. He is world renowned for operations like the one she needs. I was hoping to move her today. I am happy you arrived in time."

"Thank you, Doctor."

"You are not going to leave me, Jack, are you?"

Bennis turned to María and squeezed her hand as Dr. Peters opened the door. He looked into her eyes and was about to speak when they heard a series of pop, pop, pops coming from the hallway. Chico ducked back under the bed. Bennis saw the security guards lying on the floor outside her room and watched Dr. Peters slowly collapse in the doorway.

Scylla and Charybdis had found him.

* * * *

Jack Bennis reached for the gun beneath his shirt as a woman appeared in the doorway. She wore a red scarf and held a Russian semi-automatic Dragunov sniper rifle aimed at María Isabelle in the bed. She stepped over the lifeless body of Dr. Peters. "You have been a hard man to find, Father Bennis," she said in perfect English. "Drop your gun or she will die."

Bennis dropped his gun and raised his hands. "What do you want?" he asked moving toward the front of the bed attempting to shield María Isabelle.

"Freeze," the woman ordered. She wasn't as old as she looked on the bus. He noticed a dragon tattoo on her left hand. "One more step and I kill both of you."

Bennis heard more gunfire in the hall and then silence. "He's in here, Julio," the woman called out. "I've got him!"

"Does he have it?" a man's voice asked from the hall. A tall man with a loose fitting jacket appeared in the doorway. It was the man Bennis had labeled Charybdis. He held an AR-15 in his hands. He kicked Dr. Peters' body aside and joined Scylla. "They're all dead, Tatiana. We need to get out of here before the police arrive. Does he have it?"

"No," Bennis answered. "The money and the drugs are gone."

"Where are they?" Tatiana demanded.

"Gone," was Bennis' only answer.

"Kill him, Tatiana. If he doesn't have it, kill him and get his over with!"

"No, Julio. It's a matter of honor. We were sent to get the money and the drugs. If he won't tell us where they are, we'll take him to the pier and let *El Jefe del Diablo* deal with him. I think he will be able to make him talk. After a little physical persuasion from *El Jefe,* he will be happy to talk."

"What about the woman?"

Tatiana smiled. "Kill her. She is of no use to us."

Jack Bennis raised his hands as Julio aimed his weapon at María Isabelle. "No! No! Please! Wait!"

But a series of shots rang out, and Bennis watched in shock as both Tatiana and Julio flew back into the white wall, dropping their rifles and leaving a trail of splattered blood against the wall. At least five bullets ripped through Julio's loose fitting jacket hitting him in the center of his chest. Tatiana's head exploded as she bounced off the wall and her red scarf floated to the floor.

Bennis turned. Beneath the bed Chico lie in a prone position with the pistol Bennis dropped gripped in his hands. In the bed María Isabelle removed a .44 Magnum pistol from the blanket she had shot through. She looked at Bennis. "My brother left me this just in case. He also taught me how to use it."

Chico's voice from beneath the bed echoed off the wall. "My father taught me to shoot. I'm a pretty good shot, aren't I, Padre?"

Bennis scratched his head and smiled. "You're both damn good shots. Thanks. Now let's get the hell out of here and see if we can get María Isabelle to that specialist in New York."

* * * *

Staten Island, New York

After Lucy Bauer left, Cavanaugh spent the next hour and a half trying to calm Fran down. She was understandably upset that the killer had threatened their family. At times like this, he agreed with whoever said there are two ways of winning a discussion with a woman, but none of them work. He assured her that Morty Goldberg had arranged for twenty-four- hour coverage of their house. He pointed out the police car stationed across the street. But Fran would have no part of it.

"Do you think a cop in a car drinking coffee and eating donuts is going to stop this maniac who has been breaking into churches undetected? We live next to a damn cemetery in case you didn't notice! Even I could get into this house without being seen."

There was some loud talk, some tears, and some hugs before it was agreed that Fran would take little Stephen to her sister's in Brooklyn.

While Fran was packing, Cavanaugh called Chief of Detectives Goldberg. He told Goldberg that Lucy Bauer had also received a threatening call from the killer.

"What did he say?" Goldberg asked.

"Pretty much what he said to me about staying out of his business, but he warned her explicitly not to go to the police. He repeated that she had it all wrong and if she printed another word about him or went to the police, he would kill her, too."

"I'll send someone to watch her."

"No, Morty! She's scared to death. She doesn't want the police involved. She agreed to get off Staten Island for a while. She's going to tell her editor that she has a lead and is going undercover to follow it up."

"That sounds like another Tom Cavanaugh cock and bull story."

Cavanaugh laughed. "You know me too well. It was the best story I could come up with. She was really pretty scared. She came to me for help. If she wouldn't go to the police, I convinced her to go somewhere where she wouldn't be found and not to write any more articles about this maniac."

"Where is she going?"

"The truth is I didn't ask. I thought it better that way. Where are we on the case?"

"There is no we. You are off the case! I thought I made that clear the last time we spoke. This is a police matter, and you're no longer one of us."

"Okay, okay! I get it, but Bateman's sister, Katherine Ames, or whoever she is, hired me. For old times' sake, Morty, can you tell me if you were able to locate Monica Melrose. I think she may know something about the pictures Ames is looking for."

"I can tell you for certain Monica Melrose will not talk to you."

"I can be pretty persuasive. I got Lucy Bauer to lay low and not publish any more stories about this killer, didn't I?"

"You would have to do a lot better than that, Tom. We located Monica Melrose early this morning. She was sitting on a bench on the corner of Tompkins Avenue and Virginia Avenue in Rosebank. She was dead."

Cavanaugh closed his eyes and remembered the last time he had seen her. "You said she was on a bench, not in a church. Maybe it's not the same killer."

"Oh, it's the same person. Her eyes were in her purse along with the beer-soaked bread."

"But she wasn't left in a church. Why would the killer change his MO?"

"He's playing with us again. The bench is located in front of a small Baptist church. On top of the church front is a quote from 2 Corinthians that says, 'Look not to the things that are seen but to the things that are unseen.'"

Cavanaugh was silent for a moment. He frowned and shook his head. "It doesn't make sense to me, Morty. Why would he leave her body outside the church? He left all the others inside. What makes Monica Melrose different?"

"Monica Melrose's maiden name was Liebowitz. She was Jewish."

"Of course, that might be it! So we are dealing with some kind of religious fanatic who thinks it is his business to kill these people."

"I don't know what *you* are thinking, *kemosabe*, but *we* are still trying to fit the pieces together. He may have finally made a mistake in this instance. Tompkins Avenue can be a busy place at all times of the day, and across the street is a pharmacy. We are hoping somebody may have seen something or something was picked up on an outdoor security camera."

"Let me know if you find something," Cavanaugh said.

"I wouldn't hold my breath if I were you," Goldberg replied as he hung up.

* * * *

Chapter 19

Staten Island, New York

After Fran left with Stephen to stay with her sister, Cavanaugh sat for a long time staring at the notes he had written about the murders. It was an old habit he developed when working on the police force. The notes were scribbled in a small marble notebook he carried with him at all times. It was filled with the names and addresses of possible suspects, details of the different murders, and dates and locations of the murders. Scanning through his sloppy notes, he realized the killer was smart. He managed to get into churches and leave the bodies of his victims without being noticed. If he or she was as clever as Goldberg seemed to think, Cavanaugh doubted the police would find witnesses or video tapes showing him posing Monica Melrose's body on the bench by the Baptist church.

He looked through his list of suspects. What was the significance of the churches? Maybe his initial reaction to Monica Melrose's placement outside a church was wrong. What if the murders had nothing to do with the churches? Was the killer using them as a distraction or were they a part of his motive?

Two names stood out to Cavanaugh: Mario Impellizzieri and Katherine Ames.

Was Impellizzieri using the religious theme to distract from a personal vendetta he had with the victims? He was known to be ruthless, but despite numerous attempts to arrest him he proved to be made of Teflon. Nothing would stick to him. Was Bateman's murder based on revenge? Were the Melroses' deaths attempts at silencing them for information they may have uncovered about him? Was Mondego's killing a business venture to eliminate competition and acquire additional venues for his enterprises? Could the church murders be a manipulative deception allowing him to retaliate and eliminate enemies?

But what about Katherine Ames? If she wasn't Bateman's sister, who was she? And why would she hire Melrose and now him to find some pictures? What was in those pictures? She was directly involved in some way with three of the victims. How did she play into this situation?

And where was his brother? He had been gone for some time. Cavanaugh doubted Jack Bennis would ever find Chico. In all likelihood the boy was dead. Colombia can be a rough place. According to Goldberg, the police were looking for him. He could only imagine what trouble he had gotten himself into this time.

Cavanaugh got up and stretched. All the questions he was asking himself gave him a headache. He walked into the kitchen and poured himself a cup of coffee. It was cold. He decided to brew himself some tea. While it was brewing, he turned on the television. A beautiful Asian woman was reporting on the gruesome murder of a world renowned artist known simply as Dianna. According to the newscaster, Dianna was vacationing in a small resort town called El Valle in Colombia. Preliminary police reports indicated Dianna had been tortured. Dianna was the recipient of the Robert von Doussa International Art Award, the Deborah E. Russell Outstanding Artist Award, the Edward Flaherty Lifetime Achievement Award and the National Arts Award for Outstanding Contributions to the Arts.

Cavanaugh watched as pictures of Dianna's work flashed across the screen. When he heard the tea kettle whistling, he turned the television off just as Irish art critic Kathleen Flynn from Dublin University was explaining Dianna's rapid success and lamenting her tragic loss to the art world. Pouring himself a cup of tea, he thought how fleeting success was and how much evil there was in the world. The things that are seen are, indeed, transient. He felt sorry for Dianna, but glad that at least his brother was in Cartagena and nowhere near El Valle.

* * * *

The sky was darkening. Cavanaugh was sick of the rain. With Fran and Stephen gone, he walked through the house with the nervous energy of a hungry squirrel. He had to get out of the house and do something. Goldberg warned him to stay away from the murder investigation so that eliminated his questioning Mario Impellizzieri. But Katherine Ames was a different matter. Whatever her real name was, she hired him to find pictures Bob Bateman allegedly had taken. He looked at his watch and the clouds overhead. Now was as good a time as any.

He walked to his car. The police officer in the patrol car across the street was talking with someone on his cell phone. He never looked up to see Cavanaugh get in his car and drive away.

When he got to the address Katherine Ames had given

him, the rain had started again. He parked at a meter on Bay Street and jogged to Bateman's apartment building. It was one of a series of old, rundown three story houses.

A big chestnut tree stood in front of Bateman's building. It reminded him of the times he and his brother had played a game they called "Killer." They found chestnuts, drilled a hole through them, and placed a shoelace through the hole. Then they would take turns hitting each other's chestnut until one of them broke. The winner would become the "Killer" and would absorb the number of other "kills" the opponent had. To make the chestnut harder, players would coat their chestnuts with shellac or any other material which would make their chestnut harder. In Cavanaugh's case, he used his mother's nail polish to coat his chestnut. Once he had ten "kills" to his credit when he beat Gerry Gilmartin in a match. Gerry also had ten "kills" so, when Cavanaugh's chestnut won, he gained Gerry's ten "kills" to give him a total of twenty "kills." Cavanaugh remembered ultimately losing to his brother who had coated his chestnut with shellac and clear nail varnish. Eventually, his brother lost to Johnny McGrath whose chestnut, "Blackie," amassed an unbelievable 209 "kills." The rumors on the street were that somehow McGrath had managed to drill a hole through a rock, but nobody could prove it, and the kids just stopped competing against him. Things were a lot simpler back then.

There was no lock on the front door of the building. The glass pane by the door knob had been broken. The smell of dried urine hit him immediately. On the cracked linoleum floor two empty syringes lay in the midst of fast food wrappers, cigarette butts, a half-eaten orange lollipop, and a used condom. There were few names on the mailboxes in the vestibule, but the name Karl Trask was there. His apartment was listed as 3C.

The stairs creaked like Cavanaugh's knees. On the second floor he had to step over the body of a man covered in vomit clutching an empty bottle of Night Train Express. Graffiti marked the walls. If Katherine Ames did pay for Bateman's apartment, she couldn't have paid that much, he thought.

The faded letter "C" dangled from a scratched wood door on the third floor. The door was locked, but Cavanaugh used an old credit card and easily entered the apartment. It was dark and dirty. He could see papers had been thrown all over the place. The drawers from a dresser were lying on the floor. Bateman's clothes were strewn around the room. The mattress had been tossed aside. Looking for a light switch, he stepped on a glass frame. Then he heard the swish of something behind him. Pain seared through his head, and all went black as he fell to the floor.

* * * *

Cali, Colombia

Jack Bennis waited with Chico at Alfonso Bonilla Aragón International Airport for a private plane to take María Isabelle to New York. Captain Marian Fraumeni of the Colombian National Police was with them. The arrangements for the departure had been arranged by Dr. Peters. Captain Fraumeni expedited the flight and the necessary papers to allow Chico to accompany them. Father Bennis had contacted her from the hospital and explained what had occurred. When the police arrived at the hospital they found a total of fourteen people shot to death. The number included two doctors and a nurse as well as Scylla and Charybdis. None of the patients were harmed. The information Bennis gave the police about Tatiana and Julio's planned meeting at the pier with *El Jefe del Diablo* led to a raid which resulted in the notorious and elusive *El Jefe's* arrest and the confiscation of over fifteen million dollars' worth of cocaine scheduled to be shipped to Miami, Florida. The police went out of their way to facilitate the emergency flight to New York. A nurse and a doctor were assigned to accompany María Isabelle.

Father Bennis shook the diminutive captain's hand as they boarded the plane. "I don't know how to thank you enough, Captain Fraumeni, for all you have done for us."

"No, Padre, I must thank you. On behalf of the people and government of Colombia, I thank you for all you have done. Thanks to your efforts we have been able to disrupt one of the most dangerous cartels in Colombia. This is the least we can do for you. We have already made arrangements for the three of you to clear customs in New York and to be transported directly to the hospital. As soon as you leave, I will contact my friend, Detective Goldberg, to tell him you are on the way. You should have clear sailing. *Vaya con Dios, mi amigo.*"

Bennis leaned down and kissed Captain Fraumeni gently on her cheek. "There is an old Irish blessing my mother used to say that I would like to leave with you. It goes something like this, 'May the good Saints protect you and bless you today and every day, and may troubles ignore you each step of the way.' May peace be with you always."

A few minutes later the plane took off on a direct flight to New York.

* * * *

Chapter 20

New York, New York

Jack Bennis looked down at his brother lying motionless in the bed. Cavanaugh's head was heavily bandaged. He was hooked up to a respirator and a number of intravenous lines and contraptions. His eyes were closed. Fran Cavanaugh and Detective Morty Goldberg stood at the side of his bed.

"What happened? How long has he been like this?" Bennis asked.

Goldberg pulled Bennis into the hall. "Tom was hired by a woman whose identity we don't know. She hired him to find photographs in a room rented to a Karl Trask, whom she claimed was really Robert Bateman, a convicted sex offender, who was killed in a church burning months ago." He went on in a hushed voice explaining how Cavanaugh told him the killer called him and threatened him and his family. "Fran took the baby and went to her sister's in Brooklyn. I assigned a patrol car to keep watch on him. You know your brother. He tried to sneak out of the house. Fortunately, police officer Jefferson followed him to the flop house where he found him lying in a puddle of blood. If it hadn't been for Jefferson, we might have lost him. It's still not clear the extent of the damage. He received a severe blow to the head. My guess is it was a bat or a golf club. I spoke to his doctor before you arrived. He was young, but he seemed to know what he was talking about. They did a CT scan when he came into the emergency room. He has a skull fracture and there was some bleeding in the brain and contusions. They performed an emergency procedure to remove the pressure on his brain. He's been in an induced coma now for a couple of days. They are focusing on minimizing secondary damage due to inflammation, bleeding, and reduced oxygen supply to the brain. It's going to be touch and go for a while."

Bennis glanced over Goldberg's shoulder. A short, stocky doctor was rapidly approaching them. The doctor looked to be in his late sixties or early seventies. He was wearing blue blood-stained surgical scrubs. The lines in his face looked like they had been chiseled there. He moved quickly, but his eyes looked tired. "Which one of you is Father Bennis?" he said in the voice of a man used to giving orders.

"I am," the priest answered.

"They told me you'd be here. I am Doctor Lewis. The woman you brought in is in intensive care. I removed a bullet in close proximity to her spine. The bullet was badly decomposed and created an abscess which led the woman's body to go into septic shock."

"The woman has a name, Dr. Lewis. Her name is María Isabelle Rodriguez," Bennis said.

Dr. Lewis looked at Bennis as if he were speaking another language. "The woman's condition is critical. She is receiving oxygen to stabilize her breathing and heart function. She is being treated with antibiotics and intravenous fluids in addition to vasopressors to help increase her blood pressure. She has a severe case of septicemia, which can cause blood clotting resulting in lung, kidney, and liver failure. Although I successfully removed the bullet, it is uncertain at this time if the woman will ever walk again, but I will be frank with you, Father, the woman may not die from the bullet, but the septicemia may very well kill her. I have done all I can for her. I think it is time you pray to that God of yours."

Father Bennis said, "He is your God, too, Doctor."

Dr. Lewis let out an audible huff, turned and rapidly walked back down the hall.

Goldberg's eyes followed Dr. Lewis as he walked away. "Interesting man," he said, "although I doubt he will receive any honors for best bedside manners."

Bennis looked back into Cavanaugh's room. Fran was sitting next to him holding his hand. The woman he loved was in the intensive care unit on another floor fighting for her life, and his brother was in an induced coma due to a severe head injury. He closed his eyes as a tear trickled down his cheek and whispered to himself again, "My God, my God, why have you forsaken me....I cry out by day, and you answer not; by night, and there is no relief for me."

Morty Goldberg reached over and patted the priest's shoulder. "The psalmist continues to say he didn't turn his face away from him, but heard him. Have faith, Father. We'll find the bastard who did this to your brother."

Jack Bennis wiped his cheek and nodded to the detective. "And if you don't, trust me, I will."

* * * *

Fran stayed at the hospital that night. Jack Bennis chose to go back to Staten Island and stay at his brother's house. He met Chico in the hospital lobby. He was asleep clutching his Muisca spear as if it were a security blanket. Goldberg drove them home and filled Bennis in on the confusing details of the so-called "Stations of the Cross" murders. As they drove on the Brooklyn-Queens Expressway, Bennis commented, "It doesn't make sense. If you are right, Bateman was left in a Pentecostal Church, Melrose in a Catholic Church, Mondego in a Methodist Church, and now Monica Melrose at a Baptist Church. What's the connection? The only church with the Stations of the Cross is St. Peter's."

Goldberg held his hands on the 10 and 2 position and looked straight ahead. "From what your brother told me, this *New York Times* reporter wanted to make a name for herself and decided giving the killer a fancy *nom de plume* would sell more papers, build up her reputation, and get the killer to talk to her."

"That hasn't worked out that well for her, has it? Besides the churches, is there anything else the murders have in common?"

"Yes, all the victims had their eyes removed. I'm not sure if it means anything, but there was a quote from Corinthians over Monica Melrose's head about not looking to things that are seen but to things that are unseen."

From the back seat, Chico stuck his head between the men. "That's disgusting! Why would anyone want to cut someone's eyes out?"

"Keep your seatbelt on, Chico," Goldberg ordered.

Traffic slowed down to a crawl. There was a disabled truck in the right lane. An awkward silence enveloped the car. As they squeezed past the truck, Bennis thought how the things we see are transient, but what we don't see is eternal. Suddenly, he spoke out, "If your right eye causes you to sin,

172

tear it out and throw it away. For it is better that you lose one of your members than that your whole body be thrown into hell."

Goldberg and Chico looked at Bennis as if he had lost his mind. "It's something Matthew quotes Jesus saying in the New Testament," Bennis explained. "Is there anything the victims had in common that may have caused them to sin through their eyes?" Bennis asked.

The Chief of Detectives stared straight ahead. "Father, with all due respect, I don't know what you mean by 'sin.' Sin is pretty subjective, isn't it? What is a sin to one person may not be to another."

"Humor me, Detective Goldberg. We are talking about a serial killer here. This is not a moral or philosophical debate. Is there anything this killer could think that his victims sinned with their eyes?"

Goldberg drove past the Metropolitan Detention Center. "Well, Bateman was a convicted sex pervert who dealt in child pornography. The Melroses had a lucrative side business of making porno films in their own home. I don't know about Mondego. He owned a couple of bars on the Island."

"Did anything significant happen in any of them?"

"Well, to tell the truth, they are not the most respectable places on Staten Island. One of them is called 'The Bucket of Blood.' It's been known to serve minors and a while back two teenagers died of drug overdoses there involving fentanyl. It is possible, I guess, that the killer thought Mondego saw what was going on and allowed or encouraged it."

Chico chimed in from the back seat, "Maybe the killer was trying to help these people get into heaven by cutting out their eyes and leaving them in church."

Goldberg shook his head. "I don't know. Your brother seemed to think Mario Impellizzieri may have something to do with the murders. He was somehow involved with all the victims."

"It's just a theory, Detective. My brother and I often differ on things. Were there any other similarities besides the eyes?"

Goldberg drove in silence as the lights on the Verrazano Bridge came closer and closer. "Well, there are a couple of things we haven't released to the press. This is strictly confidential, Father, and you have to promise not to breathe a word of it to anyone."

"My lips are sealed and so are Chico's." Chico nodded his head up and down like an out of control bobblehead doll. "I'm just trying to get a handle on this," he said. "From what I have learned thus far, I think the killer is on some kind of a mission and the fact that he or she seems to be escalating the murders makes me think he is enjoying it. I thought a fresh pair of eyes might help."

As they crossed from Brooklyn into Staten Island, Morty Goldberg filled Bennis in on the numbered index cards, the pieces of beer-soaked bread, the salt, and the corn flakes. "Well, that's all we have. Detective Perez had you as a significant person of interest, but after you took off and the murders continued, we had to look elsewhere. So far Mario Impellizzieri and his twin sons are our chief suspects, but they seem to have alibis. I think you know one of the brothers who is a priest at St. Peter's."

"Do you mean Father Steve? Everybody loves him at St. Peter's. I can't see him as a killer."

"His father is Mario Impellizzieri, a known crime boss. You know what they say about the apple not falling far from the tree. He has a twin brother named Stephen who is a barber with a checkered past. Each of them has an alibi for a different one of the murders. It's possible they planned this together. What do you think?"

Jack Bennis rubbed the scar over his eye. "I don't know. It doesn't feel like a group effort to me. There is too much consistency. It's obvious the killer is smart and cunning. He's been able to get into locked buildings with a body without being seen. He's also getting bolder. From what you've told me, he's gone from concealing his victim to displaying his latest victim on a traveled street across from a pharmacy. I doubt you will find video. He most likely disabled any cameras. I believe because of the churches, there is some kind of religious theme to this, but I can't put my finger on it. I feel there is a battle going on inside him. Part of him wants to be stopped. But there is another part of him that is urging him on. He's enjoying the killings and their frequency is likely to increase. The taunting with the corn flakes and the threatening phone calls to stay out of his business make me think he is dissolving, falling apart. The more this happens, the more likely it is he will make a mistake. The question is: how many more victims will there be before he makes that mistake?"

* * * *

Chapter 21

Staten Island, New York

After Goldberg dropped Father Bennis off at Cavanaugh's house, Bennis set up Chico in the guest room. As soon as his head hit the pillow, Chico pulled the covers over and, still clutching his Muisca spear, fell asleep faster than he could tie his shoelace. Bennis went down into the kitchen, poured himself a glass of Glenlivet single malt scotch, and stared out the window. Darkness covered most of the cemetery next door, but he knew it was there. He sat at the kitchen table and thought about what had happened in the past few weeks.

Life is full of surprises. What was it his mother used to say? She loved repeating Thomas à Kempis' quote, "Man proposes; God disposes." All he was sure of was that the things of this world are transient. Was Nietzsche right? Was God dead and had we killed Him? He went to Colombia to find a runaway boy. He found the boy, but in the course of trying to find him a number of people died. He thought of the artist Dianna who traveled to a remote vacation spot only to be tortured to death because she helped him.

It didn't make any sense. Whenever he tried to help

people it seemed other people got hurt. What kind of priest was he if wherever he went he brought havoc and destruction? He read the letters of Mother Teresa and knew she questioned her faith and belief in God while bringing hope and love to others. He didn't think about the fact he had rescued five boys from human traffickers, disrupted a major drug operation, planted the seeds for a refuge for runaway children, or been instrumental in the capture of a notorious drug cartel boss and the seizure of over fifteen million dollars of cocaine destined for distribution in the United States. He wished he could believe Mother Teresa's thought that while what we are doing may seem like only a drop in the ocean, the ocean would be less because of that missing drop.

His thoughts were on the people who died and on María Isabelle and his brother who were fighting for their lives in the hospital. He was about to pour himself another Glenlivet when his cell phone rang.

It was Fran, his sister-in-law.

"Jack, you've got to come here quick. Tom's awake. He pulled out the ventilator and his IV tubes and wants to leave. The doctors and nurses are trying to strap him down. There's no talking to him. He's not making any sense."

* * * *

By the time Jack Bennis got to the hospital, his brother was asleep. The guard rails on his bed were up and his arms were tied down. "They have given him some kind of sedation," Fran explained. "He kept insisting he was fine and that he had to get out of the hospital."

"What did the doctors say?"

"They want to keep him here for a few more days for

observation and a few more tests. I'm glad my sister is able to watch Stephen at her house."

Bennis looked at his brother. He knew how much Tom hated hospitals. They had often joked about Cavanaugh's nosocomephobia, fear of hospitals. It was a common fear, but Cavanaugh's anxiety was real. He was always an independent person. Giving up control to medical professionals was something he resisted. "That's why they call it a practice," Cavanaugh would say. "It's because they haven't gotten it right yet. I don't want them practicing on me."

"I'll stay with him, Fran. I've seen him like this before. Do me a favor and go home and stay with Chico. He's in your guest room. I'll talk to Tom when the sedative wears off. I left Chico alone, and I'm worried about him. Trust me, I'll speak to the doctors, and we'll work something out."

Reluctantly, Fran left. Bennis pulled a chair closer to Cavanaugh's bed. He knew it was a losing battle. He carefully released the straps on his brother's arms, held his hand, and prayed for a miracle.

* * * *

Jack Bennis was deep in prayer when he felt a tap on his shoulder. He looked up and saw the purple hair of Detective Perez. He felt a chill race through his body.

"Father Bennis," Perez said, "I need to apologize to you. I heard what happened to your brother. To be honest, I wasn't unhappy about it at first. But it made me realize I've been taking out my anger toward him on you. I apologize."

"No need for apologies, Detective. You were doing your job. I didn't make things easier for you when I left the country."

Perez looked at Cavanaugh. "I wish I could get past my hostility toward your brother, but I can't. The past has a way of catching up on you."

"It does with all of us. I have to admit Tom has a way of getting to people, but he's not the same person he was before he became a father."

Perez pulled over a chair. "Actually, Father, I came to speak with you. Your brother is impossible to talk to."

"I know what you mean. He can be very difficult to deal with."

A groggy voice from the bed responded, "I heard that...."

Bennis patted his brother's hand. "At ease, Tom. Detective Perez is here to speak with me, not you. What can I do for you, Detective?"

She took out a notebook. A huge shadow appeared in the doorway. It was Perez's partner. She explained how Bennis was no longer considered a suspect or a person of interest. "We are pursuing another avenue of investigation now. What can you tell me about Father Steve Impellizzieri? You worked with him at St. Peter's."

"Steve is a good priest. Everybody seems to like him. It's like he has his own fan club. The rumor is maybe someday he'll eventually become a cardinal."

"Yeah, I got that a lot. But what's he really like? What do you know about his family and his decision to become a priest?"

Bennis felt his brother gripping his hand a little tighter. "Steve doesn't talk much about his family. I didn't even know he had a twin brother until tonight. I can't tell you why he became a priest. You will have to ask him that yourself. God calls each of us in different ways."

Perez's eyes went from Bennis to Cavanaugh and then back to Bennis. "The way I look at it, Father Steve and his brother were born in Sicily. Family is a big thing in Italian families, and it is especially strong and tight in Sicilian families. There is a bond in Sicilian families that we don't necessarily have here. They stick together through thick and thin. Everybody knows everybody's business. To have a priest in the family is an honor. It brings prestige and power to a family. At the same time, the mafia is very much alive and active in Sicily. What better way to gain power, knowledge, and respectability than to have a priest in the family? Knowing the right people is a valuable asset."

Bennis squeezed his brother's hand. "I think you may be grasping at straws, Detective. I can't speak for Father Steve, except to say I have always found him to be an honorable and good priest. There is an Italian phrase that you need to beware of in your investigations. *Cui scerri cerca, scerri trova* - Who looks for a quarrel, finds a quarrel."

Perez stood and glanced at her massive partner in the doorway. "I think the Impellizzieri family is covering for each other. And I think this Father Steve is in it with his father and brother. There is another Italian phrase that I've seen repeated time and time again. *'Ntra greci e greci nun si vinni abbraciu* - There's honor among thieves."

Jack Bennis stood. He was a foot taller than Perez. He extended his hand. "I will help you in any way I can, Detective, but it's not my job to judge people. I leave that to a higher Power."

Perez shook his hand, a little tighter than necessary. "The way I see it, Father Bennis, is I am that higher power, and you and your brother can help me by staying out of my way."

As she and her partner disappeared down the corridor, Bennis heard his brother struggling to get up. When he turned, his brother was staring at the doorway. He said in a strained voice, "Pompous bitch!"

* * * *

Cavanaugh looked dazed. His speech was slurred. He kept blinking as if he were trying to clear his vision. "Jack," he whispered, "you've got to get me out of here. They are going to kill me."

Bennis leaned over and pressed the button for the nurse. Within seconds, a thin brunette nurse with sparkling dark eyes and a smile that would melt butter appeared. She looked past Bennis and looked directly at Cavanaugh. "Hi, Mr. Cavanaugh, my name is Christine. How may I help you?"

"I need to get out of here."

"I'm sorry, sir, but you had a severe head injury. It's what we call a traumatic brain injury. The doctor ordered an MRI for tomorrow to see if your condition stabilizes. Depending on the results, you may need rehabilitation."

Cavanaugh struggled to sit up. The room seemed to be spinning. He felt like there was a little man with a hammer pounding away inside his skull. "Listen, nurse whatever your name is, I need to get out of here. I'm not taking any damn MRI. I'm a police detective and I need to get back to work! I don't know why I'm here. The world is filled with evil people. Somebody has to take care of them so good people can go to Yankee games with their families."

Bennis patted his brother's head. "Take it easy, Tom. I promised Fran I'd work this out."

Cavanaugh pushed his hand away and stared at him. "Who the hell are you? How do you know my name?"

181

"I'm your brother. Do you remember what happened to you?"

"Jack? Is that you? I was ... I was .... I don't know." He held his head with his hands and grimaced. "I ... I can't remember. I think I was at a baseball game."

Christine turned to Bennis. "He really needs to stay here. He's displaying some of the classic symptoms of traumatic head injuries like amnesia, disorientation, slurred speech, and confusion. He needs that MRI so we can better determine the extent of his injury. The brain injury may be temporary or it could result in long-term complications or even death."

Bennis held his brother down. "Christine," he said, "could you please get some help. We are going to need to strap him in again."

The nurse looked at the straps and then his chart. "He was supposed to be restrained. How did he get out of his restraints? I am going to have to report this. If someone did not restrain him, heads are going to roll."

"No need for that. I'm the culprit. I thought I could take him home like he wanted. I can see now that that was a mistake. I seem to be making a lot of mistakes lately. I apologize. I thought we could take care of him at home and ease his anxiety. I can see I was wrong. He needs to stay here until we get a better assessment of his injury."

Nurse Christine frowned. "They told me his brother is a priest. You should have known better."

"Christine, I don't know how to tell you this, but priests are human and make mistakes. Now please get someone to give him something to calm him down and help restrain him again."

* * * *

Chapter 22

The next few days were hectic for Father Bennis as he shuttled back and forth between María Isabelle and his brother. Both appeared to be improving. Dr. Lewis called his operation "an unmitigated success" and "a groundbreaking achievement." Her sepsis was responding to treatment and the doctor believed she would walk again. But she would need a lot of rehabilitation.

Cavanaugh's doctor was more cautious. The swelling in his brain had subsided and aside from headaches and vertigo he was progressing well. He still had trouble walking and had no memory of the incident. He didn't like being in the hospital, but he accepted it as a means to get better.

Together with Detective Goldberg, Bennis visited the apartment where Cavanaugh had been attacked. He learned the weapon that hit his brother was a softball bat. There were no fingerprints on the bat, but there were traces of Cavanaugh's blood on it.

The question remained: who hit Cavanaugh in the head? If it was the killer, why didn't he finish the job and kill him? The room had been ransacked. What would the perpetrator have been looking for? Could it be the pictures

Cavanaugh was hired to find? Did the attacker find the photos? What was the significance of the pictures?

"If there any pictures, they're not here. Either they never were or the killer or whoever hit your brother in the head has them," Goldberg said.

The detective and the priest walked across the street to a restaurant that used to be called The Cargo. Bennis and his brother had eaten there in the past a few times. The food was good and back then the outside of the building was painted like an American flag and inside a huge characterization of Rudy Giuliani leading a charge on horseback hung over the bar. The place had changed since then as almost everything else had. It had been refurbished and over the bar a painting of a naked woman and a shark and an octopus or snake replaced the former New York City mayor. Bennis knew Goldberg would not touch any of the food there, not because it wasn't good, but because of his strict dietary rules. They sat in a booth by the window and ordered black coffee.

"I imagine you questioned people in the bar about what happened," Bennis began.

"We did, and we got the usual answer. Nobody saw anything."

Bennis sipped his coffee. It was good. Goldberg held his cup and looked out the window onto Bay Street.

"There's something about this whole thing that feels familiar."

"What do you mean?" Goldberg asked.

"I can't put my finger on it, but it's been troubling me since you told me about the facts of the murders."

"I haven't been to see your brother. How is he doing?"

"He's gradually improving, but still can't remember what happened. His speech is better and his long term memory is back. He is still a little dizzy when he stands, but even that is improving."

Goldberg looked at Bennis and smiled. "I always thought he was a little dizzy when we worked together."

"I hope to be able to bring him home later today. Have there been any more leads in the murders?"

"No. We are monitoring the Impellizzieris. We have no idea who or where Katherine Ames is, and Lucy Bauer seems to have disappeared. The good thing is there have been no more murders."

"Maybe the killer is finished."

"From your mouth to God's ears."

But then, as they raised their coffee cups in agreement, Goldberg's cell phone rang.

* * * *

From the look on Goldberg's face, Bennis knew it wasn't good news. He watched as Goldberg nodded, and replied, "Yes," "I see," "Where exactly?" The phone call took a few minutes. Then Goldberg put his coffee cup down and said, "I'm sorry, Father, but I have to go."

"What happened?"

"There's been another murder. It appears our killer is not finished."

"Who was it this time and was it in another church?"

"The body was found by a group of teenagers attending a going away party for their friend in St. Luke's Lutheran Church's McCarthy Hall. Apparently, there was a lot of drinking going on at the party and a few of them decided to have some mischief and broke into the church. There's where they found her laid out in the center aisle before the altar."

"She? The victim is a woman?"

"Yes. This time there was a lot more damage to the face when he removed the eyes. The ME thinks she was alive when he removed them. We are going to have to wait for possible fingerprints and dental records, but from the general description it appears it might be that *New York Times* reporter, Lucy Bauer."

* * * *

Jack Bennis went from the diner on Staten Island to the hospital in Manhattan to visit his brother and María Isabelle. He found his brother sitting up in bed holding hands with Fran. Cavanaugh smiled when he saw him. "They just told me I can go home today," he said. "They are preparing
the discharge papers now."

Fran explained, "Doctor Shushansky said he's not out of the woods yet, but the swelling has gone down and as long as he promises to take it easy and avoid additional head injuries he should be okay."

"I think Fran as a crush on young Dr. Shushansky."

"I do not!" she laughed.

Bennis looked at the two of them. They were happy in spite of what had happened. They had each other. And they had Stephen. He started to think about him and María Isabelle when Cavanaugh asked, "Where have you been? I thought you would have come earlier."

"I wanted to check out the place where you were hit. Goldberg took me there this morning. You're lucky you were hit with a softball bat. I'm surprised your hard head didn't break the bat."

Cavanaugh frowned. "I still have no memory of

anything that happened."

Fran patted Cavanaugh's hand. "Dr. Shushansky said amnesia is fairly common in some head injuries, and it should resolve itself in time."

"The important thing is," Bennis said, "that you look better and you're getting out of here shortly. God is good."

"Have there been any additional leads on the murders?" Cavanaugh asked.

Bennis hesitated, but at his brother's persistence he told him that Goldberg just got word that another body was found by a group of teenagers in St. Luke's Lutheran Church.

"Whoever this killer is," Cavanaugh laughed, "he's definitely ecumenical. We have a Pentecostal church, a Catholic church, a Methodist church, a Baptist church, and now a Lutheran church. Who was the victim this time?"

"They're not sure. Her face was pretty messed up. They think she was alive when he started on her eyes. I imagine she fought back."

"She? Who do they think it might be?"

"They need to check fingerprints and dental records, but Goldberg said she fits the description of that reporter, Lucy Bauer."

"No! No! That can't be! She told me she was going to lay low. She was scared. The killer threatened her, too."

"Maybe he found her," Bennis said. "This guy may be a nut case, but he's smart and cunning."

Cavanaugh swung his legs over the bedside. "I need to get dressed. I need to get out of here. I need to see her. I got her into this mess. It's my fault. The bastard tortured her, didn't he?" He started crying, "It's all my fault! It's all my fault!"

* * * *

Chapter 23

Staten Island, New York

After Dr. Shushansky and nurse Christine reviewed the discharge plans with them, Cavanaugh and Fran drove back to their home. There they joined Fr. Bennis and young Chico at the dining room table. It was good to be home, but Lucy Bauer's death weighed heavily on Cavanaugh. "If I didn't ask her to help, she'd still be alive," he kept repeating.

Jack Bennis' thoughts went back to the artist known only as Dianna who helped him in Colombia and paid for it with her life. "What's done is done," he said. "There's a reason for everything. God has a plan. What it is, I certainly don't know. What I do know is we can't change the past. So let's put our heads together and find this killer."

"How?" Fran asked. "The police haven't been able to find him or her. How are we supposed to find him?"

"Maybe we've been looking at this the wrong way. Maybe it's not about revenge or power," Bennis suggested. "There is some religious theme to this. The killer deliberately leaves his victims in churches. That has to be significant. Why not just dump the bodies in the woods or some desolate place? He is taking a chance breaking into churches. There must be a reason."

Cavanaugh held his hands on his head and grimaced. "Like he's offering his victims up as some sort of sacrifice? I don't buy it. With the exception of Lucy, all his victims have been low-lifes."

"Not as a sacrifice," Bennis said turning to Chico. "What was it you suggested when Detective Goldberg told us about the murders in the car coming back from the hospital?"

Fran looked at Chico as if she had forgotten he was there. "Maybe you should go and watch some television, Chico. This isn't appropriate talk for you to hear."

"No," Bennis said, "I think Chico might be on the right track. What was it you said?"

"When you told me Jesus said if your eye causes you to sin it would be better to cut it out and throw it away. I thought maybe the killer was trying to help these people get into heaven by cutting their eyes out and leaving them in churches."

"That's the most ridiculous thing I've ever heard," Fran declared. "That's crazy!"

Cavanaugh and Bennis looked at each other and nodded. "The killer probably is crazy."

"And I think he wants to be caught," Bennis added. "He's been leaving us clues along the way. We just have to put the clues together."

"How are we going to do that?"

Bennis leaned back and rubbed his face and the back of his neck. "I know two people who might be able to help. They are very knowledgeable about church history and religious practices. One of them is Monsignor O'Brien, and the other one is a priest who is unfortunately very angry with me, Father Vivaldi, the pastor of St. Peter's Church."

* * * *

Explaining how he walked out on his assignment at St. Peter's to go to Colombia to find Chico wasn't easy. Somehow it seemed to be the right thing at the time, but looking back on it now, Jack Bennis had a better grasp at the situation he created for Father Vivaldi. Cavanaugh added that he learned from Goldberg and Lucy Bauer that Vivaldi was so angry that he informed the police, the archdiocese, and the press that he suspected Bennis' involvement in the murder of Dave Melrose.

"Have you spoken to him since you got back?" Fran asked.

"No. I've been putting it off for as long as possible. Gene Vivaldi has a temper. I don't know how to best approach him."

"Do you think he can help?"

"He's a smart man with a degree in comparative religions. Between him and Monsignor O'Brien's broad experiences, I think they can give us a better insight into the motive behind these murders."

"Then what are we waiting for? Let's go talk to him."

"Fran, you don't understand. I can't just walk in on him and ask him to help. You don't know him. I've seen his temper. I can see how we might end up getting into a brawl in the sacristy."

"Who said anything about you going there alone? We'll all go. Tom, Chico, and I will be with you. He wouldn't dare do anything in front of me. And he can see Chico, the reason you left."

"Yes, Padre," Chico said. "I will tell him what you did to save us. You saved our lives. Those men were bad. They were making us do bad things. If it will help, I will give him my Muisca spear. You said it is worth a lot of money."

Jack Bennis stared at them. He shook his head. "I

can't ask you to do this."

Fran stood up abruptly. "It's settled. No more talking. I'll get the car. We are all going, and I'm driving."

* * * *

When Monsignor O'Brien entered the rectory parlor and saw Fran, Cavanaugh, Chico, and Fr. Bennis, his face lit up. "Sure you're a brave man, Jack Bennis, to show your face around here. But I'm glad to see you. You're a sight for sore eyes." He then turned his attention to the others. "I recognize your brother here, and this lovely woman must be his wife. You're going to have to introduce me to this handsome young man, but that can wait. Fr. Vivaldi is on his way down. Have a seat and be comfortable."

A minute later, Father Vivaldi came into the room. He was smiling when he saw Fran and Chico, but his face turned red when he saw Bennis. "You've got some nerve coming here, Bennis. Get out of my church immediately!"

Fran stood and waved a pointed finger at the pastor. "How dare you speak to my brother-in-law like that! You have no idea what he went through to get here and what he accomplished while he was gone. And before we go any further, let me correct you. It's not your church; it's our church."

Vivaldi stood in front of them momentarily speechless.

Fran continued, "Now sit down and listen! Jack came here to apologize and ask for your help. If you truly are a man of God, you'll listen and get your testosterone under control and not act like a hot-headed child who's mad because he didn't get his way."

Vivaldi's hands were shaking. He looked at each of

them. The presence of the woman and the young boy troubled him. Beads of sweat formed on his brow. Monsignor O'Brien gently guided him into a chair. "Hear them out, Gene. Jack came with his family. Let's listen to what he has to say."

The veins in Father Vivaldi's forehead were pulsating, but he sat and folded his arms. He listened as Jack Bennis explained why he left. Chico interrupted him to tell Vivaldi how Padre Bennis rescued five boys from human traffickers. He told the pastor how bad men made them do bad things, and if it weren't for Bennis they might have been killed. Bennis started to apologize for leaving as abruptly as he did, but his brother interrupted him to point out in the course of his rescuing the boys he stopped a drug ring, established a home for runaways, and was instrumental in the arrest of a notorious drug lord and the confiscation of fifteen million dollars' worth of cocaine.

Jack Bennis tried to downplay Chico and Cavanaugh's praise. As they talked Fr. Vivaldi's shoulders seemed to relax. He unfolded his arms and leaned forward. "I didn't come here to make excuses. I was wrong," Bennis said, "and I ask your forgiveness and your help in the investigation of the murders that have recently taken place in churches on Staten Island."

"How can we help?" Monsignor O'Brien asked.

"The fact that the killer is leaving his victims in churches makes me believe there is some religious element to the murders. I know Father Vivaldi studied comparative religions in the seminary and hoped he could explain the significance of similar objects found at the scene of each murder."

"I read about the removal of the eyes. Do you think the killer is taking Jesus' directive literally when he said if your eye causes you to sin, cut it out?"

"There is reason to believe that might be the case," Cavanaugh said.

"But there are other things found on the victims that haven't been publicized. We were hoping you might be able to help explain them."

Both Monsignor O'Brien and Father Vivaldi's eyes narrowed. "What things?" they both asked.

Cavanaugh looked at his brother and nodded. Bennis told both men about the beer-soaked bread and the salt. The men looked at each other, and then Father Vivaldi said, "Honestly, I know of no religious service or ritual that would use those things. I am sorry I can't help."

Bennis sighed, "It was a long shot, but thanks anyway."

Monsignor O'Brien made the sign of the cross and whispered, "*Peccatum comedenti.*"

Everyone looked at him. He folded his hands and closed his eyes. An uncomfortable silence fell over the room. Cavanaugh broke the quiet. Turning to his brother, he said, "He's talking gibberish again. What the hell is a *peccatum comedenti?*"

"It's Latin," Father Vivaldi said, "I'm not sure, but I think it has something to do with sin."

Monsignor O'Brien's face changed. His eyes narrowed and the mirth in them vanished. "*Peccatum comedenti.* My father told me stories about them that his father had told him. They thought themselves spiritual healers. From what you've told us, I believe the killer you are looking for is a depraved Sin-Eater."

* * * *

All eyes focused on Monsignor O'Brien. He looked at each of them and explained that hundreds of years ago, Sin-Eaters followed a ritual to cleanse the dead of their sins by absorbing their sins into themselves. They would place the deceased on a board or table and then place some kind of bread and beer or wine on the body. By eating the bread and the drink they believed they were digesting the deceased's sins, thereby absolving the soul of the dead person.

"I don't understand," Cavanaugh said. "This is hogwash. Why would anyone in their right mind want to take on the sins of another person? I've got enough sins of my own without taking on the sins of others."

"Greater love hath no man than to lay down his life for another."

"With all due respect, Monsignor, your life is one thing, but your soul is quite another thing."

"The people who practiced this ritual," Monsignor O'Brien said, "were usually poor people, beggars who had nothing to live for. The Sin-Eater would be given a meal and a little money so the person who died with unforgiven sins could get into heaven."

"This Sin-Eater thing doesn't make sense. Why would this nut job be killing bad guys so that they could get to heaven?"

"A lot of things in this world don't make sense, Mr. Cavanaugh. *Boni pastoris est tondere pecus non deglubere.* It is a good shepherd's job to shear his flock not to flay them."

"So if I read you right, Monsignor, this Sin-Eater seems to be concentrating on people who are involved in criminal activities. He is eliminating these people, but at the same time he thinks he is absorbing their sins."

"If you are correct, Monsignor," Bennis said, "we have a very serious problem here. There are a lot of evil people in this world and if he thinks he is absorbing their sins he may become increasing evil himself."

Little Chico spoke up. "But if he is getting rid of all the bad people, isn't that a good thing?"

Monsignor O'Brien looked at the young boy. A tired smile crept over his face. "*Non facias malum ut inde fiat bonum*. You should not make evil in order that good may be made from it."

Cavanaugh leaned next to his brother and whispered, "The old guy might be onto something here, but I sure as hell wish he'd speak English."

* * * *

Chapter 24

When they arrived back at Cavanaugh's house, Chief of Detectives Morty Goldberg and Officer Jefferson were waiting for them. Cavanaugh hopped out of the car in a rush to tell him about the possible motive they learned from Monsignor O'Brien. As he got out of the car, however, he lost his balance as a fit of vertigo overcame him, and he collapsed into the arms of his brother and Chico.

Once inside, Jack Bennis guided his brother to his favorite chair while Fran took Chico with her to get him a glass of water. "The doctor told you to take it easy, Thomas. He said you might be feeling a little dizzy for a while."

"I'm okay. Just leave me alone. We have to tell Morty what we found."

Goldberg stood next to him. "I know how upset you were when I told you the killer stuck again, and we thought the victim might be that *New York Times* reporter. I came here to tell you we were wrong. It wasn't Lucy Bauer that was killed. We checked fingerprints. The woman had a record as long as your arm."

"If it wasn't Lucy, who was it?"

"Her name was Aleksandra Bronkovitz."

Cavanaugh shrugged. "I never heard of her. Does she

have any connection with the others?"

"Aleksandra went by a number of different aliases including Jean Narby, Laura Boyd, Jennifer McManus, Karen Brown, and Katherine Ames."

"You've got to be kidding me! Kathy Ames?"

"I wish I were. I spoke to the police in Cincinnati. As near as we can figure it out, she was the lover and accomplice of Bateman, a real Bonnie and Clyde couple. She left him when she discovered he was into child pornography, but came to New York hoping to change him and win him back. She lied about being his sister and paying for his room. Bateman used the alias Karl Trask to avoid police warrants for him in Cincinnati. We would have tracked him down in time. Melrose must have found him and told her he was using pictures he took to blackmail someone. She wanted those pictures maybe because she was in them or maybe to find out who he was blackmailing so she could pick up where he left off."

Bennis shook his head. "Oh! What a tangled web we weave when first we practice to deceive. Do you think she hit Thomas and took the pictures?"

"I don't think so, Father. She wasn't that big and whoever hit Tom was pretty strong. My bet is the killer hit him and took the pictures if there even were any."

Cavanaugh took a drink of water and frowned. "Why didn't he kill me then like he did the others?"

"Maybe, Thomas, because he didn't see you as being evil. You didn't fit into his pattern. My guess is she might be in those missing photos."

"What pattern? What did you find?" Goldberg asked.

Fran, Bennis, Cavanaugh, and Chico proceeded to tell Goldberg what they learned about Sin-Eaters. They explained that Sin-Eaters were known to perform ceremonies in the seventeenth and eighteenth centuries to take on the sins of the deceased. They performed rituals to cleanse the dead of their sins. In some cases they placed bread and beer on the dead body and then consumed some of it. The idea was that the dead person's sins were digested by the Sin-Eater, not only saving the dead from hell, but also from wandering the earth as a ghost. The Sin-Eaters themselves were usually poor outcasts who were shunned by others and considered repulsive and repugnant because they carried the unabsolved sins of others and were destined to burn in hell when they died. Consequently, they avoided others until they were called to help.

"We think our killer is a modern day Sin-Eater, who has altered the traditional ritual," Father Bennis explained. "He is focusing his attention of people he considers evil, a plague on the community. He thinks by eliminating them, he will be saving them and the rest of the community. He cuts their eyes out because he feels they have sinned with their eyes."

Goldberg sighed, "If you're right, he's going to have a heck of a lot of work to do. He may run out of churches before the runs out of potential victims."

* * * *

Fran put on a pot of coffee and brought out cheese and crackers for everyone. Goldberg, Cavanaugh, and Bennis sat around the dining room table and discussed the case. Fran pulled over a chair and joined them. Chico moved to Cavanaugh's favorite lounge chair. Officer Jefferson stood watch at the door. Fran asked, "Why doesn't Officer Jefferson join us?"

"He's fine where he is," Cavanaugh said and turned to

Goldberg and asked, "Why did you bring that guy with you? Do you know he threatened to taser me when I was trying to see Jack?"

Jefferson answered, "I was just following Detective Perez's orders."

"That's what the German officers said at the Nuremberg Trials."

Goldberg spoke up. "Officer Jefferson is an excellent, conscientious police officer. I wish we had more like him. Jefferson's a damn good officer. He was following Detective Perez's direct order. I brought him with me so you could thank him."

"Thank him? Have you lost your fine Jewish mind? Thank him for what? Threatening me with his stupid yellow taser?"

"No, Tom. For saving your life. If Jefferson had not followed you into Bateman's apartment and found you, you probably would have bleed to death before anyone found you. Jefferson saved your *goyishe* life."

Cavanaugh looked at Jefferson standing at parade rest by the front door. "I didn't know," he said. "I don't remember what happened. You say he's the one who found me?"

"He saw you sneak out of your house and followed you. I wouldn't make this up. I thought you should know."

Fran rushed to Officer Jefferson and gave him a big hug. Father Bennis shook his hand and invited him to sit with them. Jefferson checked with Goldberg who nodded assent. Cavanaugh slowly rose and offered his hand to Jefferson. "I'm sorry, kid," he said. "I didn't know."

Jack Bennis looked at his brother and said, "It's no crime to be kind to one another. 'Forgive us our trespasses as we forgive others.'"

"Okay, okay. I don't need a lecture. I said I'm sorry.

No need to beat a dead horse."

Chico called out from the lounge chair, "You're not a dead horse, Padre."

Everyone laughed. Then they sat together and tried to analyze the killings in the light of the Sin-Eater facts. As they spoke, Officer Jefferson Googled "Sin-Eater" and relayed that they were fairly common in Europe and the British Isles in the 1700s and 1800s. The Catholic Church eventually excommunicated Sin-Eaters. The last known Sin-Eater died in the early 1900s.

Cavanaugh said, "I still think Mario Impellizzieri has something to do with this. If he was in those pictures, Ames or whatever her real name was could have been blackmailing him. Maybe they were of him and her in some compromising positions. If he's in the middle of a divorce, he wouldn't want those pictures getting into the wrong hands."

Goldberg started clicking his pen again. "What about the parents of the children Bateman exposed himself to? I remember you said one of them had a violent temper."

Fran brought Cavanaugh's marble notebook to the table. He flipped through the pages until he found Jack O'Hanlon. "This guy O'Hanlon's a high school physical education teacher. They say he has a temper. He's been reprimanded for it a few times."

Bennis looked at his brother's notes. "It says here his wife works at Staten Island University Hospital. She is also a Eucharistic minister at St. Peter's. I know them. In fact, I spoke to them the night I found Dave Melrose's body."

"So," Goldberg said, "they were both at the church the night Melrose's body was found. The husband has a temper. His daughter was approached by a pervert at the ferry terminal. The way I see it, they had reason to be angry with Bateman for what he did to their daughter."

"I don't know, Morty. From everything I learned about Mrs. O'Hanlon, she seems like a really nice person. I don't think she's involved in this."

"Tom, they had motive. The wife works in a hospital. She has means to obtain hypodermic needles. Fentanyl is easy enough to obtain. Together, they could easily have moved the body into the church."

Jack Bennis shook his head. "I don't believe they are murderers. Mrs. O'Hanlon is a Eucharistic minister at St. Peter's. They are good, caring people."

"With all due respect, Father, wasn't Judas one of Jesus' apostles? How did that turn out?"

"I had a long conversation with them that night, Detective Goldberg. I don't believe they could have done it."

Chico called out from the lounge chair, "Maybe they put the dead guy in the church before they talked to you."

All eyes turned to little Chico. He was coiled up in the chair. Goldberg asked Father Bennis, "What did you talk about that night?"

All eyes shifted back to Bennis. He touched the scar above his eye, but said nothing.

Goldberg repeated his question. "Father, what did the three of you discuss?"

"It was a private conversation, Detective. I would rather not discuss it."

"This is a murder investigation, Father. What are you holding back?"

"Nothing. I just don't feel comfortable disclosing things said in confidence."

"Excuse me, Chief," Jefferson interjected. "All the info I got on Sin-Eaters indicates they were poor, uneducated, and shunned by most people. Mr. and Mrs. O'Hanlon don't seem to fit that profile."

Goldberg continued clicking his pen. "Officer Jefferson, this murderer has deviated from the traditional role of previous Sin-Eaters. He's choosing people he believes are evil, and he's killing them and cutting their eyes out. This Sin-Eater is a different character." He reached over and snatched Cavanaugh's notebook. "I'm taking this with me. There may be more information in it that we can investigate more fully."

Cavanaugh started to stand, but became dizzy and fell back into his chair. "You can't do that, Morty. That's my property!"

"I'll send it back in the morning. You can't do anything now anyway. I told you that you were off this case. It's our job now. Officer Jefferson will watch the house until I send relief for him." Then Goldberg stood with the notebook in his hand, thanked Fran, wished everyone a good night, and left.

* * * *

Fran took Chico up to the guest room and told Cavanaugh she was going to read a little in bed. When they were alone, Cavanaugh suggested they have a nightcap. Bennis poured himself a Glenlivet on the rocks and brought Cavanaugh a bottle of Becks. They sat in silence for a minute until Cavanaugh asked, "Why didn't you tell Morty about the meeting you had with the O'Hanlons? Is it one of those 'bound by Confession' things?"

"No. It wasn't about the Sacrament of Penance. I regarded it as a kind of counseling conference. I think of it as a matter of patient confidentiality."

"But they're not your patients."

Bennis took a sip of his scotch.

"You know, Jack, sometimes I think you are really screwed up."

"Is this the pot calling the kettle black? Who wanted to kick the police officer who saved his life out of his house because he once tried to follow the orders of a superior officer?"

"That's not fair, Jack, and you know it. Besides...." Cavanaugh hesitated to take a long gulp of his beer. "Besides, I know what you were talking about that night."

Bennis frowned. "You are so full of it your eyes are brown. How would you know?"

"You were discussing their neighbor who's been acting strange lately. He used to be friendly and outgoing, but now he's reclusive and avoids people. His wife died in a hit and run accident about a year ago, and then one son committed suicide and the other son died of a drug overdose."

"How do you know all this? I never told you."

"Jack, remember I used to be a detective, and a damn good one if I do say so myself!"

Bennis' jaw dropped, and he stared incredulously at his brother.

"Relax. I'm not clairvoyant. I met Mrs. O'Hanlon at Lee's Tavern. She was asking for you. She was worried about you because you seemed to suddenly drop out of sight. I told her you were looking for a lost boy. Then she told me all about her meeting with you. The old guy really faced a lot of heartaches."

Cavanaugh paused and took another gulp of beer. "You know, Jack, the more I think about it, the more the old guy seems to fit the profile of a Sin-Eater. He's smart, has isolated himself from others, and has faced a hell of a lot of problems."

Bennis twirled the ice cubes in his glass. "I've been

thinking the same thing. I think I'll visit him tomorrow to see what I can learn."

"Be careful. I wish I could go with you, but I know I can't with this head of mine. Do you think the O'Hanlons will tell Goldberg or Perez about him?"

"I doubt it. They're good people and don't like talking about others and judging them." He stopped and finished his drink. Then he looked at his brother and said, "Now that I think of it, Thomas, why didn't you tell Detective Goldberg about the neighbor?"

Cavanaugh finished his beer and smiled. "Simple. It was none of my business."

* * * *

Chapter 25

The following morning, Jack Bennis rose early and went to St. Peter's where he asked Father Vivaldi's permission to assist in Monsignor O'Brien's 9:00 Mass. Permission was granted. Bennis felt good saying Mass again. He listened to Monsignor's homily with familiarity and anticipation. He never knew what Monsignor would say.

Monsignor O'Brien began by talking about wedding traditions in Ireland, Africa, and the United States. He spoke about a colorful stained glass window in one church that newly married couples loved to have their picture taken in front of. He drew laughter from the congregation when he pointed out how appropriate it was for them to be photographed in front of the window because the words at the bottom of the window were, "Father, forgive them for they know not what they do."

He felt from years of experience working with couples that marriages fluctuated between "I would die for you" to "If you cough one more time, I will strangle you." Jack Bennis smiled when Monsignor couldn't resist using another Latin phrase, *"Amor et melle et felle est fecundissimus"* – Love is rich with both honey and venom.

Then he segued to the Gospel of St. John where Mary tells Jesus at a wedding feast in Cana that they are running out of wine. "You would think it was an Irish wedding," he said. "Jesus' response was, 'Woman, my time has not yet come.' But he does what Mary wants. He knows his mother and he performs his first recorded miracle. He changes water into wine."

Monsignor drew a few more laughs when he commented, "Sure I know we could have used him at a few parties I've attended in the past." But he went on to concentrate on how Jesus honored his mother. Even though it wasn't his time, he did what his mother wanted. Like many women, Mary didn't say it specifically, but he knew what she wanted him to do, and he did it.

At this point, Monsignor digressed into a story about his own mother and how when she told him his room was a "sorry mess," he knew what she wanted and how he better do it or face the "bloody consequences."

He held onto the sides of the lectern and said, "The fifth commandment is about honoring your father and mother. Honor in our world today has been twisted. People honor things like money, cars, luxurious homes, fame, criminals, popularity, political parties, drugs, alcohol or whatever. Today's world honors false gods. Honor your father and mother. It's simple. It's all a matter of honor. Perhaps the important question we need to ask ourselves is what do we honor? Are we honoring the right things?"

Jack Bennis stood as Monsignor O'Brien shuffled slowly to the main altar. Bennis' head was spinning. Honor thy father and mother. He honored his mother. But the first person he killed was his father. He thought back to that day when he saw his father raping his little sister. His father held a knife to his sister's neck. She was crying. Bennis snuck up behind him and wrapped an extension cord around his neck and pulled back as hard as he could. He twisted the cord until his fingers hurt and his father stopped struggling.

When he released the cord, his father's limp body fell to the floor. It was then that he saw his father's knife imbedded in his little sister's neck. Her blank eyes stared up at him. He never got that image out of his mind.

The choir started singing "How Great Thou Art." He tried so hard to forget the past, but it kept rearing its ugly head. It was an accident, and yet it wasn't an accident. He was glad his father was dead. He was glad he killed him. The father he honored was the father of all of us, Christians, Jews, Muslims, and everyone else.

At the end of Mass, Bennis stood in the narthex or vestibule of the church greeting parishioners with Monsignor O'Brien. Roberta O'Hanlon expressed joyful surprise when she greeted him. "When did you get back, Father? We missed you."

"It's good to see you, Roberta. How are Jack and the girls?"

"You know Jack. He's coaching the baseball team after school and the girls are doing well. Charlotte is in the school play and Jacklyn is loving kindergarten."

Bennis leaned a little closer. "And how is your neighbor? I've been thinking about him. Is he any better?"

"No. We hardly ever see him. He's become a recluse. He used to be such a kind and outgoing person, but now we never see him. Jack says we tried, but I still worry about him. He never answers his door. I've tried calling him, but my calls go straight to voicemail."

"Do you think it would help if I went to visit him?"

"I don't know if he would talk to you, but it's worth a try. It couldn't hurt."

* * * *

Rumors were that the two-story red brick garden apartment complex on Grymes Hill where Jack and Roberta O'Hanlon lived was originally constructed by Donald Trump's father. Today most of the apartments were condominiums. Cavanaugh thought the rumors were "fake news." Jack Bennis didn't really care. All he cared about right now was going to try to talk to a suspected Sin-Eater and then to going to the hospital to see María Isabelle.

Richard Wallowmire lived in a studio apartment next to the O'Hanlons. Situated on the second highest point on Staten Island, some of the apartments had a beautiful view of the New York Harbor and the Verrazano-Narrows Bridge. Wallowmire's apartment looked out on a large open area of grass.

Jack Bennis knocked on Wallowmire's door. No answer. He knocked again. Again, no answer. On his third attempt, he called out as he knocked, "Mr. Wallowmire, my name is Father Bennis. I'm from St. Peter's Church. The O'Hanlons were worried about you. They asked me to see how you are."

At first, there was no answer. Then he heard a series of locks being opened. The door opened slightly. The security chain was still on. A head peeked out. The eyes were what struck him first. They were sad, not exactly terrifying, but definitely not peaceful. The balding head had lines and scars that crisscrossed his face. "You really a priest?" the mouth asked in a harsh, muffled voice.

"Yes."

"I don't remember you from when Betty and I went there with the kids."

"I was working in Cartagena, Colombia. I just recently returned."

"That Castillo San Diego de Barajas still there or did

they tear it down and build more housing for drug addicts?"

"It's Castillo San Felipe de Barajas, and it's still there. It offers a great view of the Caribbean. I worked at St. Peter Claver Church."

"Do they still have that coffin of St. Theresa in the back?"

"The body of St. Peter Claver is encased in the main altar. Is the test over? I am a real priest. Can I ask you how you know about Cartagena?"

"I guess you're legit. I worked with the merchant marines on tugboats down there a long time ago. It was a good job, but I missed my wife and sons."

"May I come in or shall we continue to talk through the door."

The head withdrew, and Bennis heard the chain being released. As the door opened, Wallowmire said, "You can't be too sure nowadays. I hear there are a lot of bad things happening around here."

Bennis walked into the room. It was dark and dusty. There was a metallic smell Bennis recognized all too well. It was blood. A chill swept over his body. He turned and looked at Wallowmire. A thin beam of sunlight lit up one side of his face. "Can I get you a beer and some bread," he said.

"No, thank you. I came because Mr. and Mrs. O'Hanlon are worried about you." Wallowmire took a newspaper off the couch and motioned for Bennis to sit. He was a lot bigger than Bennis expected. "The O'Hanlons are nice enough people, but they should mind their own business. They are too damn nosey."

Bennis sat. "You know my brother's name is Thomas Cavanaugh. He's a private investigator. He had a call recently from someone who told him to mind his own business."

Richard Wallowmire stood in front of him. He loomed

over him like a tall oak tree. "I take it this isn't a social visit, is it?"

"It's whatever you want it to be."

The big man clasped his hands. Even in the darkness, Bennis saw they were massive. He cracked his knuckles one at a time. As he moved his head, the beam of sunlight danced across his face bathing it from lightness to darkness and back again.

"Do you carry that magic stole of yours to hear confessions?"

"I don't need it, but I have it. Would you like to receive the Sacrament of Penance?"

"Why not?" he said and sat down with a thud next to Bennis as the priest took his stole out of his pocket and placed it around his neck.

"Bless me, Father," Richard Wallowmire began, "for I have sinned...."

* * * *

Father Bennis spent the next two hours listening to Richard Wallowmire's confession. He freely confessed to each of the killings. "They were evil people," he said. "They sinned with their eyes so I removed their eyes. I was following scripture. If you sin with your eyes, it is better to cut them out than to be cast into the Gehenna of fire. They were evil. They needed to be eliminated. Someone needed to eliminate them, so I did. But I didn't want to be responsible for sending them to hell, so I absolved them of their sins."

The priest's hands were sweating. The acrid, metallic smell was nauseating. But he persisted. "Were you the one who attacked my brother?"

"I didn't kill him. He's not one of the evil ones. But I

warned him to stay out of my business. He didn't listen."

Wallowmire went through each of the murders in detail. He seemed to enjoy reliving the murders. He used drugs he found in his son Gerald's room. He used a hypodermic needle with a mixture of the heroin and fentanyl. He approached his victims when they were alone and injected them with the heroin and a lethal dose of fentanyl. He took the bodies back to his apartment and performed his ritual. "I don't know what happened with the Ames woman. When I got her back here, she was still alive and started to struggle. The fentanyl didn't work on her like it did for the others for some reason. Maybe she had built up a tolerance for it. I don't know. Maybe it was a bad batch."

He told the priest how he extracted the eyes of his victims in his bathtub using a simple box cutter. It was messy, but not as bloody as he originally thought. He carried his victims to his kitchen table where he performed his ritual. He said he used whatever bread products he had available and used beer because he liked it better than wine.

Wallowmire explained the reason for choosing each of his victims. After the deaths of his family, he felt he had nothing else to live for. He felt a deep guilt for his wife's death. Betty was driving to church when she was killed in an automobile accident. He blamed himself for her death because he decided to take the boys fishing that day instead of attending church services with her.

Her death affected the whole family. Between the death of his mother and the pressure of school, Gerard, who was a student at MIT, hanged himself. And then Gerald died of a drug overdose at a fraternity party at the Bucket of Blood. Wallowmire felt he had nothing to live for. He was contemplating suicide when two things happened. First, he opened up the family Bible to complete the family record. He started entering his wife and sons' information when he noticed the name Richard Wallowmire. The family record listed his death as April 23, 1906. Wallowmire recalled his father talking about his great-grandfather who was from Sunderland, England, and was famous for something. Wallowmire's own birthday was April 23. Was he named after his great-great-grandfather?

Curiosity led him to Google Richard Wallowmire, and that's when he learned about Sin-Eaters. His great-great-grandfather was a well-known nineteenth century Sin-Eater. Then he opened the Bible, and it fell open to Matthew Chapter 5 – "If your right eye causes you to sin, tear it out and throw it away. For it is better that you lose one of your members than that your whole body be thrown into hell."

That was when the idea hit him. There was so much evil in the world. Perhaps he could eliminate it and save some souls in the process. He remembered reading about a man named Bateman who exposed himself to a group of young girls at the ferry terminal. He should have gone to prison, but a lawyer named Melrose got him released on a legal technicality. That was when he decided Bateman must die and so must Melrose. They were evil men. Then he read that Montego was fined for serving minors in his bar and realized his bar was where his son Gerald died of an overdose of heroin and fentanyl. He must die, too. When he went to Monica Melrose's house to convey his condolences, he discovered she and her husband were involved in producing hardcore pornographic films. She pleaded for her life and told him about Kathy Ames and the photographs Bateman had in his apartment. He went to the apartment to find the pictures. When he found the photos, he decided she must die, too. It was all logical to him. It was like setting up dominoes all in a row and then pushing one. One thing led to another. Monica Melrose told him all he needed to know. He leaned closer to Father Bennis and said, "There is no honor with evil doers. They are all alike."

"My brother didn't know Kathy Ames' address. How did you find it?"

"I followed her from Cavanaugh's office. It was really very simple. I didn't know who she was at the time, but after I saw the pictures, I knew."

Wallowmire stood up and asked, "May I get you a glass of water or something? My mouth is dry. I fear I have talked too much."

"No, thank you," Bennis said. He watched Wallowmire go into the kitchen and heard the water running. When he returned, Wallowmire stood over the priest again. He held something in his hand. It wasn't a glass of water.

"Now give me your absolution," he demanded.

"Are you truly sorry for your sins and do you resolve with the help of God's grace to sin no more."

Richard Wallowmire swayed back and forth in the beam of sunlight. He went from light into darkness. Bennis saw the object in his hand was a box cutter. Wallowmire chuckled, "Of course not! I am not sorry, and I have no intention of stopping. There is still so much work to do. There are a lot of evil people in the world, Father."

"You can't be serious. You have no power to forgive sins. Only God forgives sins. Priests have the power to forgive sins only because God has given it to them by virtue of their reception of Holy Orders. Placing bread soaked in beer on the body of a dead person and then eating the bread does not absolve their sins."

"But I am serious – deadly serious. I have more work to do. I have no intention of stopping. It is my duty."

"Then I cannot grant you absolution."

Wallowmire flipped the box cutter from hand to hand. Bennis started calculating the distance between the two of them. Wallowmire had the advantage because he was bigger and above him. Wallowmire stepped back suddenly. "Then get out of my house!"

He faded into the darkness of the room. "I enjoyed our little conversation. I know you can't tell anyone about what I told you. You are bound by the seal of confession. Hold everything in your mind, Father, and know that you know who I am, what I have done, what I plan to continue to do, and that you can do absolutely nothing about it because your God has bound you not to speak a word of what I have told you to anyone." The door of the apartment swung open, and Wallowmire shouted, "Now get out of my house before I change my mind about you!"

* * * *

Jack Bennis walked slowly back to his car. Richard Wallowmire was without any doubt the Sin-Eater. He freely admitted it; he almost boasted about it. He was proud of what he did. He gave intimate details of each murder, and he disclosed his plans to continue his killings. What was even more disturbing and frightening, however, was that Wallowmire knew Bennis was bound by the n not to acknowledge to anyone anything he told him.

Bennis' head was spinning when he reached his car. How could he allow Wallowmire to continue killing people? In Wallowmire's eyes, the people he murdered were evil. He believed he was ridding the world of sinners while saving their souls at the same time. He had appointed himself as judge and jury.

The priest knew information that would lead to the arrest and conviction of the Sin-Eater, but he could tell no one. Wallowmire had put Bennis in a horrible predicament. It is the absolute duty of a priest not to disclose anything a penitent tells him while confessing his sins. Bennis couldn't tell the police. He couldn't tell his brother. He had to hold the information given to him to himself. He wasn't allowed to even give clues about what he was told.

It is a sacred obligation of a priest not to betray the sinner by word or sign or by any manner whatsoever in any way. Bennis was handcuffed. He knew what Wallowmire planned to do, but could do nothing to stop it. He felt like his head was splitting open. He needed help. Wallowmire had placed an unbearable burden on him.

Instead of going to the hospital to visit María Isabelle, he turned the car around and headed back to St. Peter's. He needed to seek the wisdom and counsel of an experienced priest whom he trusted. He decided to pick the brain of Monsignor O'Brien.

He found Monsignor in church praying. Bennis asked if he could speak in private to him about something that was troubling him. They went into an open confessional, and Bennis explained his situation without mentioning any names. Monsignor sat and listened. At times, Monsignor was so still Bennis felt the older man had fallen asleep. But he hadn't.

After he told him the predicament he found himself in, Monsignor looked up. "Sure it's a difficult conundrum you find yourself in, Jack, but you know what you must do. You and I are bound by the seal of confession. There is no easy way around it. It makes no difference whether you granted the person absolution or not. What the penitent tells us we cannot communicate to anyone else. *'Non est ad astra mollis e terris via'* - the road from earth to the stars is not easy, but *'facilis descensus averno'* - the way to hell is easy."

Bennis' hands were sweating and his head felt like it was ready to burst. "But how can I in due conscience sit back and watch him continue to kill people? I must be able to do something to stop him!"

"Oh, Jack, sure there is something you can do. You can pray. You can pray with all your heart, your mind, and your soul. Then you must leave it in God's hands. Remember the prayer, 'God, grant me the serenity to accept the things I cannot change, the courage to change the things I can, and the wisdom to know the difference.' A priest's job is never easy. Canon law is specific. The sacramental seal of confession is inviolable. We, as priests, are forbidden to betray in any way, for any reason, a penitent even under the threat of our own death or the death of others. Think of it as St. Thomas Aquinas did. The priest hears confession not as a man, but as God hears it. We represent God in the confessional."

The two men sat in the closed room in silence for a while. Then Monsignor O'Brien spoke again. "Sure I don't know if I've helped you, Jack. The good Lord knows it's a heavy burden the person has heaped on you. But He will give you the strength to deal with it. Leave it in His hands. I don't know if you remember Father Mychal Judge. He was a Franciscan friar who served as a New York City Fire Department chaplain. He was killed during the 9/11 attacks on the World Trade Center. Fr. Judge had a prayer that he used to say: 'Lord, take me where You want me to go. Let me meet who You want me to meet. Tell me what You want me to say, and keep me out of Your way.' Sure I know you want to do something, but in this case, leave it to God and the only thing you can do is pray and keep out of His way."

Jack Bennis sighed. He wished he had Monsignor's faith and confidence. He stood and thanked Monsignor O'Brien. As he was leaving, Monsignor called after him, "*Non ergo turbetur cor vestrum. Dum vita est, spes est.*" A slight smile crept across Bennis' face. He knew the Latin and what it meant. "Let not your heart be troubled. While there is life, there is hope."

* * * *

Chapter 26

María Isabelle was asleep when Jack Bennis visited her in the hospital. He pulled over a chair and sat beside her. She was pale and thinner. Her hair needed to be washed. There were a few strands of gray in her hair and lines in her face he had never seen before. She had been through hell, yet she looked beautiful to him.

He recalled how they first met in Cuba, how she cared for him when he was shot, how he brought her with him to the United States, and how he fell in love with her. He reached over and held her hand. It was cold.

He didn't hear the nurse enter the room, but he felt her presence. He turned and looked up at a tall blond nurse. She smiled and said softly, "I'm Laura Jean, María's nurse. You must be Father Bennis. María has spoken a lot about you. She has been through an awful lot. It is good to see her resting."

"How is she progressing?"

"Better than expected. We plan to take her to physical therapy tomorrow so it is good she is getting some rest."

"Thank you, Laura Jean. I was just leaving. Please tell her when she wakes that I was here."

Walking down the corridor of the hospital, he felt like

the world was collapsing on him. Multiple images and situations bombarded his brain. María Isabelle ... Richard Wallowmire ... Morty Goldberg ... Cavanaugh ... Monsignor O'Brien ... his father ... the unidentified next victim ....

The memory of Richard Wallowmire's confession haunted him. He knew the killer. He knew he planned to strike again. He didn't know who, when, or where the Sin-Eater would kill again. How could he hold back, in good conscience, this information from the police? Would he be an unwilling accessory to the next murder? An even more pressing question was would he be able to withhold what Wallowmire told him from his brother? Cavanaugh knew where he was going. Would he lie to him and say Richard Wallowmire wasn't home? He believed two wrongs never make a right, and he was bound by the seal of confession. "Leave it to God," Monsignor O'Brien advised. "Do not trouble yourself. It is in God's hands." That was easier said than done.

Bennis sat in his car deep in thought. Where was God when Chico and the other boys were kidnapped? Where was He when the artist Dianna was tortured to death? Where was He when his brother and María Isabelle were almost killed?

He felt a deep emptiness in his soul when he started the engine. He grasped the steering wheel and repeated once again, "My God, my God, why have you abandoned me?" Had he lost his faith? Did he no longer believe? He stared at the cumulus clouds above. A falcon glided effortlessly across the sky. No, he still believed. They that hope in the Lord shall renew their strength. They shall take wings as eagles. They shall run and not be weary. They shall walk and not grow weak. Blessed are they who have not seen and still believe. He believed. It was the only thing in his life that made sense. It gave him strength.

Wallowmire was willing to absorb the sins of others, damning himself to everlasting torment in order to eliminate evil doers, thinking he was saving their souls. It didn't make sense. Wallowmire was delusional. His world had crumbled before him. He had nothing to live for. He was what his brother would call "a nut case," but Bennis saw him as a deeply troubled man.

Jack Bennis had killed before. He knew what it felt like. He didn't like it, but he was good at it, damn good. He hoped and prayed that those days were past. Could he sit back and let God sort it out? Or would he be part of the solution? Driving out of the hospital parking lot, the words from the Old Testament Book of Ecclesiastes flashed across his mind again. "For everything there is a season, a time to be born and a time to die, a time to kill and a time to heal...." He wondered to himself, what time was it for him? And would he have the courage to do the right thing?

* * * *

Jack Bennis dreaded going back to his brother's house. After visiting María Isabelle in the hospital, he went back to St. Peter's and had a long talk with Fr. Vivaldi. The pastor made it clear to him that he was softening, but insisted he didn't want Bennis staying at the rectory until "this thing" with the "Stations of the Cross Murders" was over. Bennis knew he could always crash at his brother's house. He had his own room there, and Chico was staying there. Fran and his brother always welcomed him. That wasn't Bennis' main concern. He dreaded the cross-examination his brother would put him through. Maybe it was the years Cavanaugh spent as a homicide detective. Bennis knew Cavanaugh knew he intended to question the

O'Hanlons' neighbor. Cavanaugh would hound him for information, and he couldn't tell him anything about Wallowmire's confession. Cavanaugh could be like a ravenous dog with a bone. He wouldn't let up until he had answers.

When he arrived at the Cavanaugh's house, the front lights were on, and it looked like the living room light was on, too. Bennis said a quick prayer that Thomas would be asleep and carefully unlocked the front door. All was quiet, almost too quiet. The only sound he heard was the ticking of the clock in the living room and the dull hum of the refrigerator in the kitchen.

His room was upstairs, but he feared he would wake someone so he settled into Cavanaugh's favorite lounge chair and closed his eyes. Before he knew it, the smell of bacon and coffee woke him. It was morning.

Tom Cavanaugh looked down on him. "Wake up, sleepy head. What time did you get in last night? I never heard you."

"It was late, Thomas. I didn't want to wake anyone."

"We're all up now. Fran is cooking bacon and eggs. Chico is in the kitchen eating everything in sight. For a little kid, he sure eats a lot. Did you ever think of feeding the poor kid? Stephen's been up for hours. I'm surprised you didn't hear him crying."

"I must have been in a deep sleep."

Cavanaugh pulled over a chair. "So? How did it go?"

Bennis' mind was spinning like a roulette wheel. "Well, I visited María Isabelle in the hospital. She was sleeping so I didn't disturb her. Her nurse told me she is doing well and they are planning to take her for physical therapy this morning."

"That's great, but I meant how did it go with the

O'Hanlons' neighbor?"

"I met him. He was in the Merchant Marines. He worked for a while in Cartagena."

"Yeah, but what did he say about the murders?"

"The man has had a lot of tragedies in his life."

"Yeah, but what do you think about him and the Sin-Eater? Do you think he's the guy?"

Bennis rubbed the scar over his eye and struggled to get up. "You know that bacon smells good. I could really use a cup of coffee, but first I have to pee."

"You're doing it again, Jack. You're avoiding the question. Do you think he could be the killer?"

"Thomas, I really need to go to the bathroom. Maybe we can talk about it later."

"Oh, I get it! It's another of those private counseling services you provide that you won't talk about. I'm your brother, Jack. You can tell me anything!"

Bennis rolled his eyes, looked at Cavanaugh, and smiled. "If I don't go to the bathroom now, I just might ruin your favorite chair." While he was in the bathroom, he heard the phone ring. When he came out, Fran had a plate of bacon and eggs ready for him and a cup of hot coffee. Chico was attacking a stack of pancakes like a starving lion. Cavanaugh sat in the living room talking on the phone. When he finished his conversation, Cavanaugh joined them at the kitchen table. He looked confused. "That was Goldberg," he said. "He says they think they found the murderer."

Bennis almost choked on his coffee. "They did?"

"Yeah. He said the notes he took from me helped a lot."

Bennis knew his brother had not seen Wallowmire. He would have no notes about him. The priest took another sip of coffee and said nothing.

"To tell the truth," Cavanaugh said, "I'm really surprised. Perez and the Hulk arrested the guy early this morning."

"Who is it?" Fran asked.

"That teacher guy, Jack O'Hanlon."

This time Bennis did choke on his coffee. "They arrested O'Hanlon? Why? How did they figure it was him?"

"Well, the way Goldberg tells it, they read in my notes about his violent temper and that his daughter was traumatized by Bateman at the ferry. It turns out O'Hanlon had no alibi for any of the murders."

"That's no proof. That's all circumstantial. What reason would he have for the other murders? It doesn't make sense."

"Yeah, but that's the way it works sometimes. The guy who looks like he's innocent turns out to be the bad guy."

"I know the O'Hanlons. They wouldn't do these things. Mrs. O'Hanlon is a Eucharistic minister. I spoke with them the night I found Melrose's body. I think they've arrested an innocent man."

Chico mumbled something, but his mouth was so full of pancakes, nobody understood him.

Cavanaugh poured himself a cup of coffee. "To be honest," he said, "I didn't think he was a likely suspect either after we heard all that Sin-Eater stuff from that old monsignor, but Goldberg tells me they searched O'Hanlon's car and found a six pack of beer, some stale bagels, a blood stained box cutter, index cards, and some fentanyl in the trunk. They feel sure he's the guy."

Jack Bennis looked down at his uneaten bacon and eggs. He felt sick. Wallowmire was smart and crafty. He must have planted the box cutter, beer, fentanyl, and bagels in O'Hanlon's car after he left him. If God was going to work this one out, he thought, God was taking His own sweet time. Maybe God needed a little help from him.

* * * *

It all seemed pretty simple. Jack O'Hanlon had been set up by Wallowmire. As a man, Bennis wanted to confront Wallowmire and physically wring a confession out of him. As a priest, however, he felt he needed to comfort Roberta O'Hanlon. What must she be going through? He imagined Detective Perez and her gigantic partner barging into their apartment in the middle of the night or the early morning hours. Roberta had her daughters to care for, and her husband was suddenly ripped from their home and arrested for multiple murders.

Bennis called Mrs. O'Hanlon. He felt the panic and frustration in her voice. "How could they think Jack killed anyone? You know him, Father. Sometimes he loses his temper at times, but he could never kill another human being. He's not a violent person. He's just not that kind of person."

They talked for a while. Her children were at school. She didn't know what she should do. The police didn't listen to her. She told the children their father had to go to work early. "I know I lied," she cried, "but how could I tell them their father was arrested for murder? I don't know what to do."

Bennis rubbed the scar over his eye. "Do either of you have any enemies? Did anything unusual happen recently?"

"No, Father. We get along with everyone. The kids have been doing great in school. I told your brother how Charlotte is in the school play. She is so proud of herself. And Jacklyn is having the time of her life in kindergarten. Jack was enjoying practice with his team. Last year they made it into the semi-finals. This year he felt they had a real chance of going all the way."

Bennis felt like he was walking a tight rope over the Grand Tetons. "Did Jack or you have any confrontations with anyone recently?"

"No, Father. Everything has been fine." She paused a moment and then added, "Well, it really wasn't a confrontation. We both laughed about it after."

Bennis gripped his phone tighter. "What happened, Roberta?"

"Mr. Wallowmire knocked on our door last night and told us you had come to see him. Thank you for doing that, Father. We were worried about him. For some reason, however, he seemed upset and told us to mind our own business. Jack said that goes to show you that when you try to help some people, it sometimes doesn't work out. We dismissed it as the rantings of a lonely, old man and decided to leave him alone. Actually, we laughed about it over a glass of wine after kids went to bed. Some people just don't want to be helped. Jack and I agreed to honor his request and chalked it up to experience."

Bennis nodded. He recalled how Jesus told his disciples that if people will not listen to them to "shake the dust" from their feet and move on. In Jack and Roberta O'Hanlon's case, however, it might have been too late. For some reason, Wallowmire decided to implicate them in the murders. Was Wallowmire being vindictive because the O'Hanlons, like his own brother, did not "mind their own business"? Or was he being cautious just in case Bennis decided to tell someone about his confession?

There was only one way to find out. Jack Bennis decided to visit Richard Wallowmire again.

* * * *

Chapter 27

Father Bennis waited until dark. He didn't want any witnesses to his meeting with Richard Wallowmire. He parked his car a quarter of a mile away and walked through the shadows to Wallowmire's apartment. There was a cool breeze in the air. The moon was hiding behind dark clouds.

He didn't know what exactly he would say to Wallowmire, but Bennis' personal code of honor did not permit an innocent man to be punished for the crimes of another. He hoped he could talk sense into Wallowmire. He wasn't particularly optimistic, but he still had hope.

He slipped in and out of the shadows. Lights were off in most of the condominiums around him. The O'Hanlons' apartment was dark. The children were probably asleep. It was late. He wondered what Roberta told them about their father. How did she explain his absence? Did the kids at school talk about him? Did they tease Charlotte and Jacklyn? Bennis knew kids can be cruel. Jack O'Hanlon's arrest was on the news. The *New York Post* ran a headline, "Stations of the Cross Murderer Caught." How do you protect children from gossip and slander about their parents? Richard Wallowmire's actions hurt a lot of innocent people. The world might not miss a Bateman, but some people might. What kind of a code of honor did Wallowmire follow that allowed him to hurt innocent people? He had to be stopped.

Bennis blended into the darkness. He had been carefully trained in clandestine operations. He moved with the stealth of a panther. When he reached Wallowmire's door, he knocked softly. Then he froze. He felt something near him. He turned. No one was there. Maybe it was the wind. Maybe it was a bird. He knocked again. A little harder. Again, no answer.

He stiffened. There was something behind him. He couldn't see it, but he felt its presence.

He lifted his hand to knock again, but a powerful hand suddenly gripped his arm. A voice whispered in his ear, "No one's home."

Bennis swung around. The face was hidden in the dark, but he smelled beer on its breath. It cautioned softly, "If you keep knocking like that, you'll wake up the dead, or you just might join them."

Bennis squinted into the darkness. He recognized the voice. The hand released its grip on his arm. "Thomas, is that you?" he asked.

"Who did you expect? Santa Claus?"

"What are you doing here?"

"I could ask you the same question, but we both know why you're here. You should never play poker, Jack. I can read you like a Dr. Seuss book. I'm your brother and a damn good detective, I might add."

"Ex-detective!"

"Let's not quibble over words. Let's get the hell out of here now and go somewhere we can talk. I don't know what you expected to do here, but I came to keep you from doing something stupid! You don't have to thank me now. You can thank me later."

.

* * * *

They drove down the hill past Wagner College to an all-night diner on Hylan Blvd. They bickered back and forth all the way. "What are you doing following me? You should be home in bed. You are still not completely healed."

"Look who's calling the kettle black this time. Who's dressed like a ninja warrior sneaking around at night?"

"I wasn't sneaking anywhere. I was going to speak with someone."

"Come on, Jack, you're a priest. Thou shalt not lie. I saw you sneaking around."

"What were you doing here?"

"I've been watching this house for hours. I figured you'd come looking for him after you heard O'Hanlon was arrested. Call it surveillance. I'm good at it. Did I ever tell you I was a good detective? A damn good detective!"

Jack Bennis' hands were sweating. "I didn't tell you anything."

"You didn't have to."

When they reached the restaurant, the brothers settled into a booth by the window. A young waitress came over to them and offered them a menu. Jack Bennis looked up. He recognized the waitress. It was Judy Vernon, a Eucharistic minister at St. Peter's. "Judy," he asked, "is that you?"

The waitress looked at him and blushed. "Father Bennis? I didn't recognize you without your Roman collar."

"How have you been? I heard your husband was sick. How is he?"

Judy Vernon looked around. The diner was almost empty. "Ron got an infection in his knee and has been out of work for months. I had to go back to work to make ends meet."

"I'm sorry to hear that. I was wondering why we

hadn't seen you at the nine o'clock Mass in a while."

Judy turned. Behind the cash register, the owner of the diner, Mikhalis Panagotas, stood, arms folded, glaring at Judy. "We'll manage, Father. I wish I could talk more. I heard about Roberta's husband, but the boss is tough. What can I get for you?"

Cavanaugh spoke up ignoring the menu. "Just bring us a pot of coffee for now, Miss."

After the waitress left, Bennis started to explain. "Judy's husband, Ron, hurt his knee on a construction site and developed an infection...."

Cavanaugh reached across the table and grabbed his brother's arm. "Stop it, Jack! I really don't care about Judy and Ron's problems. I want to know about why you were prowling around in the night like a ninja warrior."

Bennis pulled away and started moving the pepper and salt shakers. "Remember, Thomas when they used to have record machines in diner booths? You would put a quarter in and pick a record to play. For some reason my favorite songs were the Platters' 'The Great Pretender' and 'All I Have to Do Is Dream' by the Everly Brothers."

"Jack, I don't know what you planned to do tonight. I have an idea but you're going to get yourself in deep trouble if you don't let go of whatever it is."

Judy came back with their coffee and left. Bennis stared at his cup of coffee and watched the steam rising from the dark liquid. Cavanaugh stared at his brother. Bennis nestled the cup in his hands and said, "I wish I could tell you, Thomas, but I can't."

"Okay, I get it. Well, not really, but I won't push you. I just don't want you getting into serious trouble. I know you are upset that that O'Hanlon guy got arrested. But you have to let the police work it out. You need to stay out of it."

"I don't think he did it, Thomas."

"Maybe he did. Maybe he didn't. I get it. You want to help. But crawling around in the dark of night isn't going to help."

Bennis didn't say anything. He sipped his coffee and stared out the window. When he finished his coffee, he said, "I need to get my car."

Cavanaugh said, "Promise me you won't do something stupid." Bennis mumbled something, and Cavanaugh turned to call the waitress over. A tall man who looked to be in his sixties entered the restaurant. He wore a dark navy blue peacoat and a black baseball cap. He stared at Cavanaugh as if he recognized him. He slowly took his hands out of his pockets and cracked his knuckles. His hands were massive. He started walking toward them as Cavanaugh heard his brother say, "Judy, may we please have the check?"

The man in the peacoat stopped at their table. "Good evening, Father Bennis," he said in a husky voice. "You're out late tonight."

Bennis looked up and stared into the face of Richard Wallowmire.

* * * *

The color in Jack Bennis' face disappeared like water going down the drain. His heart skipped a beat. He looked at his brother and then back up at Wallowmire. He didn't say anything.

"And this must be your brother," Wallowmire said extending his hand to him. "It is a pleasure meeting you again."

Cavanaugh frowned. "I'm sorry, friend, you have me at a loss. I don't remember meeting you."

"It's not important," Wallowmire smiled displaying a line of crooked, yellow teeth. "I seemed to be blessed with a memory for faces. My name is Wallowmire, Richard Wallowmire."

Bennis started to squirm out of his seat. "We were just leaving, Mr. Wallowmire."

"Please, call me Richard. No need to leave right now. The night is young. Let me buy you both a cup of coffee."

The priest rose and grabbed the check. He stood breast to breast with Wallowmire who did not back away. Wallowmire had the distinct odor of beer on his breath. Wallowmire extended one of his massive hands to take the check. "Here, let me pay for that. It is a pleasure meeting you again."

Bennis pulled the check back and moved past Wallowmire without saying a word. Cavanaugh stood. "It's late, Mr. Wallowmire. Thank you for your offer, but I need to take my brother home."

Wallowmire glanced at the diner clock. "Yes, indeed, it is late. I am just coming home from my business. I like to get a bite to eat before I retire for the night."

"What kind of business are you in Mr. Wallowmire?"

"Please call me Richard. Mr. Wallowmire makes me sound too old."

"Okay, Richard."

From the check out, Jack Bennis called to his brother. "We need to go, Thomas."

Cavanaugh hesitated. Wallowmire smiled. "Have a good evening, Mr. Cavanaugh. May I call you Thomas? You seem so much friendlier than your brother."

"As my mother used to say, 'You can call me anything, but late for breakfast.'"

"Ha, ha. That's a good one. I will need to remember

that one." And then he added, "It's a shame about Jack O'Hanlon, isn't it?"

"You know O'Hanlon?"

"Yes. He was my neighbor. Lovely family. Seemed like a nice man, but he did have a temper. It's hard to believe he would kill people, but you really never know someone, do you? "

Standing next to Mikhalis Panagotas at the checkout counter, Bennis called, "Thomas, we really need to go! Now!"

As they got into his car, Cavanaugh asked, "Who is that guy? He seemed like a nice guy, but a little creepy. I don't remember ever meeting him, but I heard his name someplace. "

Jack Bennis stared out the window. He said nothing.

"Wait a second. He's the one Mrs. O'Hanlon told me about when I met her at Lee's Tavern, isn't he?"

Bennis clasped his hands together as if in prayer. "I don't know. I wasn't with you at Lee's."

Cavanaugh nodded his head up and down. "Now it makes sense. I thought you were going to the O'Hanlon's apartment, but you weren't. You were going to Wallowmire's apartment, weren't you?"

"You're the detective."

"And a damn good one, too, if I do say so myself."

"Just get me to my car. It's been a long day, and I'm tired."

"You sure are in a grouchy mood. Richard told me he was just coming home from his business. What kind of business is he in? I think he might have had a few drinks before coming to the diner. Did you smell alcohol on his breath?"

"You sure are in a talkative mood. What is this? Twenty Questions?"

"All right, all right, I'll shut up and take you to your car, but I'm following you home just in case you decide to become a night-stalker again!"

* * * *

Chapter 28

Cavanaugh followed his brother home from the Grymes Hill apartments. He loved his brother and, most of the time, enjoyed his company. He and Fran had set up a room for him in their home. Still, he couldn't wait for Bennis to move back to the rectory. Two are company, three are a crowd, and with Chico staying with them, he felt, four were a mob. He wanted his home back.

But something was bothering his brother. He seemed distracted, anxious, withdrawn. Cavanaugh never saw his brother react to another person as he did to Wallowmire in the diner. Ever since he went to visit Wallowmire, Bennis changed. He was evasive, uncommunicative, morose. This wasn't like him. Cavanaugh used to tease him that he could talk so much that he could talk someone into going to hell in such a way that they looked forward to the trip. Now, Bennis didn't want to talk.

Cavanaugh suspected his brother's behavior had something to do with Richard Wallowmire. Bennis went to visit him initially because he seemed to fit the qualities of a Sin-Eater. When the police arrested Jack O'Hanlon, Bennis insisted he was innocent.

Then tonight, he finds his brother, dressed in black,

knocking on Wallowmire's door in the middle of the night. Why? Why was he shocked to see Wallowmire in the diner? Cavanaugh saw the look on his brother's face when Wallowmire came to their table. Why did he try to avoid him? What had Bennis discovered that caused his drastic change in behavior?

As he crawled into bed that night, Cavanaugh convinced himself that Bennis knew somehow that Wallowmire, not O'Hanlon, was the Sin-Eater. And if he did know, why didn't he speak up? How could he let an innocent man be arrested for murders he did not commit? Cavanaugh's individual code of honor would not permit that, but his brother was a priest! How and why would a priest permit an innocent person go to jail for crimes he did not commit?

Lying on his back, Cavanaugh stared into the dark ceiling. He was a good detective - a damn good detective. There must be a logical reason for his brother's actions. His headache began to return. He ran through a host of different scenarios. Finally, he reached the only conclusion there could be. Father Bennis was somehow bound by the ancient seal of confession. Wallowmire had set O'Hanlon up. He had planted evidence in his car. The blood stained box cutter, the beer, the bread, the index cards, and the fentanyl had been placed there by Wallowmire. The police had all the evidence they needed to arrest and convict O'Hanlon. If this was the case and his brother was bound to silence, Cavanaugh resolved that he himself would have to find something to clear O'Hanlon and apprehend the real Sin-Eater.

He fell asleep wondering how in the world he was going to do this.

* * * *

In the morning, Fran woke Cavanaugh up. She sat on their bed and placed little Stephen on his chest. Cavanaugh smiled seeing his son crawling around on his chest. He savored being a father. He never thought a baby could bring him so much happiness. He tickled Stephen and listened to his son's giggles. He looked up at Fran and read anxiety in her eyes. "We have a problem, Tom," she said.

He cradled his son in his arms and asked, "What happened?"

Fran shook her head. "I'm sorry, Tom. I know he's your brother and I know how much you care for each other, but we have to do something."

Cavanaugh frowned.

"What are we going to do with Chico? We can't just keep him here. Your brother left early this morning to go say Mass at St. Peter's. The boy needs to go to school. I don't want to be mean, but we can't just have him hanging around the house all day."

Cavanaugh sat up in the bed as the phone on the night table rang. "What time is it?" he asked.

"It's almost 9:30. You had a good sleep. Do you want me to get the phone?"

"No. You take Stephen. I'll answer the phone. It might be Goldberg." He swung his legs over the side of the bed. "You're right, Fran. We need to make some plans. Let's all talk it over later. I know something's bothering Jack, but we do have to talk about Chico."

Fran made a huffing sound, took Stephen, and left the room. Cavanaugh reached over and grabbed the phone. An agitated female voice shouted at him, "You lied again! I thought I could trust you, but you lied again. You are a manipulative son of a bitch!"

It was Lucy Bauer.

"What are you talking about, Lucy?"

"I read the papers, Cavanaugh. They caught the Stations of the Cross Murderer! What happened to your promises of an exclusive? I have to read about his capture in the paper and see it blasted all over the TV? What happened to the exclusive? Now I have to play catch up. I promise you I won't be so kind to you when I write my next article!"

"Hold on! Calm down. First, I had no idea where you were. But even if I did, I think they arrested the wrong man. You interviewed the O'Hanlons. Did you think he was the murderer? I know I didn't. I think he was set up by the real murderer."

He went on to explain how the police found a bloody box cutter and fentanyl in the trunk of O'Hanlon's car. "There is more to the story than cutting out his victims' eyes. The police didn't tell the press the killer left half-eaten beer-soaked bread on his victims."

"Why would he do that?"

"We think he was following some kind of old ritual. My theory is he cut out their eyes because all his victims sinned in some way with their eyes either by what they saw or did or allowed others to do."

"I don't understand. Why would he leave beer-soaked bread?"

"That's where it gets really weird. We think he is a Sin-Eater. Somehow he thinks the bread absorbs his victims' sins and by eating the bread himself he absorbs their sins thereby allowing them to avoid eternal punishment."

Lucy Bauer was silent for a few moments. Then she said, "That's insane!"

"Yeah. I think so, too. But our killer just might be a bit crazy himself."

"If it's not O'Hanlon, who is it?"

"I have a feeling I met the killer last night when I was with my brother at an all-night diner, but I have no proof. The police want this case over with quickly. They have been getting a lot of pressure from the community and the press. Given the evidence they found in O'Hanlon's car, and the fact he has no solid alibi for murders, they think they've got their guy. Jack and I, however, think otherwise. The problem is the killer is smart, and the evidence he planted in O'Hanlon's car is damn incriminating."

"You were with your brother?"

"Don't go there, Lucy. He refuses to say anything about this. I may be wrong, but I think it is a seal of confession thing."

"A what?'

"Look it up. I'm too tired to explain. It's something like you not revealing your sources, only he can't even give a clue to what he knows."

Cavanaugh cautioned her not to breathe a word of what he told her. He explained how he believed the killer almost killed him, hitting him over the head with a baseball bat. He reminded her that the killer warned both of them to mind their own business. Then he added, "I'm beginning to believe implicating O'Hanlon might have something to do with his not minding his own business."

When he finished his conversation with Bauer, Cavanaugh sat on the edge of his bed and recalled how Richard Wallowmire told him he was coming home from his "business" and how he smelled like he had been drinking. He stood up slowly to avoid getting dizzy. He wondered if Wallowmire was returning from another murder. He remembered Goldberg warning if they were right about the killer's motives he would run out of churches before he ran out of potential victims. Was Wallowmire returning from another kill? If he were, who was it this time? Wallowmire was smart and crafty, but, from his behavior in the diner, Cavanaugh felt he was getting more and more cocky and arrogant. Wallowmire was proud of himself, almost boastful. He was getting careless. It was only a matter of time before he would slip up.

As Cavanaugh started getting dressed, his mind was a whirling kaleidoscope of unanswered questions. Who would be his next victim? How were they going to prove O'Hanlon's innocence? How were they going to be able to stop a deranged Sin-Eater?

*   *   *   *

Father Bennis knelt in the back of St. Peter's and prayed. Richard Wallowmire was going to kill again. In his mixed-up mind, he thought he was doing a good thing. He had to be stopped. The priest stared up at the crucifix over the altar. What could he do? He couldn't tell anyone what he heard in Wallowmire's confession. Monsignor O'Brien advised him to leave it in God's hands. Bennis knew he couldn't control the future. He knew in his brain that the worst fears are imaginary fears. But this was a real fear. He knew Wallowmire intended to continue his killing spree. He believed that if bad things happen, God promises to get us through. How many times had he told his parishioners that God will never take us where His grace will not sustain us? If He brings you to it, He will get you through it.

But Father Bennis was still a man. He felt the fear, dread, anxiety, and grief over what he anticipated Wallowmire doing in the future. They were palpable, intense feelings. He prayed that he had enough faith to leave it in

God's hands. "Not my will, but Yours be done," he repeated over and over again in the hope that he could let go.

He clutched his hands tighter and tighter together. He felt sweat dripping down his forehead and down his back. He felt the presence of his God slowly seeping into him.

Then a sudden, gentle tap on his shoulder startled him and brought him back to the present. He turned. It was Father Steve. "I didn't mean to frighten you," he said, "but I wondered if I could pick your brain for a few minutes."

Bennis looked around. They were the only ones in the church. He slid over. "I don't have much of a brain to pick, but sure, help yourself."

Father Steve managed a smile. "I'm worried, Jack. I had a dream last night."

"Steve, I've got to tell you upfront. I'm not too good at interpreting dreams. I'm not like Joseph who could interpret the Pharaoh's cupbearer and baker."

"I'm not really sure what the dream was about. It's kind of fuzzy now, but it was scary."

"I get those dreams often."

"That's not it. My twin brother called me this morning. He had a disturbing dream last night, too. He couldn't remember what it was all about either, but it scared him. It woke him up. You don't know my brother, Jack. Nothing much scares him. We hadn't spoken to each other in years. Why would the both of us have terrifying dreams the same night?"

"I honestly don't know, Steve. Interpreting dreams is way beyond my pay grade. I've read how identical twins may have some kind of unique bond that gives them a special connection. They say some twins seem to know each other's thoughts and can sense when one or the other twin is in danger. It's all anecdotal. There is no scientific evidence that

I know of, but I've heard some twins claim to be able to actually read each other's minds."

"I don't want to read my brother's mind. I've told you we are quite different. But I can't get the thought out of my mind that something bad is about to happen."

Jack Bennis looked back at the crucifix hanging over the altar. "I heard a confession the other day that unnerved me. Obviously, I can't speak about it, but it bothered me so much I went to Monsignor for advice. His advice was to put it out of my mind and not worry about the future. No one knows what the future will bring. A bad dream may just be a bad dream. There's no sense worrying about things that haven't happened. As Doris Day would say, '*Que sera, sera.* Whatever will be will be.'"

"Who's Doris Day?" Father Steve asked.

"Sorry about that. She was a singer before your time. The point I was trying to make is the future is not ours to see. And whatever the future holds for us, God will help us deal with it. I don't know if this helps you with your dream, but my advice is to try to stay in the present. After his wife died, I still remember a New York sports reporter who would sign off his radio show with, 'Yesterday is a canceled check. Tomorrow is a promissory note. Today is the only time we have so spend it wisely.' I think it's part of human nature to worry about things that haven't happened. I know I do. The Bible is full of people who did. My best advice is to try to stay in the present. It makes no sense worrying about something that may or may not happen."

Father Steve sat in silence for a few minutes. Then he thanked Bennis, got up, genuflected toward the tabernacle, and slowly walked away.

Jack Bennis sat back and stared at the altar. Slowly, images of Richard Wallowmire began to return. He felt confident he gave Father Steve good advice. He only hoped he could follow his own advice and rid himself of the nagging negative emotions he felt about the future.

* * * *

Cavanaugh went to his office to think. The odor of donuts from the coffee shop it used to be still lingered in the air. He sat at a plain folding table he used as a desk and tried to figure out a way to catch the Sin-Eater and exonerate Jack O'Hanlon.

His headaches had stopped, and he only felt a little dizzy when he made sudden moves. His memory of being hit over the head came back, but he never saw who hit him. All he remembered was the sound of the bat and the crunch when it hit his head.

If Wallowmire was the Sin-Eater, he was smart and careful. But he was also needy. He wanted to be recognized for what he was doing. That was the reason for the numbered index cards and the cereal on his victims. Religion obviously played a role in the murders, too. In Cavanaugh's eyes, the killer actually thought he was doing the world and his victims a favor.

Part of Cavanaugh wanted to applaud Wallowmire, but another part realized he was dangerous and acting as judge, jury, and executioner. He needed to be stopped. Just then the telephone rang. Cavanaugh recognized the garbled, husky voice immediately. "I warned you to mind your own business. You should have listened to me," it said.

"You're the one who hit me, aren't you?"

"I only meant to knock you out. I didn't intend to kill you. I only kill evil doers. You should have listened to me and minded your own business."

Cavanaugh wanted to tell him he was working a job

for Kathy Ames and that he was doing his own business when he was hit, but he realized he would be talking to the wall. Instead, he asked, "Why did you kill Kathy Ames?"

"I don't need to explain myself to you. But if you found the pictures I found in Bateman's apartment you would know. She was evil, Mr. Cavanaugh. She was a very evil woman."

"Why are you calling me?"

"I wanted to apologize for hurting you, and I also wanted to alert you to my latest sacrificial offering."

"Offering? You are crazy! Is that what you call your murder victims?"

"Let's not debate semantics, Mr. Cavanaugh. As your mother would have said you can call it anything you like. I call it sacrificial offerings."

"Listen, Mr. Wallowmire, I know who you are!"

"Mr. Wallowmire?" the voice laughed. "I don't know any Mr. Wallowmire. You may call me Richard, Thomas. It's so much friendlier and more personal than the 'Stations of the Cross Murderer,' don't you think? But we deviate from the main point of my call. If you do not find my latest sacrificial offering soon, the smell will be difficult to get out of the church."

"Who did you murder this time?"

"That, Thomas, is for you to find out."

"And how the hell am I supposed to find that out?"

"Use your head. Let your darker side give in to the power of the music that I bring to you, and you will find my latest sacrificial offering."

And with those parting words, Cavanaugh heard the line go dead.

* * * *

Chapter 29

Maybe it was pride. Maybe it was a sense of satisfaction. Maybe it was simply filial competition. He would never know for sure. He knew he should have notified the police immediately, but he had no proof. It was his word against his. The police had their man. He knew how it worked. Without proof, he would be opening a can of worms they wouldn't want to deal with. So, Cavanaugh hopped in his car and drove to see his brother at St. Peter's Church.

Cavanaugh found Father Bennis in his old room thumbing through a stack of mail on his desk. "What's up, Jack? Has Vivaldi decided to let you back?"

Bennis turned to his brother. "He said not until they caught the killer, and, according to the police and the press, they have."

Cavanaugh moved into the room. "We both know they haven't. Not yet at least. I had a call from him a little while ago."

"What? He called you?"

"Yeah. You were right. I know why you were so upset last night. The real killer is Richard Wallowmire."

The tall shadow of a man appeared in the doorway. He was dressed in a sweatshirt, dungarees, and sneakers.

"Excuse me," he said, "I don't mean to bother you. I was just ...."

"I know you from someplace," Cavanaugh said.

Jack Bennis stood and introduced them. "Thomas, this is Father Steve. You've heard me talk about him."

"Yeah. Now I remember I saw you after a funeral talking to an old lady."

"Where are you headed, Steve?" Bennis asked.

"I'm on my way to the hospital to visit a friend. What's all the commotion about?"

Cavanaugh explained. "I just got a call from the killer. It's not the O'Hanlon guy they arrested. The guy's name is Richard Wallowmire. He's a neighbor of O'Hanlon. I figure he planted that evidence on O'Hanlon."

"Have you notified the police yet?"

"No. I wanted to tell my brother first. Apparently the guy left his latest victim in a church somewhere. We are going to try to figure out where."

"Well, good luck with that. I really have to get going. Have a great day."

Cavanaugh turned to Bennis. "He seems like a nice guy."

"Father Steve is. Everyone in the parish loves him. Now when are you going to call the police?"

Cavanaugh explained how he had no real proof it was Wallowmire on the phone, but he mentioned things they had talked about in the diner. He was sure it was Wallowmire.

"Where did he say he left his victim? If he killed again and the police are holding O'Hanlon they will see O'Hanlon couldn't be the killer and he was set up."

"That's just it, Jack. He didn't say. He told me to figure it out and then he gave me a line from *Phantom of the Opera*. He said if we didn't find the body or what he called it a 'sacrificial offering' soon it would stink up the church."

"What was the line?" Bennis asked.

"Let your darkest side give in to the power of the music that I bring and you will find my latest offering."

Bennis sat on his bed. He rubbed the scar over his eye. "There are no real opera houses on Staten Island. He said it was a church. 'The power of the music.' That's it. It has to be St. Hildegard Episcopal Church on Monroe Street. It has one of the largest pipe organs in the country. The body must be in St. Hildegard's." He handed Cavanaugh the phone. "Call Goldberg," he shouted. "We have no time to lose."

As Cavanaugh dialed Goldberg two men appeared in the doorway. "What's all the fuss about?" Monsignor O'Brien asked.

"My brother just received a call from the serial murderer. He's struck again."

"Who is it this time?" the other priest asked.

Bennis looked confused. "Father Steve? I just saw you in civilian clothes a few minutes ago. I thought you said you were going to visit a friend in the hospital."

"You couldn't have seen me. I've been in the chapel praying with Monsignor all morning long."

"Then who did I see? I could have sworn it was you."

"You must have seen my brother. We look identical. Even our mother had trouble telling us apart."

"I can't believe it. He looked exactly like you."

Monsignor O'Brien said, "*Fere libenter homines id quod volunt credunt* – Men generally believe what they want to."

Cavanaugh turned from the phone and did a double-take when he saw the two priests in the doorway. "I just spoke with Goldberg. I don't know how to tell you this, but he said Mario Impellizzieri has gone missing. Somehow he avoided the surveillance team they had on him. He's in the wind. They are sending police to St. Hildegard's to check it out. If there is another victim there, he thinks he knows who it might be."

"It's my father, isn't it? It's that dream we had. Does my brother know?"

Bennis said, "He left before we figured out the church might be St. Hildegard's, but I think he may have heard the killer's name."

There was a look of panic in Father Steve's voice and eyes. "If he knows, he will kill him. My father taught us from an early age that no trait is more justified than revenge. Stephen believes it is a code of honor to seek revenge. You have got to stop him!"

Cavanaugh grabbed the phone again. "Change of plans, Morty. Meet us at Wallowmire's apartment on Grymes Hill. Bring backup. I think he is about to be killed by Impellizzieri's son Stephen."

* * * *

Police cars were already on the green in front of Richard Wallowmire's apartment complex when Bennis and Cavanaugh arrived. A black Ford Fusion skidded to a halt next to them, and Lucy Bauer got out. "What's happening?" she demanded.

"What the hell are you doing here?" Cavanaugh asked.

"I heard it on my police scanner. I figured something important was happening."

Gun shots suddenly rang out. A bullet ricocheted off Bauer's car. Another hit her side view mirror. Bennis, Cavanaugh, and Bauer ducked behind Bauer's car.

"What's happening?" Lucy asked.

Cavanaugh shook his head. "What kind of a reporter are you? Someone's shooting at us in case you didn't notice."

Kneeling behind the Ford's trunk, Cavanaugh watched Detective Perez's huge partner stumble out of Wallowmire's front door and tumble down a few steps. He lay there motionless. Then he watched as Perez leaped from behind a patrol car screaming as she rushed toward her partner.

More bullets came from the front window of Wallowmire's apartment kicking up dirt and grass around Perez. Suddenly, Cavanaugh dashed from around Bauer's car and headed toward Perez.

"Thomas, get down! What do you think you are doing? Get down!" Bennis shouted.

Cavanaugh tackled Perez before she reached her partner. "Get your filthy hands off me!" Perez cried. "My partner's been shot. He needs help!"

Cavanaugh ignored her screams and pulled her back out of the line of fire. Holding the struggling Perez, he turned to see his brother dodging bullets from Wallowmire's apartment. Bennis reached Perez's partner and stooped down behind the massive detective. He seemed to check his wound and whisper something to him. Then, he rolled away and ran toward the open door of the apartment.

"What's he doing?" Perez screamed. "He's going to get killed!"

"Don't, Jack! Don't!" Cavanaugh shouted as he watched his brother disappear into the building.

More gunshots rang out from within the building. Then silence. Complete silence. Dead silence. It seemed like time stopped for a moment.

Then suddenly, in a heartbeat, everything started moving. A police SWAT team charged the building with bulletproof shields and assault weapons. Police medics rushed to the downed officer. Perez pulled away from Cavanaugh. She ran to her partner who was being administered to by the emergency medical team. More police cars and vans and emergency vehicles arrived tearing up the green in front of Wallowmire's building. Curious neighbors started coming out from their homes like hungry hedgehogs at night.

Cavanaugh stood like a lonely statue staring at the building. Then, as if in a dream, he started walking toward the open door of Wallowmire's apartment. Officer Jefferson met him on the way and walked with him. At the front door, a SWAT officer held up his hands to stop Cavanaugh. Jefferson waved him off. "He's okay, Joe. Let him in. He's one of us. His brother is in there."

Cavanaugh wandered into the apartment. The smell of gunpowder was overwhelming. Police were already marking off the area. Everything was being recorded. By the window, Cavanaugh saw the bloody body of a man dressed in a sweatshirt, dungarees, and sneakers. He recognized Fr. Steve's brother, Stephen Impellizzieri. There were brass gun shells all over the room. But where was Jack Bennis?

Officer Jefferson guided Cavanaugh through the maze of empty bullet casings. As they moved deeper into the apartment, Cavanaugh saw photos of tugboats mingled among family pictures. The metallic, slightly sweet smell of blood mixed with urine and vomit gradually replaced the odor of gunpowder.

At the door to the kitchen, Officer Jefferson turned to Cavanaugh and said, "Are you sure you want to do this?"

Cavanaugh took a deep breath. "Yeah. I need to," he said.

In the kitchen a body lay on the table. It was twitching like it was in pain. Its head was turned away from the medic. Cavanaugh saw blood flowing from a jagged hole where an eye had once been. The man on the table was covered in blood. It looked like he had been tortured. On the floor by the medic's foot, a displaced slimy eyeball wobbled back and forth. The man on the table seemed to be talking to a man on his other side. Cavanaugh felt relief lifted from his heart like a heavy burden. The man on the table was talking to his brother, Father Jack Bennis.

* * * *

When Cavanaugh and Bennis emerged from Wallowmire's apartment, Chief of Detectives Morton Goldberg was conducting an impromptu briefing with a group of TV, radio, and newspaper reporters. Alongside of him, Detective Perez stood silently at parade rest. Her eyes were red and swollen. Officer Jefferson stood in front of Cavanaugh and Bennis in the doorway as they listened to Goldberg dealing with the hungry press.

Goldberg's voice was calm and relaxed. He spoke in a steady matter-of-fact, unemotional manner. Reporters jammed microphones and tape recorders in his face as he spoke. He told them a police officer had been wounded and two men killed in the Grymes Hill apartment. The names of the victims were being withheld until next of kin were notified and a thorough analysis of the crime scene conducted. He referred all questions to the District Attorney's Office. At the present time, he told them he had no additional information to give them, but he promised to release a complete statement as soon as possible.

The reporters threw a barrage of questions at him in rapid succession.

"Who was killed?"

Goldberg stared at the reporter and replied, "I believe

I addressed that question."

"Was this shooting related in any way to the Stations of the Cross Murders?"

"I have no additional information to give you at this time."

"What is the name of the police officer who was shot?"

"I have no additional information to give you at this time."

"How serious is his condition?"

"I have no additional information to give you at this time."

"The apartment where the shooting took place belongs to a Richard Wallowmire. Was he one of the victims?"

"I have no additional information to give you at this time."

"What connection does Wallowmire have with Jack O'Hanlon who lived next door?"

Goldberg raised his hands. "Ladies and gentlemen," he said in a calm but slightly louder voice, "As I have told you, I have no additional information to give you at this time."

A reporter from CNN shouted, "Were Wallowmire and O'Hanlon involved in the series of church murders?"

Goldberg stared at the reporter for a few seconds and then replied, "I have no additional information to give you at this time."

"When can we expect additional information?" an ABC reporter asked.

"I answered that question in my initial statement."

A young reporter in the back called out, "Is this shooting related in any way to the body found in St. Hildegard's earlier today?"

Goldberg started clicking his pen. "As I stated before, I have no additional information to give out at this time."

An avalanche of additional questions erupted.

"Whose body was found in St. Hildegard's?"

"Where exactly was the body found?"

"Was the person murdered?"

"Did it look like the work of the serial killer?"

Cavanaugh turned to his brother and whispered, "I don't know how Morty deals with these idiots. I would have told them all to piss off a long time ago."

Bennis had a faraway look in his eyes. "I'm going to sneak out of here and go to the hospital to see María Isabelle. She was supposed to have her first physical therapy session today. Can you get a ride with someone? I'll meet you back at your house. Tell Goldberg I need to talk to him."

Cavanaugh turned and saw his brother disappear behind some hedges. On the green in front of them, Goldberg continued to give the reporters the same response, but the tone of his voice was no longer patient. Finally, as most of the police vehicles left and police tape had been placed on the apartment, Goldberg stated, "This briefing is terminated. Have a good night, ladies and gentlemen."

The group of reporters gradually dispersed leaving only Lucy Bauer, Goldberg, and Perez. Cavanaugh came down the steps with Officer Jefferson and told Goldberg his brother wanted to talk to him after he got back from the hospital.

"I have a couple of questions I'd like to ask him myself," Goldberg said.

"Why don't we all meet at my place tonight to celebrate the end of this nightmare and talk without the press parasites?" He looked at Lucy Bauer and added, "No offense, Lucy."

"None taken," she said, "as long as I get that exclusive you promised."

Goldberg checked his cellphone and nodded. "We still have some work to do here. We'll meet you at your place tonight, Tom. After I get preliminary reports from forensics and the coroner, I think you will have a pretty juicy exclusive, Ms. Bauer."

* * * *

Chapter 30

Father Bennis found María Isabelle sitting up in her hospital bed. Two tall well-built men stood with a short, stocky doctor speaking to her. The taller of the two men had a shaved head and wore a bullet proof vest reading POLICE ICE. The other tall man's jacket read POLICE HSI. Both men were armed. Bennis recognized the doctor immediately. He was María Isabelle's surgeon, the renowned Doctor Lewis. There were tears in María Isabelle's eyes.

"What the hell is going on here?" Bennis asked walking straight to María Isabelle.

Dr. Lewis turned to Bennis defiantly. "I had to call them. She is an undocumented immigrant. I performed an intricate operation on her, but my license is on the line here. I saved her life, but she does not belong in this country without proper documentations."

The two U.S. Immigration and Customs Enforcement agents avoided Bennis' stare. "What do you think you're doing here? I brought Ms. Rodriguez here with the permission and assistance of the Colombian National Police."

The man with the POLICE ICE vest explained, "We got the call from the doctor here, Father, and we had to investigate. ICE is a bureau of the Department of Homeland Security, and we enforce immigration and customs laws to protect our country from terrorist attacks."

Bennis' face turned red. The veins in his forehead pulsated. "You can't be serious, agent. María Isabelle came here because she was gravely ill. She had been shot by an assassin of a drug organization in Mompas, Colombia. Look at her! She is no threat to anyone. She almost died from her bullet wounds and can barely walk. She is no terrorist!"

The man with the Homeland Security Investigation (HSI) jacket said, "In the course of checking Ms. Rodriguez's background, we discovered her brother, Santiago Rodriguez, aka Chago, is a Colombian drug lord."

"This is ridiculous!" Bennis shouted. "Her brother was arrested and is in La Modelo Prison in Bogotá!"

The ICE agent stated in what sounded like a memorized speech from the ICE manual, "ICE is dedicated to detecting and dismantling transnational criminal networks that threaten the American people and threaten our industries, organizations, and financial services. Drug trafficking is a serious threat to the lives of our citizens and the strength of our economy."

Dr. Lewis folded his arms and looked up at Bennis. "I know the law, Bennis." He pointed a stubby finger at María Isabelle. "She is an illegal alien. She has no authority to be in our country. The role of ICE is to identify, arrest, and remove aliens who represent a danger to our national security or are a risk to public safety as well as those who enter the United States illegally or otherwise undermine the integrity of our immigration laws and our border control efforts. Her close family ties to Colombian drug traffickers necessitates that she be deported."

Bennis held María Isabelle's hand. She was sobbing.

"Your patient has a name, Doctor! It is María Isabelle, and she has more honor and integrity than most people I've met recently. She is a human being who deserves respect. I promise you, we will fight any deportation procedures. In the course of our legal battles, you will most likely be revealed as the callous, insensitive, selfish individual you have shown yourself to be! Now get out of here before I lose my temper!"

Dr. Lewis turned abruptly and marched out of the room. The taller ICE agent spoke softly, "I'm sorry, Father. We are just doing our job. We will be in touch."

The HSI agent handed Father Bennis his card. "If there is anything I can do to help," he said, "please call me. We apologize."

After the agents left, Bennis pulled over a chair and sat next to María Isabelle. He dried her tears with his handkerchief and held her hand. "It will be all right," he reassured her. "We'll work something out."

She looked at him. Her voice was sad. "I love you, Jack Bennis."

He grasped her hand a little harder. "And I love you, too. Don't worry. We will work this out."

Her sparkling blue eyes looked up at him. "Do you love me for better or for worse?"

"I do."

"Do you love me in sickness and in health?"

He smiled, "You know I do."

"Will you love me until death do us part?"

He felt his eyes watering. "Yes. I will," he said.

She stared intently into his eyes, "Are you willing to leave your God for me?"

He closed his eyes. He felt a tear rolling down his cheek. He didn't speak.

"It's a simple question, Jack. I need to know."

"We've been through this before. I feel I have been called to do God's work."

"I need an answer, Jack."

Bennis stared at her. Even in a hospital bed, she was beautiful. Her blue eyes seemed to penetrate his soul. He thought about how he met her in Cuba, how she cared for him when he was wounded, and most of all how much he loved her. They were unmistakably bound to each other by trials, struggles and love. He took a long time before answering.

* * * *

Chapter 31

Chief of Detectives Goldberg, Detective Perez, Officer Jefferson, Lucy Bauer, Fran, and Chico were sitting around the dining room table in Cavanaugh's house when Father Bennis arrived. "We were waiting for you, Father Bennis," Officer Jefferson said. No one else spoke. Goldberg occasionally clicked his ballpoint pen. Perez chipped away at her purple nail polish. Bennis lowered his head and pulled over a chair. He looked tired. He clasped his hands together as if in prayer. Bauer patted her fingers on an invisible keyboard. Chico scanned the faces around the table waiting for someone to speak. Finally, Fran called out, "Tom, are you coming or do we have to drag you in here?"

Cavanaugh walked into the room carrying a heavy tray with both hands. He put the tray down and unloaded a six pack of Becks beer, a bottle of Concord Grape Manischewitz, a bottle of Glenlivet scotch, a bottle of Reasons Cabernet Sauvignon, a bottle of Reasons White Lies, a bottle of root beer, and a bottle of diet cola. "I ordered some pizza, and I can make some of my famous spaghetti sandwiches if you like. I thought we should celebrate. We stopped the so-called Stations of the Cross Murderer."

"You're an ass, Cavanaugh," Lucy Bauer said.

"I'll second that! My partner was shot!"

"Easy, ladies! He's my husband, and please excuse me while I go get glasses and utensils my husband seems to have forgotten."

"Spaghetti sandwiches?" Chico moaned.

As Fran got up, Detective Perez continued, "How can we celebrate when my partner is in the hospital?"

"He'll be all right. The bullet couldn't penetrate his muscle-bound body. I spoke to the medic. She said he'll be fine."

"He could have been killed," Perez continued.

"But he wasn't," Cavanaugh stated. "That's something to celebrate, isn't it?"

Fran returned with plates, glasses, knives and forks. Another blanket of silence fell over the table. Chico broke the silence with a question. "What do you think happens after you die?" he asked.

"I think Wallowmire will burn in hell for what he did," Perez declared.

Goldberg poured a healthy quantity of Manischewitz wine into a paper cup. "I'm not sure I believe in a heaven or a hell. I think life is like a burning candle. When you blow on it, and it goes out, that's it. There is nothing more."

"That's cold," Fran said. "Life wouldn't make much sense to me if that were all it was. Then everyone could do anything they wanted and there would be no punishment."

"Whoever said that life is fair?" Goldberg asked. "People seem to do whatever they like nowadays anyway. There seems to be no accountability."

Cavanaugh opened a bottle of Becks. "Jack gave Wallowmire last rights before he died."

"You don't really believe that man will go to heaven after all the killing he did, do you?" Bauer asked.

"He did get rid of a lot of bad people," Fran said.

"Maybe, but, if you remember, he almost killed me, too," Cavanaugh said.

"Almost doesn't count except in horseshoes and hand grenades," Perez added.

Fran reached for the Reasons White Lies. "I wonder why some people do the things they do. I don't think we are born good. I believe there is good and evil in each of us, and it's a fight between the two of them. The one we feed the most is the one that dominates."

Jack Bennis sat in silence at the end of the table sipping a glass of scotch. Cavanaugh looked at Jefferson. "You're not drinking, Jefferson. Are you too good for us?"

"No, sir. I'm still on duty and besides I don't drink alcohol."

Fran suggested some water or a soda.

"Jefferson, what do you think happens after you die? Are you into the seventy-two virgin thing?"

"Tom," Fran said, "that's totally uncalled for and insensitive!"

"It's all right, Mrs. Cavanaugh. I get that a lot. The truth is I'm not sure I believe in a god. With all due respect to Father Bennis, I don't see how a god could allow all the horrible things we see all around us to happen."

One by one, everyone at the table looked at Bennis. He swirled the scotch in his glass around, but said nothing.

Suddenly, Chico spoke up. "I think when we die we come back again as an animal or another person. I think the pet spider monkey I had in Mompas was another person in another life."

Detective Perez giggled. Goldberg sipped his wine. Jefferson looked at the boy and smiled. Bauer poured herself another white wine. Cavanaugh popped open another bottle of beer. Bennis finished his scotch and placed his glass forcefully on the table. He looked at each person and said, "We all seem to have different ideas about life after death. Richard Wallowmire was a troubled man. He suffered a lot of loss and pain in his life. I think he actually thought he was doing the right thing in murdering those people. Like a lot of people, he took messages from the Bible out of context and reinterpreted things and twisted them to fit his needs. I don't know what will happen to him after death. I leave that to a higher power. I am not the one to judge him. I know Christ promised in His kingdom there would be many places for all who followed Him. I wouldn't be a priest if I didn't believe this."

"Does that leave me out, Father?" Goldberg said.

"No, Detective, as the song goes, all God's children have a place in the choir. I can't condemn Wallowmire. I feel sorry for him. He was a very troubled man."

Goldberg took another mouthful of his wine. "Speaking of trouble, I need to get a few things straight with everyone here."

All eyes turned to Goldberg. "Initially, I was troubled," he said, "by how Stephen Impellizzieri knew Richard Wallowmire was the serial killer when we didn't. All our evidence pointed to O'Hanlon. It turns out the body we found at St. Hildegard's was Mario Impellizzieri, Stephen's father and the biggest crime boss in town. But the problem I still could not understand was how Stephen Impellizzieri knew Wallowmire killed his father. Then we discovered Mario was a cautious crime boss. He knew what had happened to rival mob bosses. Maybe he even had a part in their demise. We'll never know. But we do know now he was cautious to the point of paranoid. We found a spy body camera on his body. It relayed information to his son. Just in case something happened to him, he wanted Stephen to get revenge. The video from Stephen's phone shows Wallowmire injecting Mario with something and then after performing his grisly ritual of cutting his eyes out and eating the beer-soaked bread from his chest before shoving him behind the pipe organ at St. Hildegard's."

"But how did he know the killer was Wallowmire?" Perez asked. "Did he know him or recognize him from some place they previously met?

"No. Apparently, they had never met. He saw his father's killer, but initially did not know who he was...."

"Until he came to the rectory at St. Peter's and heard me mention Wallowmire's name," Cavanaugh said. "I thought he was Fr. Steve, his twin brother. They looked exactly alike. He heard me say Wallowmire was O'Hanlon's neighbor." He shook his head. "I accidently gave the killer Wallowmire's name."

"That's the way I figured it, too. But I still have another problem on my hands. The gun that killed Stephen Impellizzieri was Detective Perez's partner's gun."

"But how could that be?" Perez asked. "Eric was shot before Impellizzieri was killed. We all saw him tumble out of the apartment. How could he have killed Impellizzieri?"

Goldberg looked at Father Bennis. "Impellizzieri received a very tight grouping of three center-chest shots. It honestly looked like the work of a professional. No offense intended for Perez's partner, but he was a lousy shot. We know Wallowmire couldn't have shot him. He was dying on the kitchen table. In addition to cutting out one of his eyes, both his knee caps were broken and his fingernails pried off. Impellizzieri was literally torturing him to death."

Father Bennis held his empty glass of scotch in both hands. "I killed him," he stated. "When I went to check on

Detective Perez's partner, I took his gun. When I went into Wallowmire's apartment, Impellizzieri and I exchanged shots. He wasn't a very good shot either."

"I think we all thought you shot him. We heard the exchange of gunfire after you entered the building. The fact that Detective Perez's partner's gun killed Impellizzieri was a bit of a puzzle. Of course, we will find your fingerprints on the gun and gunpowder residue on your hands. That is, if we choose to check."

"What are you talking about?" Bennis said. "I just told you I shot him."

"That's where I have another problem. Perez's partner will live, but he may have a permanent disability from his wound."

"What are you suggesting?"

"With your permission, Father, I would like to leave you out of it and give Perez's partner credit for stopping Stephen Impellizzieri. We like to take care of our own. It's part of our code of honor. He would get a commendation and be able to retire with merit. After all, he did take a bullet. But it's your decision. It would definitely avoid a lot of paper work and publicity for you."

Young Chico spoke up, "But that's a lie. Padre shot the killer. He is a hero."

Bennis poured himself another glass of scotch. He knew what a field day the press would have with headlines like "Priest Kills Serial Killer's Killer" or "Priest Avenges Serial Killer's Murderer." His past would be played out in the newspapers and on TV in graphic detail. The Catholic Church had enough problems without his adding to them. Chico's future would be jeopardized as well as María Isabelle's. He did what he knew was the right thing when he went into Wallowmire's apartment and shot Impellizzieri.

Everyone at the table stared at Bennis. He looked up and said, "Chico, I am not a hero. I did what I thought was the right thing. But I did kill a man. I am not looking for medals or commendations. I don't honestly care who gets credit for killing another human being. It's a bit disturbing to tell the truth. Do what you think is best, Detective Goldberg. I told you what happened. I told the truth. What you or others do with the truth, I have no control over. A little while ago, someone spoke about why God would allow bad things to happen. I believe He doesn't. He has given each of us free will to make our own decisions. Obviously, we do not always make the right decisions and bad things happen. Scholars and theologians have argued this throughout the ages. Ultimately, I don't know the answer. It is a mystery just as exactly what happens after death is, but I firmly believe there is a plan. I don't know what it is, but I trust in the big Guy. I don't think you can go wrong if you trust in God. In fact, I know you can't go wrong."

* * * *

Chapter 32

When everyone else left, Fran took Chico up to bed, fed little Stephen, and left Cavanaugh and Bennis alone at the dining room table. They sat in silence for a while. Bennis was sipping another glass of scotch. "Do you want me to put on a pot of coffee?" Cavanaugh asked.

"No. No thanks. The coffee will only keep me awake."

"Something's troubling you, Jack. You haven't been yourself since you came back from the hospital. How is María Isabelle by the way?"

Bennis reached for the bottle of scotch and poured himself another drink. "It's been a busy day, Thomas. I have a few things on my mind."

Cavanaugh reached over and removed the half-empty bottle of Glenlivet. "You made a pretty good dent in this bottle, but it's not going to help whatever it is that's bothering you. Speak to me. Maybe I can help."

Bennis nodded his head. "You're right. It's just that I don't know what to do. I've been thinking about Chico. He's an undocumented immigrant. What do I do with him? I was trying to help, but now they might send him back."

"Don't worry about it. Fran and I already discussed this. We decided we are going to try to adopt him and his sister."

"What?"

"We talked it over. We waited a long time before we found each other. Our Stephen was a blessing. You might say a miracle. Fran always wanted a large family, but after her ectopic pregnancy, we realized that would not be possible. Three children may not be a large family by some standards, but in today's world it is."

"Are you sure?"

"Is the Pope Catholic? Yes, we are dead serious. We looked into it. Our government does not make it easy to adopt an undocumented child. It's a complicated process. Normally, a child has to live with you in your legal custody for two whole years before you can even ask to sponsor him."

Bennis frowned, "Does that mean you would have to live in another country with Chico for two years?"

"Have no fear, brother. We hired an immigration lawyer, Mark Collier. Everyone says he's the best. I hate to put it this way, but because Chico is an orphan, it makes the process a little easier, but it's still very complicated and confusing. Since Colombia is a member of the Hague Adoption Convention, we will have to follow their adoption process. As I said, it's a complex process, but it's meant to be that way to prevent child trafficking. Mark told us there is even a way to adopt Chico's sister. We already started the process."

Jack Bennis pushed his glass of scotch away. "Thanks, Thomas. That is a huge weight off my mind. Now I think I need some sleep."

Cavanaugh got up, took the bottle of Glenlivet, and said, "The couch is all yours. Good night and don't let the bed bugs bite."

* * * *

In the morning, Bennis woke up to the smell of fresh brewed coffee and the sound of Chico running down the stairs. He rose slowly. His head felt like it was splitting open. He staggered into the kitchen. Cavanaugh was busy feeding Stephen. He looked up and said, "Good morning, sleepy head. Hope we didn't wake you up. You look like you have the wrath of God kind of a hangover."

"What's a hangover?" Chico asked.

"It's a long story, Chico," Cavanaugh said. "It means Padre has a bad headache."

"*Lo siento mucho*, Padre."

"Thank you, Chico," Bennis said as he poured himself a cup of coffee.

The kitchen door flew open, and Fran breezed in with donuts, bagels, and the daily newspapers. "It's all over the front pages," she said placing everything on the kitchen table.

Chico zeroed in on the donuts like a guided missile. Cavanaugh, Bennis, and Fran grabbed the newspapers. The headlines read, "Hero Cop Captures Killer," "Stations of the Cross Murderer Killed," and "Nightmare Ended." As Chico devoured one donut after another and little Stephen sat in his highchair sucking his thumb, they shared the news stories.

"Whatever happened to diligent reporting and basic research? I hate it when newspapers get it wrong. They are still talking about the Stations of the Cross Murderer," Bennis complained. "Wallowmire dropped his victims in different churches. There was a Pentecostal Church, a Catholic Church, a Baptist Church, an Episcopal Church, and a Lutheran Church. Some of them don't even have the Stations of the Cross!"

"That's all that Lucy Bauer's fault! She started it. She said giving the killer a fancy name would sell more papers,"

Cavanaugh exclaimed. "I told her it was wrong, but she persisted. It caught on and practically started a panic. It definitely did sell papers, but it almost got the both of us killed."

"I have to admit," Fran said, "Goldberg kept Jack's name out of the stories. And, no matter what you say about her, Tom, I think Lucy Bauer's article is by far the best. She's a good writer. She gives details in her story that none of the other papers have."

"I guess it's all over now," Bennis said folding his paper. "Goldberg told us last night that they found hypodermic needles, fentanyl, index cards, and wooden skewers in Wallowmire's apartment. There were also traces of the victims' blood in his bathtub. It's pretty clear he planted that evidence in O'Hanlon's car probably because he didn't 'mind his own business.' I imagine they'll be releasing O'Hanlon sometime today."

"You sound sad, Jack," Cavanaugh said. "Something else is on your mind."

"Since when did you become a mind reader?"

"How many times do I have to tell you, I can read you like a children's book with large print and colorful pictures."

Bennis glanced over at Chico reaching for another jelly donut. Fran understood immediately. "Put that donut back, Chico! If you don't watch what you are eating you'll dig your way to the grave with your teeth! Do me a favor and take Stephen into the playroom and watch him for a few minutes. We need to talk about something for a little while."

"Sure thing, Mrs. C," Chico said, and he lifted Stephen from his highchair, wiped his face and hands and then carried him into the playroom.

Fran turned to Cavanaugh and Bennis. "Don't look at me that way. Chico is thirteen years old. He took care of his sister and he's a responsible young man. Now what the hell is going on with you, Jack Bennis?"

Bennis clasped his hands together. It was difficult to talk.

"It's about María Isabelle, isn't it?"

Bennis looked stunned.

"Don't give me that look! I'm a woman. I know things about love. You are in love with her. Don't even try to deny it. It's written all over your face."

"That must be it," Cavanaugh said. "When I asked you about María Isabelle last night you avoided the question. What's the story?"

"There is no story, or at least not much of one. She is getting better. The operation was a success, and she will most likely be back to her old self in no time."

"Bollocks!" Fran declared. "You're in love with her, and she's in love with you. It's no secret. Anyone who has seen the two of you together knows. So what are you so miserable about? Did the two of you have a lovers' spat?"

Bennis got up and poured himself another cup of coffee. "No. We didn't have a fight. But you are right about me loving her."

"So what are you going to do about it?" Fran and Cavanaugh asked.

Jack Bennis smiled for the first time that morning. He checked his watch. "I have to get going. I have an appointment with Fr. Vivaldi?"

"So what are you planning to do?" Cavanaugh said.

Bennis rose slowly, took his coffee cup to the sink, and said, "Wouldn't you like to know? One would think you were writing a book. Well, if you are, leave that chapter out. Don't worry yourselves about it. God will provide. We'll be fine. Whatever will be, will be!"

* * * *

Acknowledgments

I believe we are a product of all our experiences. So too, this book is a product of the many people I have meet and listened to as well as the sometimes twisted imagination I have been blessed with and a lot of research. Specifically, I need to thank Dr. Larry Arann, Dr. Louis Gianvito for their help and assistance; Robert Boyd and Mary von Doussa for their editing services and encouragement; and Diane, my wife, who has put up with my writing and my "moods" for over fifty years. Thank you all.

I hope you enjoyed the read, and it gave you something to think about. I always appreciate hearing from readers. If the spirit moves you (and I hope it does), please drop a brief review at Amazon,com, FACEBOOK, Twitter, Linkedin, Goodreads, or wherever . You may also check out my website (www.georgerhopkins.com) to see some of the other books in the Cavanaugh/Bennis series.

If you would like to read more about Jack Bennis' military career and how he became a priest, you might enjoy the first book in the series, *Blood Brothers*. The story revolves around a plot to kill Fidel Castro.

If you are interested in learning how Fr. Bennis first met

María Isabelle, *Collateral Consequences* will give you the answer. The influence of the Mafia in Cuba before the revolution is part of this story.

If you would like to discover how Jack Bennis and Tom Cavanaugh discover they are brothers and not half-brothers, the answer is explained in *Letters from the Dead*. This novel deals also with cyber-bullying and the effects of the wars in Rhodesia and Somalia.

If you are interested in reading about the events leading up to Jack Bennis being shot while saying Mass, *Random Acts of Malice* will give you the answer. Death threats to a criminal judge are part of this story.

Unholy Retribution tells the story of how Fr. Bennis becomes the chief suspect in the grisly murders of innocent Muslims. This novel takes the reader from New York to Ireland and Scotland in efforts to track down the killer.

In *Chasing the Devil's Breath*, both brothers become involved in a drug war in Colombia and María Isabelle is seriously wounded.

The seventh novel in the series, *The Staten Island Butcher*, finds both brothers trying to lead normal lives only to become involved in a homeless, alcoholic Vietnam Veterans' problems and catching a serial killer who preys on young women.

I sincerely hope my books not only entertain, but supply you with information and a number of ideas to ponder and discuss.

The best of all good things to you and yours, and thank you again.

George R. Hopkins

Made in the
USA
Middletown, DE

76860066R00155